The Geisha's Granddaughter

The Geisha's Granddaughter

Chayym Zeldis

Five Star • Waterville, Maine

This novel is a work of fiction. Names, characters, places and incidents are either the product of the author's imagination, or, if real, used fictitiously.

First Edition
First Printing: August 2003

Set in 11 pt. Plantin by Christina S. Huff.

Printed in the United States on permanent paper.

Library of Congress Cataloging-in-Publication Data

Zeldis, Chayym, 1927–
    The geisha's granddaughter / by Chayym Zeldis.
        p. cm.
    ISBN 0-7862-5112-3 (hc : alk. paper)
    1. Japanese Americans — Evacuation and relocation, 1942–1945—Fiction.   2. Japanese American families—Fiction.
3. Japanese American women—Fiction.   4. Concentration camps—Fiction.   I. Title.
    PS3576.E44G45 2003
        813'.54—dc21   2003040855

For Nina . . . .

For my grandson, Michael Liam

And for the men of the
522nd Field Artillery Battalion,
U.S. Army . . .

"... the indomitable heart of life that sings "when all is lost... "
—Conrad Aiken

Chapter 1

Akira Shiraishi was a short man, slight, almost frail of build, but wiry—"a leather thong of a man," his wife Komako always said. He had leathery skin as well, darkened by exposure to the sun, and fine hair completely gone gray. From a distance, though he was not bent, he looked old; but up close you saw that he actually looked younger than his forty-two years. More than the youthfulness suggested by his unblemished, unwrinkled complexion was the fierce and fresh-spirited look in his electric-blue eyes. "Akira's eyes," a close friend once remarked, "have the look of the sea when it was first created . . ."

Akira was both by nature and intent a hard worker. Typically, he put in a ten-hour day, but there were times when he worked twelve, fourteen, even fifteen. Farming was no occupation you picked up and put down at will, like office papers or factory parts: farming had a rhythm, a deep, compelling rhythm, and once you gave it your heart and soul, it did not easily let go. As a very young child, Akira had gone to live on his uncle's farm north of Yamagata; he was certain that his love for the land derived from those early years. All his life, he had fallen asleep and wakened to memories of that pristine period, when newly separated from his mother, mother earth had cherished and consoled him.

Mariko, his mother, had been a very famous geisha, as her son came to understand much later. Forbidden marriage, she'd entered into a long-term, binding relationship with a considerably older man, a man possessed of enormous wealth and formidable influence in the highest of circles: Akira had issued from the liaison. Having been born and loved and coddled, then given away to Mariko's brother, Akira never knew precisely why. Occasionally, staring at the geisha's photograph given him by his uncle, he struggled to grasp how he'd been an obstacle to his parents.

The farm life was warm and boisterous and nourishing, with cousins and crops and animals; but several years after he came to live with his mother's brother, Akira's uncle died. The burdens of managing the farm and caring for her nine natural children fell upon the dead man's wife, who promptly decided that the obligation of raising Akira was excessive and unnecessary. Mariko and her paramour did not want the child back, so another solution was found in the person of Mariko's older brother, Toshiro, the family rebel or black sheep, depending on how you viewed it. In the last year before the turn of the century, Toshiro Shiraishi, severing ties with family, friends and country, had sailed from Japan to the United States and settled on the West Coast. Rumor had it that he'd married an American woman, a divorcée, but no one actually knew that for a fact. By the time Akira arrived from the village north of Yamagata to live with his sixty-year-old uncle, also a farmer, the wife had died.

Toshiro was a reed-thin man with scant hair and a wispy moustache, stained orange-yellow with nicotine, as were the tips of his fingers. He had a small house, which he'd built himself, set dead in the center of a web of dirt roads and paths that wound their way through his citrus groves and vineyards. He owned two dogs, four goats, some chickens and some ducks, and a rusty bicycle; talked little and smoked much. He wore simple, washed-out clothing and shoes cracked with age, but he was meticulous in his grooming and care of self, and all but fanatic in tending his property: his orchards and vineyards were cultivated with consuming zeal. On the day that Akira came to live with him, he stared at the newcomer as if observing some new species of animal and said finally: "My wife died without giving me a son, and now you show up, almost out of the blue. What an irony of fate! A boy of seven, and a man of sixty. We'll see how it all turns out . . ."

It turned out well. Not easily, but well. Toshiro was taciturn, stiff, demanding, addicted to his work. The boy was used to many voices, the diversity of play and labor, the glow of family hearth. Akira had to adapt to his uncle's silences and subtleties, to his curtness and impatience. At considerable effort, the aging man had to pry the child from himself. It took time. In the first weeks and months, suspicious of each other and hesitant about making compromises, which might have been misinterpreted as surrenders, the two kept their distance in a sparring match. But as time progressed, they grew to appreciate each other, and thus became closer. Akira came to know what he had initially sensed: that his uncle was rope braided of stout fiber, not flint; and Toshiro discovered what he'd divined at the outset was true: that the boy had within him the kernel of a real man.

It was Toshiro who taught Akira the English language. More than all else, even the almost exalted cultivation of the land, the study of this multifaceted, glittering tongue excited and inspired the eager pupil. Akira felt English unfolding in him like the petals of some exotic flower. He awaited his lessons impatiently, and his teacher, ever grateful for such hunger, instructed him with surprising patience. One night, after they'd finished the learning and Toshiro had dimmed the kerosene lamp and put the kettle of water on for tea, Akira asked his uncle why he'd left Japan and come to America.

The question seemed to rivet Toshiro to his place by the

stove. He was silent for several moments, then he said: "I went away from Japan because I didn't belong there."

Akira was puzzled. "I don't understand. What made you feel you didn't belong in Japan?"

Toshiro stared at the window, at which there was nothing but the blackness of the night. "Something told me," he replied. "Something deep inside me. Something that could not be ignored. It said to me: 'Listen well, Toshiro: you are no part of this land, this people. Even though you were born here, among them, you are different. And so you must go.' That's what the voice told me—in the very words I've repeated to you . . ."

"And you listened to the voice?"

"Yes, of course, I listened. I had no choice."

"And why did you come to America?"

"It was where I could go."

"And do you belong here?"

"I don't know."

Akira thought for a time; he searched his uncle's face. "And the voice you heard? Tell me about it."

Steam was hissing from the kettle, so loudly that the sound seemed to fill the room. Toshiro reached out a hand to shut off the flame. "When it speaks to you, my boy," he said, "you'll know . . ."

The two understood each other more with the passing years. The boy respected his uncle's newfound wish to unearth buried treasures; the man honored his nephew's need to hear an inner voice. They helped each other along the road of life. The stiffness in the man relaxed at the contact with the child; the child's softness toughened under the tutelage of the man. They worked together, and Akira acquired knowledge of the soil. They studied together, and Akira mastered the English language. At times, they even played together: catch, with a softball the man had brought from the general store in town, and quoits, and mumblety-peg with a prized jackknife that Toshiro had given Akira for his tenth birthday and taught him to use. On his twelfth birthday, Toshiro gave his nephew a bicycle.

Then the two rode together, almost as comrades. More importantly, Akira rode alone. On the dirt paths through the groves and vineyards and fields; on the back roads; sometimes on the main highway that traversed the valley; occasionally into town to the library for books, which he piled into a basket on the handlebars of his bike and took home to read. There was a school in town, but by tacit agreement with his uncle, Akira didn't attend it. There were also Japanese- and Native Americans in the town, but Akira avoided them all. Nephew and uncle were yoked to their life of solitude: it was lonely, but it gave them freedom.

Toshiro died at seventy. He hadn't been ill, but that didn't matter, it was his time to go. He'd died after the supper things were washed and put away, in his chair, by the bedroom window, reading. He simply closed his eyes for a moment to rest and did not open them again. A few days before, he'd told Akira: "I'm happy. Happy that I could overcome loss; happy that I still had the interest to seek and find . . ." On the last evening, Akira came into the house from some irrigation he hadn't finished and found Toshiro dead.

Everything Toshiro owned went to his nephew. Akira was fifteen, a boy but a man. He missed his uncle, but sought the man's spirit in all that he did. It always seemed to him that he was working and living for two: himself, and the dead man. He tended the land with zeal and pride; he went to the library more often and brought home books and read in the light of the kerosene lamp until his eyes refused to go on; he took longer and longer bicycle trips, sometimes sleeping out under the stars where he chanced to stop. He felt free, but his loneliness weighed on him; sometimes, it cut him like a knife. He wanted something, someone to be free for. When he was seventeen, he saw her, the woman he would marry. He knew that he'd marry her. His voice spoke to him for the first time and told him so.

It was nearly dusk, the hour when the sun ladles molten gold into the sky; he was pedaling homeward, the rear wheel of the bike spurting sand. Glancing idly to the right, he caught sight of her in the vineyard, her hair weaving the ruddy light into what he imagined to be a halo as she bent to prune. Without consciously willing it, he stopped. He couldn't help himself: he stared at her, and when she lifted her head and saw him there on the path, she stared back. Then Akira realized he'd seen her before, but never really paid attention. She was the daughter of the Fujiyamas, and her name was Komako.

Embarrassed, he half-nodded a greeting to her and, not waiting for it to be acknowledged, sped off. He cycled furiously. He had about a mile to go and covered the distance at such a rate that he was sheeted with sweat when he arrived. He leaned the bike against the side of the house and went to the pump to wash his face. The Fujiyamas were the neighbors to the west; they came to America around the same time that Akira's uncle did, and had three daughters, Komako being the youngest. Toshiro had maintained civil relations with them, but no more. In his view, neighbors were to be cooperated with and that was it: friendship, even cordiality, was out of the question.

Akira's mission became not to overturn his late uncle's philosophy, but to draw closer to Komako. He invented excuses for visiting the Fujiyamas. He got to know when she'd be in the groves, and he arranged to be nearby at the time.

She went to school in town: he planned his trips to the library to coincide with her schedule. Their first conversations were brief and halting; they often looked away after the initial exchange of words. But it didn't matter. Akira was certain of his feelings for her; more than that, he was sure that she felt the same way about him. The voice had said so. And Akira equated the voice with certainty. It was only a matter of time.

The Fujiyamas had always liked Toshiro and regretted the fact that they'd been unable to befriend him. They had respected his barriers and need for aloneness and kept gracefully away at the required distance. Secretly, they rejoiced when Akira came to live with him, and they were filled with admiration for the way in which he raised the child. When, at length, they learned of Akira's love for Komako, they did not hesitate to bless the union. Akira was young, but a man in every sense. He knew how to bend suffering into a tool for life; he had determination and stamina and patience. He could reason and analyze, but he understood the knowledge of the heart. And as he valued the young woman, Komako, he would cherish her when she was old. So, under a porcelain-bright sky on a late spring day, with the willows swaying and the chimes singing in the wind, Akira and Komako were married in the Fujiyamas' flower-festooned yard. Akira was nineteen; his bride was seventeen.

The marriage was real. A man and a woman joined together, and their uniting of spirits and bodies augmented their single selves. Akira's loneliness thawed; Komako's reticence melted away. The house was filled with the gliding mysteries of her presence, the aromas of her meals, her song. The farm was suffused with Akira's energy, his meticulous concern, the boundless drive of his requited manliness. He came in at eventide to the richness of his wife's mind and sensuousness of her body. The two enjoyed everything they did together, which gave them deeper individuality. The years went by more rapidly than they'd ever reckoned. They lacked for nothing—except for a child.

They wanted a child. They tried repeatedly, consistently, but to no avail. Doctors advised them, but the advice led nowhere. The wish for a baby became nagging desire and finally a fierce obsession. One morning, before they'd yet risen from bed, Komako turned to Akira and said: "Will you pray?"

Her husband was puzzled. "Pray for what?"

"Why, for a child, of course . . ."

Akira stared at her for what seemed an endless time, then he said slowly: "I do not think such prayers are answered."

"What do you mean?"

"I mean that, in life, people try to do things. They try as hard as they can, or wish. And whatever happens, happens."

"Then we are not interceded for?"

Akira sat up. He shrugged. "We do not ask for life. We have no choice: we are born, thrust into life. Death is met unwillingly by most, but it is an option. Between the two borders, we do what we can: use or ill-use or not use the strengths we are given. Our . . . Maker does not bother Himself with our cries or complaints—or for that matter, with our flattery. Our prayers are because we need them. They are straw in the wind . . ."

Komako held his face between her hands. "But will you pray for a child?" she entreated, as if he'd never spoken. "Will you? For me, my husband . . ."

He took her wrists. There was little he would not grant her. "For you, my wife," he said with a smile that was almost shy, "I will pray."

Now, as the sun sank below the windrow of cypresses to the west, Akira remembered that morning. He had, indeed, prayed at his wife's behest. Awkwardly, uncomfortably, with the conscious and indelible belief that his stammered words were straw in the wind, he had nevertheless kept his promise. That was years and years ago. Komako did not conceive. Though he never again uttered a word of prayer, Akira knew that his wife prayed every morning and night: it might be said that the sun rose and set with her supplications. But no baby was conceived. It was the one lack in their life together.

Akira sighed. He leaned on his hoe and, shading his eyes, looked in the direction of the setting sun. Through a gap in the windrow, he spotted two vehicles on the main road through the valley. Squinting, he made out that they were army vehicles. A vise squeezed his heart. It was wartime. Japanese-Americans were distrusted, even hated. The cars disappeared behind the windrow. Akira shivered. It was because his voice had spoken. Something terrible was about to happen. With a groan he could not stifle, he threw down the hoe and moved quickly toward the house.

Chapter 2

Komako knew every sound on the farm, and the engines that powered the cars in from the main road and down the rutted dirt trail that led to the house weren't any of them. She had been about to feed the fowl and then the goats and finally the dogs, which were beginning to stir restlessly at the door, when the raucous, unfamiliar noise of the vehicles made her shift in her chair. She rose from the kitchen table, sat down, and then rose again. The dogs barked; a chicken squawked: the whine of the motors and squealing of brakes were deafening. Komako stood where she was by the oilcloth-covered table. She had a sense of the ominous: some trouble or other was coming. But Komako didn't budge; trouble always arrived too soon, and did not have to be met halfway.

Before feeding the animals, Komako always prayed. Some days, she sat with head bowed at the table; other days, she gazed out the curtained kitchen window at the citrus grove nearest the house; sometimes, she knelt on the bedroom rug her mother had woven decades ago, her cheek pressed to the cloth of the quilt. Her prayers were the same each day, but they always seemed new to her—as if she'd broken sacred, virgin ground. Her words were simple and direct. She prayed for the souls of her departed parents, of the sister who'd died, and of Toshiro, Akira's uncle; she prayed for the well-being of her husband and herself; and then she asked God to give her a child. She spoke frankly to God. "Lord," she entreated, "permit me to be a part of the Creation: let me bring a child into Your world. I have knowledge of myself, Lord: I know that I will be a good mother, that I will respect my child, that I will have his good at heart, and that I will release him to his own destiny when the time comes. Lord, I ask this in my name, in the name of my husband, Akira, and in the name of the unborn child." And she added: "You won't be sorry, Lord. I promise You . . ."

That the years passed without her giving birth or even conceiving did not stop her from praying; she did not miss a single day. She prayed before she fed the animals because she felt that in feeding she both gave and got, and that was what she felt about having a child. That time was also suitable because Akira was out of the house and did not see her at prayer. She knew he wouldn't have objected and would certainly never have disparaged her, but she wished to separate her own continuing faith from his resignation and disbelief. She did not want Akira's negative attitude to dilute or taint her own unwavering fervor.

Komako had made up her mind to wait for the knock at the door, then she would meet the strangers and find out what they wanted. But the knock didn't come. The car engines had shut off—except for the nervous growling of the dogs, the yard was quiet. What had happened? Had Akira heard or seen the approaching vehicles and come in from the far groves? She felt mounting apprehension and hurried to the window. Through the parted curtains, she saw Akira. He stood almost in the center of the yard; behind him were the three uneasily squatting dogs, torn between their master's command to stay and their distrust of strangers. Once she saw that her husband was all right, Komako felt some relief. Then she could take in the rest of the scene.

Opposite Akira stood a tall, very tall, American soldier. He was obviously an officer of rank, wearing a black-visored hat and insignia on his shoulders that burned with the light of the dying sun. Just behind him was a soldier wearing stripes on his sleeves; somewhat to the right, at the edge of the yard, more soldiers waited in the parked cars. The officer had a holstered revolver at his hip; so did the sergeant to his rear. To Komako, watching from the house, the scene seemed unreal. But, like her husband, she was acutely aware of the war. They never spoke of it, but it weighed heavily on them. Whenever she and Akira drove to town in the battered pickup they'd bought several years back, they caught the stares of suspicion and animosity. For them, the war had an added, bitterly ironic twist: they were tied in the public mind to America's deadly enemy, Japan, a land which Komako had never set eyes on and Akira had departed from as a small child.

As Komako watched, the officer unfastened the top button of his uniform jacket and reached inside; he drew out a paper and handed it to Akira, who carefully unfolded and read it. Her husband's face was expressionless as he read, but even at a distance Komako could see the glitter of pain in his eyes. When Akira finished, he looked up. The officer said a few last words, then he turned, and followed by the sergeant, walked back across the yard to his car. The dogs barked furiously, rising but not budging from their places; the engines of the vehicles roared; Akira stood where he was and watched as the cars swerved in the dust and drove off.

Long after they had rounded the bend of the trail and disappeared, Akira remained standing in the yard; as if he might lose it, he had the paper given him by the officer clutched tightly in hand. Without seeing it, Komako knew what it said. The rumors had been circulating for several months: it was said that Japanese-Americans were to be removed from their homes and land, and sent to internment camps. To prevent espionage and foil sabotage, America would take precautionary measures. Some Japanese-Americans discounted the rumors; others believed them. Komako and her husband had reserved judgment. And now, at last, judgment had come.

It was a strict rule: Komako never deviated from the one prayer she offered daily. But on this day, as the dusk slowly swallowed the statue of her husband in the yard, she made an exception. Leaning up against the kitchen wall to support herself, she whispered: "I know that my husband and I have the strength to survive, Lord. Now, I ask You: give us the will . . ."

Chapter 3

The orange and lemon groves, the vineyards, the vegetable plots, the flower beds; the house and yard and the toolshed; the fowl and the goats; the back roads through the valley and twisting trails through their land; the little creek that doubled back on itself like a silver shoestring; the windrows and the shade trees: all gone. All that his uncle Toshiro had bequeathed to Akira, and all that Akira and his wife, Komako, had done with and made of it over the years since they'd married, was taken. Vanished in an instant, as if at the cruel whim of a magician's wand.

One of the three dogs, which had accompanied them, died soon after they went to the internment camp. The remaining two were listless, almost indifferent to life. In his mind, Akira called them ghosts, but never said the word aloud to Komako. In a way, Akira also considered himself and his wife to be ghosts. It wasn't only, or perhaps primarily, their material losses: it was their connection to all the years of the past and to their future. Akira didn't believe in personal prayer; he did not see himself as a religious man. But he did believe in holiness. To Akira, living with a woman was holy. So was caring for animals. So were cultivating the soil and tending the land. So was the continuity of human efforts and dreams. America had stripped him of all but his relationship with Komako, now his only real tie to life.

Each morning had always been filled with promise and challenge for Akira, and with a keen sense of accomplishment. Now, each new day greeted him with the over-whelming knowledge of his loss and crushing weight of his imprisonment. Almost without exception, he spoke only to his wife. Naturally reserved, he retreated into himself, making contact with strangers only when it was absolutely necessary. The confinement, overcrowding and constant tumult deepened his sense of isolation. Thoughts of suicide, which had never before occurred to him, flashed through his mind. But they were momentary; he did not dwell on them or consider them a real threat. Komako's presence defanged them: she alone was his solace, his pleasure, his anchor.

Several months after their internment, Komako fell ill. They went to the camp physician, who prescribed whatever medicine he had in stock. Akira brought her back to their quarters and put her to bed; she fell asleep at once. He sat by the bed, watching her face intently as, flushed and dark-lidded, she breathed laboriously. When she awakened, she tried—after her fashion—to smile in reassurance. "Have you been sitting here all this time?"

He nodded.

"It wasn't necessary . . ."

"I wanted to."

"Why don't you go out now?"

"I have nowhere to go."

"Try to meet some people. Talk to them."

"I have nothing to say."

Komako stared at him. "Akira," she said slowly, "if I am really ill. If I die—"

"You will not die."

"Akira—"

He took her hand. It was light, like a leaf—and with that perception, a sense of the soil and of growth and of all the years together on their land rushed back to him. Gently, he lifted her hand to his lips. "I will not live without you," he murmured.

"What did you say, Akira?"

But he did not tell her.

A week passed, and her fever broke. Akira was jubilant. A day later, she was out of bed and up and around again. Her husband's joy was an island in the sea of gloom and depression. They celebrated at supper with a little wine they had left. That night, for the first time in weeks, they made love. Bound to each other in body and spirit, they forgot what had been taken from them and remembered what they had. Akira felt satisfaction. In bitterness, they could yet taste the sweet. Who could say? Perhaps one day, the war and the internment would end. Perhaps one day their house and their land would be returned to them, and then the bitterness itself would end.

The night of rejoicing faded quickly into the grim pattern of their confinement. Akira carved little figures and animals out of wood, and then gave them away on impulse to children. They called him "The Toy Man"; sometimes, when he knew that he was unobserved by adults, he conversed with them. He would have loved a child of his own, but he could never pray—as Komako continued to do—for one. He spent much time writing down his thoughts and feelings in a journal he'd begun keeping not long after they'd been put in the camp. He wrote on lined paper in cheap school notebooks, and wryly called his collection, "The Encyclopedia of My Soul." On occasion, usually late at night or in the early hours of the morning, he read excerpts to Komako when they could not sleep. He helped his wife clean, and he helped her prepare their meals. He spent a lot of time watching her knit. And he spent a lot of time just watching her.

So the days went by, each dissolving into a gray blur. Akira had stopped thinking about and planning for the future, which to him was remote and illusory. When he thought of his life with Komako and what they'd been torn from, he could not bear the pain; and so most often, his mind and heart skipped back to the distant past. To his time as a small child with his rowdy cousins and the boisterous animals on the farm north of Yamagata; to his voyage from Japan to America and journey to his uncle's farm; to his boyhood with Toshiro, who had firmly but lovingly raised him to be a man. These old—Akira called them ancient—memories gave him bitter-sweet succor. They constituted a secret garden, whose worn paths he could wander with impunity. Deep down, they made him feel that existence had a worth beyond the degrading reach of man.

More than ever, Akira dreamed. Wild, exotic, spectacular dreams. If his pain was the seed, dreams were the flowers. One which recurred again and again he named, "The Washington Dream." In it, he traveled to the White House and banged on the front door. "Let me in, let me in!" he cried. "You can't go in," said the guards. "But I must," Akira persisted. "I must ask why America has done this; why she has punished me?" The guards shook their heads: "Go away!" they ordered. But Akira kept banging on the door. "I came here when I was a child," he cried. "I grew to manhood in America, I tilled her soil. Became one with it. I married in this land. Would have a family here, if only—" The guards stared at him. "If only what?" they asked. But Akira could never answer.

The other dream that came back over and over was of his mother, Mariko. Her hair was done up in rigid geisha-style, piled like pitch-black coal above and to the sides of her expressionless, white mask of a face. She was dressed in a lavender silk kimono, decorated with red, pale green and black geometric shapes, and she held an open violet parasol above

23

her head. She was alone, in a bare, windowless, yellow-walled room, through whose only door he had just entered. He was happy, because he felt she could not flee from him. Half-awed, half terrified, he moved closer. "I am Akira," he said faintly, "your son." In a tiny, strained voice, she inquired: "What's that?" He repeated, this time more confidently: "Akira. I am Akira, your son." And he added, with insufferable pain: "You sent me away. To the farm near Yamagata. Don't you remember?"

Now she moved towards him. Her blank, chalk-white face, the scalpel-like preciseness of her eyebrows, her eye makeup and the exotic, flame-red color painted over her lips, which looked like burst blood vessels, frightened him. "Akira," she murmured, reaching her free hand stiffly towards his head. Dizzy with expectation, he held his breath, but she refrained from touching him. "So many years," she sighed, "and you haven't grown a bit. Why is that?" He flushed. "My longing for you," he stammered, "has kept me a child. But now—" Her black-cherry eyes stared at him. "Now, what?" she demanded. For answer, he held out his arms to her.

She stepped back. "Don't—" he pleaded, glancing over a shoulder to make certain she could not reach the door without his intercepting her. But the door was no more: the room was without exit, without escape for either of them. He was exultant. At last, it would be finished: the phantom would become flesh, the void would be filled. No longer was he afraid to speak. "You can't hide anymore," he told her. "You must tell me why you sent me off. And you must accept me; you must claim me as the son you bore." She had retreated to the far wall. A spasm of fear squeezed his heart; for an instant, she appeared to be a mural executed with consummate skill on the yellow background. But then he saw with re-

24

lief that she was real. The parasol was gone, she clutched a fan in its stead. He saw that she breathed and moved the fan. He thought he even heard her sigh.

So the time had come. He advanced across the parquet floor. He would know mother-love: the mystery would be manifest. As before, his arms were out. But now he would embrace her, press his face into her bosom, unleash the unshed tears, let his heart at long last have its way. She was so close now. He gazed up. Glimpsed her elaborate hairpiece, the sash of her kimono, the fan in her tiny fingers. "Mother," he whispered, reaching to clasp her waist. "Mother," he said again. Above him, the fan fluttered.

And she vanished.

Chapter 4

Akira had vanished.

It was a standing rule that when either left their household for any length of time, he or she would inform the other. But Akira had been gone for hours, without having said a word to his wife. As the afternoon wore on, Komako grew more concerned. During the last hour, she had opened the door several times to look out, and once she'd even stepped outside to peer this way and that for some sign of her missing husband. She had considered asking other inmates if they'd seen him, but she and Akira had so little to do with their neighbors that it was awkward, almost unfair, to bother them in time of need.

Komako wasn't really worried; he could not leave the camp, and there was actually little chance of something serious happening to him within its confines. But she had something to tell him, something of so momentous an importance that every second's delay distressed her. She wasn't absolutely certain, but she was sure the moment had come to involve her husband. She seemed to have no place for herself; nervously, she paced the room, and again went to the door to open it a crack and glance out. At the bottom of the three wooden steps, the dogs lay disconsolately in the dirt; they sensed her presence, but didn't stir. People walked to and fro, dragging their bodies as if underwater. Next door to the left, an infant cried. Komako's heart raced. No sign of Akira. If only he'd return so she could tell him . . .

He had been so gloomy lately. For some days after her re-
covery from the illness, his spirits had been lifted. But then,
once more, they began to slide. She thought the last couple of
days were worse than ever. She pictured him sitting around,
staring into some world only he could enter. He ate poorly,
almost without appetite. His hard-won sleep was broken by
nightmares. She heard him moan; sometimes, he wakened
with a terrible cry. "What did you dream?" she asked. But
he'd never say. Instead, he'd hug her. "I'm sorry I disturbed
you," he'd whisper. "Go back to sleep." So she'd weighed
telling him her news for over a week. But now she needed to.
What she believed had to be true. What had seemed impossible all the years had come to pass. She'd held back from announcing it long enough.

She touched the doorknob, but moved instead to the
window. Beyond the barbed wire at the camp's perimeter, the
fields were gray and the sky over them cindery. Only one
figure was visible in the compound; as she watched, it came
nearer. Her heart hesitated and then sang. It was Akira. She
knew his walk, his every movement. She continued to watch
as the figure, gray and bowed desolately, approached their
quarters. Then she turned and went swiftly to the door.
"Akira," she said hoarsely, "I didn't know where you'd gone
off to—"

He shut the door. "I was out walking," he said with cha-
grin. "Ten times around the perimeter . . ." He winced.
"Sorry I forgot to tell you."

She ignored the explanation. "Akira," she said breathlessly, "Akira, my darling, I'm almost certain that I'm pregnant—"

She had pictured herself laughing wildly with triumph.
But instead, she flung herself into his arms and burst into
tears.

27

Chapter 5

The officer was very tall, somewhat gaunt-faced, and engrossed in studying the document in front of him on his desk. Akira knew the man was well aware of his presence, but did not choose to acknowledge it just yet. So he stood helplessly, watching the officer pore over the paper and glancing from time to time over the man's shoulders to the large photograph of the president on the wall behind him and the American flag to one side. Except for the over-loud ticking of a clock, the room was silent. To the left stood the junior officer who had ushered Akira into the office, also waiting, also as helpless as he.

On stepping into the room, Akira had immediately recognized the officer at the desk: the unusual height, the heavy-boned face, the set of the heavy shoulders on which the silver leaves of lieutenant colonel now rested. Akira remembered that day at dusk in the yard, the army cars rolling in, the official order with which he had been served. He would never forget. The lieutenant colonel had been a major then. Smug, oblivious to others' pain, officious—chances were that he'd relished discharging his duty. For a split second, Akira had the urge to turn his back on the desk and leave. But the feeling was only for an instant. He knew why he had come. He knew why he would never change his mind.

The lieutenant colonel raised his eyes. They were flinty, filled with the look of a man who can at will make out blank checks drawn on the lives of those under his command. His fingers toyed with the edge of the paper. He cleared his throat. "Your name?"

"Shiraishi, Akira."

"You wish to serve in the United States Army?"

"I do."

"Sir—you will address me as sir."

"I do, sir."

"Your reason or reasons?"

Akira felt his cheeks go hot. "My wife, Komako, is pregnant, sir. I wish the child to grow up free. Not—" He halted.

"Not what? Speak up."

"Not a prisoner, sir. Like I am."

The lieutenant colonel's eyes remained expressionless; his face seemed fused with the unmoving bulk of his body. He glanced over at the junior officer. "Jackson, process this man."

"Yes, sir."

The lieutenant colonel glanced back at Akira. "What's the name again?"

"Shiraishi, sir. Shiraishi, Akira."

"Mine's Edwards. Good luck to you, soldier."

"Thank you, sir," said Akira in an even voice. But he quickly turned aside his head so the officer would not see his tears.

Chapter 6

Like milk from a pitcher, moonlight slid through the window and splashed over the bed. Akira was asleep, with his head turned to the wall; the light made white marble of his cheek and neck. Komako and her husband had gone to bed early and made love. Gentle, appreciative, understanding love that deferred pain and suspended time. When they were spent, they'd kissed and said good night. Akira had drowsed off almost at once; his wife remained awake. She was awake now, propped up on one elbow, gazing down at the ghostly pale skin of Akira's face. Except for the fragile stirring of his lips as he breathed, he did not move, did not seem alive. Every once in a while, Komako leaned over and with extreme care, so as not to disturb him, listened to him breathe; once, she put her ear to his rib cage so she could hear his heart.

They had gone to bed early because Akira was leaving for the Army Induction Center in the morning. The alarm clock was set for four A.M., and he would catch the bus that left camp at five. His suitcase, packed and shut and bound for safety with a leather belt, stood near the door. A little kit bag for his shaving things, other toiletries and last-minute odds and ends rested on a chair; Komako would put the lunch she'd prepared for him inside and draw the strings tight when they awoke. On the back of the chair hung his jacket and hat; beneath it, freshly polished, were his heavy work shoes. They'd have fifty minutes together from the moment the alarm went off to the minute he stepped out of the door; ten minutes were allotted for the walk to the main gate of the camp, from which the bus departed.

The two of them had talked much about Akira's decision to join the army. Komako had been against it. "Now," she told him, "when at last I am pregnant with your child, you'll leave. I don't understand."

"It's because you are pregnant with my child," he countered, "that I'm going."

"But you must stay—to protect me and the baby."

He shook his head. "I must go to do that," he said.

"Why should you fight for the Americans after what they've done to us?"

Akira held her to him. "America took away my manhood," he told her. "By serving, I'll get it back."

She was silent.

"Do you understand, Komako?"

"No," she wept, "I don't."

"You will," he said.

But she didn't. Even on the eve of his departure, she did not really fathom why he was leaving her and their unborn child. She was afraid. The war was a terrible one; its casualties were numberless; there were rumors that it would never end. Why did he have to enlist? What if he came back maimed, half-destroyed? What if he were missing for years? What if he never returned at all? For an instant, panic seized her. She wanted to prod him, to shake him, to waken him and make him change his mind. Perhaps she hadn't explained enough, argued enough, pleaded until he saw her point? But she knew better. She knew the matter was closed, finished for good; it was too late to alter anything.

So she fell back into her pit of resignation. She reclined and softly ran her hands over her thighs and breasts and rising belly. Then she slid down between the sheets and turned and

31

pressed herself close against Akira; she stretched an arm across his chest. He looked cold as snow in the unearthly glow of the moonlight, but his body was warm and alive. She stifled a sob.

Chapter 7

Though it was early morning, the sun over the valley was bright enough to flood the kitchen with light; it fired the glass panes in the cabinets, glinted in the pots on the stove, sparkled over the linoleum on the floor, which Komako had just finished washing. Doing the floor was nearly the last in the long line of household chores that began at six-thirty, after Akira had finished his breakfast and left for work. Mitzko was still asleep; there was time for a break. Absently, she drew a hand across her damp forehead and seated herself at the table. The coffee in the cup was lukewarm, the way she'd learned to like it because of Akira. As she drank, she listened to the birds in the tree outside the window. Sometimes, their song was sweet enough to carry her heart away to a realm where there was no sorrow, or perhaps it was just that Komako was free enough to let her heart go.

Sadness was a part of life, woven into its fabric. Komako knew that, so she rarely complained. She also knew that she had much for which to be grateful: Mitzko, who was a healthy, vivacious two-year-old; Akira, who had returned unscathed—at least physically—from his army service; being released from the internment camp after the end of the war; Akira's employment; the living accommodations they'd received as a part of his pay. They yearned for their expropriated house and land, which had not been given back to them, but they chose not to dwell in a tent of mourning. Life was too precarious and too short to waste on what could never be.

Komako finished the coffee and rose. In the room's pristine silence, the birdsong seemed to swell. Empty cup in hand, she went to the window. Beyond the willow, alive with the restlessness of the birds, the freshly raked yard gleamed: at its center, ringed by flower beds and a low wire fence, was a majestic royal palm; past the yard's far perimeter was the spacious rear lawn of the general's house. Komako shaded her eyes from the sun. To the right, guarded from view by a line of meticulously shaped cypresses, were stables and riding ring; to the left were the tennis courts; to the front of the house was the swimming pool. Komako, Akira, and their daughter, Mitzko, occupied the tiny, slate-roofed gardener's house behind it all. Komako thought the house charming; Akira considered it adequate for their needs; with reverence, Mitzko called it their "willow house."

At the sink, Komako washed and rinsed her cup and set it in the rack to dry. She had still to do the blue-tiled bathroom, but she did not move from the sink. The look in Akira's eyes that morning—a look that appeared in them all too often— kept her prisoner. It was a look different than any she'd ever seen, an expression so terrifying that she could not meet it with her own eyes. She shivered. The truth was that her husband had come home from the war a changed man. Sound of body and of mind, yes: but something had happened to his heart, or to the mysterious essence that is called a man's soul. He had written to her all the time he'd been overseas, written long letters describing his experiences and state of mind— much as he'd done in his "Encyclopedia." Just before the German surrender in 1945, his letters had reduced themselves to one- or two-paragraph notes that told her he was well, how much he loved her and the baby he'd never seen, how greatly he longed to be back. The letters were sincere, but they were almost all the same. They did not tell her what

34

was happening to him, and Komako sensed that they avoided something he could not bring himself to write about.

She'd resolved to ask him when he returned. But the look in his eyes—the look she'd seen that morning when they got up—stopped her. He had been through an experience he could not share, something he would keep as his own because he could not communicate it, even to her. Yes, he was her own Akira, sensitive and serious and industrious; he loved her and Mitzko as much as a man could love his family; he'd coped with their losses and steered his energy towards the future. But he'd been altered. Something had touched his core—and damaged it beyond repair. Komako always helped her husband with everything; this was the first time in their relationship that she felt helpless.

There was the bathroom with the pale blue tiles, "the sky room," Mitzko called it, to do, and the laundry which had piled up; the storage room needed ordering and the vegetable garden had to be weeded. Still, she couldn't move. Remembering Akira's look paralyzed her, made her feel she would never move. But then, from the alcove off the kitchen that had been made into a child's bedroom, she heard Mitkzo's voice calling. It was sweeter than the calls of all the birds in the world.

Komako left the kitchen sink and hurried towards it.

Chapter 8

The time when it began to get dark—evening, her mommy and daddy called it—was the best time of all. Day was too bright and night was too dark. But evening was just right. The hard edges of things rubbed off. The birds fell asleep in the willow, her favorite tree. The dogs curled up by the front door. From the stables, the whinnying of the horses stopped. All the buildings and fences and paths disappeared in growing shadow. Like a breath of relief, a special hush came over the world. Then the fireflies came out. She reached for them in the dusk, but never meant to catch them. It was just a game—and they understood. She loved the time of evening. Like her mother's arms, it made her feel safe.

But it wasn't evening yet. There was still time to go. She could tell by the sun, which hadn't even touched the tower with the weather vane up on top of the general's house. A while ago, her mother had asked her to water the flowers in the beds to both sides of the front walk. Except for the times she'd stopped to glance at the sun or think about the fireflies, she had worked steadily.

"Mitzko—"

Her mother's voice came from the kitchen window. Mitzko set down the watering can and turned. "Here I am, Mommy."

"Yes, I can see you now. Have you finished the beds?"

"Not yet, Mommy. I've only done one side—I have the other to do."

"If you're tired, Mitzko, stop now and do the rest in the morning. It'll be dark soon, anyway."

"I'd rather finish, Mommy."

"All right, Mitzko. I leave it to you."

Mitzko picked up the half-filled watering can. Actually, she was tired, but she hated quitting. Once she'd set a task for herself, she liked to see it through. Besides, she'd be outside when the sun sank behind the big, castle-like house of the general and the evening covered everything with its violet quilt. She emptied the can, and started for the faucet by the toolshed to refill it. It was then that she caught sight of the man coming down the main path. She halted and watched for a moment and then went towards him.

It wasn't her father, she knew that. The man was a stranger, but something drew her to him. She even left the watering can behind, under the unopened faucet. She was shy by nature and tended to be wary with people, but she marched forward with eagerness, almost with urgency. When she reached the flagstones of the path, she stopped. The man stopped too. Didn't move. Just stopped in his tracks and looked down at her. Unabashedly, she stared back.

The stranger was about her father's height, perhaps a tiny bit taller. He had thin, black hair that seemed to shrink from his forehead, very dark eyes, and a reddish-brown scar that zigzagged down one side of his face and curved to split his chin into what looked like two halves of an apple. The scar didn't frighten her, though; it seemed natural, as if it belonged to what he was. Neither did his clothes repel her. They were old and worn, but they seemed just right for him: an old army jacket (she knew all about army jackets, her father had one) with a shoulder-patch which looked familiar, though she couldn't quite make it out, a shirt that was missing a button, baggy army trousers repaired at the knees, and heavy shoes of the sort her father often wore. She saw all of this, but she didn't know what to say. Didn't really know if she should say anything.

He solved the problem for her. "You must be Mitzko," he said.

"I am," she said without hesitation and with a pride she didn't understand.

"Well, I've heard all about you."

"You have? Who told you?"

"Why, your father did. He even showed me your picture—that is, when you were a baby."

"Then you must be my daddy's friend."

He nodded. "Your father and I are friends, indeed. Good friends."

She stared up at his scarred face, which did not scare her, into his pained eyes, which did not alarm her. His voice was soft and mellow, like the fading light: she listened to its notes like the tones of a chiming clock. She remembered snatches of conversation between her parents. Then, again without hesitating, she said: "You are Chuo."

"Yes, I am Chuo."

"Chuo from the army."

"I am Chuo from the army."

"Welcome to our home, Chuo."

There were tears in his eyes; she did not miss them. "I am honored to be here," he said. He put out a hand.

And she took it.

Chapter 9

Komako heard her daughter's voice and then caught the sound of the man's. At once, she left the pot of stew she was cooking on the stove and hurried to the window. She was just in time to see Mitzko take the stranger's extended hand and drop it, as if the two had been formally introduced to each other by some invisible presence. Then the man, stooping slightly, grasped the handle of the satchel at his feet on the path; he smiled down at Mitzko and the two of them, walking together as though they were old friends quite used to it, came forward toward the house.

Komako had little time to think, let alone consider. She scarcely managed to untie her apron strings and hang the apron on a hook, smooth her hair down into place, and turn the flame under the stew to low before the expected knock came at the front door. She hadn't really seen the man; her glimpse from the window had informed her of little more than that he limped badly on his right leg. Seeing him from close up startled her. It wasn't his physical appearance at all: the way people looked physically—even if they were maimed or disfigured—rarely disconcerted her. It was rather that the scarred stranger clad in a worn out uniform jacket and carrying a decrepit satchel gave off the aura of an apparition. It was a quality—almost a signal—that she picked up instantly; it made her feel that this man had left the most vital part of himself elsewhere, and was presenting no more than a shadow.

"This is Chuo," said Mitzko gaily, turning to the stranger for confirmation.

The man bowed his head. "Chuo Kurimoto."

"He's Daddy's friend," piped Mitzko.

"And you are Komako," said the stranger, "Akira's lovely wife. I am truly honored."

Komako found her voice. "I am honored as well. Welcome. Please come into our home."

Mitzko followed at his heels and closed the door. "He saw a picture of me, Mommy. When I was a baby. Daddy showed it to him."

When Chuo smiled, the scar writhed as if trying to escape his cheek. "Akira showed me your picture too, Mrs. Shiraishi. Many times. He said: 'This is my Komako. She keeps me going.' Please don't think me presumptuous, Mrs. Shiraishi, but when he said that, it kept me going as well."

"Have you come from far away?" Komako didn't know what to call him—Chuo or Mr. Kurimoto—so she called him neither.

"I've come all the way from San Francisco . . ."

"Then you must be tired. Why don't you wash up and then have some tea? My husband will be home any time now."

The stranger was silent. He closed his eyes for an instant. "Akira," he murmured in a just-audible voice. When he opened his eyes, Komako took his satchel and then his jacket.

"I'll show you where the bathroom is," said Mitzko.

As the two went off, the man limping behind the child, Komako set the satchel down in the storage room and slipped the jacket onto a hanger. Reaching up to put it on the rack, she saw its shoulder-patch. It was the same as the one on Akira's uniform jacket. The two men had served in the war together. In the same battalion. They were part of the same

40

mystery. For a moment, she remained frozen with an up-raised arm. Akira would come home to reunite with the man he'd spoken of as his "blood brother." Komako didn't know precisely what that meant, or where it would lead.

But she was afraid.

Chapter 10

Mitzko had been excited when her father and mother transferred the contents of the storage room in the house to the toolshed outside around the back and set about making the former into a bedroom. They'd brought in a used pull-out sofa and old armchair from the general's stock of unwanted furniture and household goods meant to be given away; Komako had contributed a standing lamp she didn't care for; and Chuo himself, wincing as he bent to his work, had built a bookcase. Wanting very much to be part of things, Mitzko had donated the braided rug that lay on the floor at the foot of her bed.

Somehow, that hadn't been enough. "I want to give Chuo something more," she told her mother.

Komako was scrubbing the kitchen floor. "What, for instance?" she asked without looking up.

"Oh, I don't know. I can draw some pictures, maybe. His walls have nothing on them."

Komako wrung the rag into the pail. "You'd better ask him," she said.

Mitzko had. That very evening. Mitzko often shared evenings with Chuo, because he, too, knew what a special time evening was. Her approach had been tactful. "Blue is a nice color for the walls in your room," she told him. "But the walls are bare."

"I know."

"Why don't you choose some pictures?"

He shrugged. "I guess I've not found anything I like."

"Suppose I drew you some?"

At once, the shy little smile that came with the lightness of a butterfly onto his lips appeared. "Would you?"

"Oh, yes!"

"Then I'd put them up."

She had worked late. Past the hour she went to bed. Had begged her mother for the extra time. The next morning, before the bus arrived at the main gate to pick her up for school, she'd knocked at his door. She was jubilant, but the force of her emotions kept her from speaking. Thrusting the drawings into his hand, she said: "These are for you." And then she'd turned and run out of the house and onto the flagstone walk all the way to the gate, her book bag flapping at her back.

Now, Chuo had her pictures. All of them. One of the valley, with the clouds in the sky; one of the general's red-brick house, with its shuttered windows and slate roof and its tower and rooster weather vane; one of the wooden hut that her father had built for her up in the branches of the tree near the stable; one of the birds in the willow; one of Komako and Akira holding hands, with the dogs at their feet, in front of her own house. And there was also the picture she'd drawn last, the one she'd worked on the hardest, the one in which she'd deliberately used the brightest colors: her portrait of Chuo himself, clad in his army jacket and wearing the crumpled felt hat Akira had given him just after he'd arrived.

All day, she was restless at school; she watched the clock and fidgeted in her seat. When the last bell rang, she was first out of class and onto the bus. Again, this time in reverse, she ran from the gate to the house. Her mother called, but Mitzko didn't respond. Chuo did not answer her knock, but his door was slightly ajar and she boldly pushed it open. She felt a thrill of pleasure and relief. All the pictures had been hung. Chuo's own portrait was in a place of honor over the sofa bed. Suddenly, a hand touched her shoulder. She started.

It was Chuo. "Thank you," he said. "Now, it really looks like a room."

"Now," Mitzko told him, "it looks like home."

She was glad that he'd come to live with them. From the first, she had cared for him. She felt that she understood him better than anyone else did. She liked being with him. Chuo could make anything. Chairs, tables, cabinets, bookcases, lamps, kites, toys of every kind. He'd made her puppets and rag dolls and even a spinning wheel that really spun wool. He was a carpenter; he knew all about electricity; he knew everything about pipes and plumbing; he knew how to grow flowers and vegetables, and how to take care of trees; he could sew; he could cook wonderfully, which Komako sometimes let him do; he was an expert fisherman and often fed the family with his catches; and though Mitzko had never seen it, he told her that he could hunt and ride a horse and drive a car. He always told her the truth. She never lied to him. They were friends.

Chuo knew all about nature, and he explained to Mitzko. He had brought with him a pair of army binoculars, and the two of them went out into the countryside to watch birds and animals. To Mitzko, these expeditions were enchanted: they were sacred. Once, on an outing, Mitzko asked him if he had a family. "Besides ours," she added.

"I grew up with an aunt and uncle in San Francisco," he answered. "They died many years ago." He paused for a moment to shade his eyes from the sun, which was climbing towards its zenith. "I never really knew anything about my family in Japan; Aunt and Uncle never talked about them. Actually, I considered myself their child."

"But I mean, were you ever married?"

"I was."

Mitzko frowned. "Where is your wife?"

The binoculars hung on a strap around Chuo's neck; absently, his fingers grazed them and fell away. "She died. In childbirth. While I was overseas in the army." He was silent; then he said: "Your father knows. He was with me."

"What was your wife's name?"

"Akiko."

"Akiko . . ." Mitzko murmured, as if the syllables told her something about the dead woman. She looked up at Chuo and then burst into tears. She was ashamed of herself. "I shouldn't be crying," she stammered.

He patted her head. "It's all right, Mitzko," he said. "Cry all you wish."

They went far that day—all the way to the creek, which took them until noon to reach. Mitzko had prepared a lunch, and they sat on the bank of the stream and listened to the water gurgle as they ate. There were dragonflies with iridescent wings in the air (Mitzko thought them second-best to fireflies) and birds all about. Between bites, they shared the binoculars. After lunch, they spotted crayfish and minnows in the creek. Chuo brought out a packet with a fishing line inside, but Mitzko had no interest in fishing that day. "Let's just walk," she said, "and talk." Chuo nodded approval.

They followed the stream for a time, but didn't speak. The sun sloped westward. Clouds stirred lazily, like driftwood. The drone of unseen insects soothed their minds. Silence— not talking—seemed to suit them. Where the creek turned northward, they turned west, out of the pathless fields and onto a dirt trail skirting the edge of an orchard. Through the glossy green leaves of the trees, Mitzko could see the ripening fruit. Chuo had halted and she did too. He was peering through the binoculars. "There," he said, handing her the binoculars, "on that highest branch. See the raven. He looks like a lump of coal."

Mitzko saw the bird and laughed. Then, glancing up him, she said softly: "You must have loved Akiko very much."

"I still love her," he said.

On the way back, they found bird nests and an anthill, and observed lizards and a snake. By the time they reached home, the sun was firing the rooster weather vane on the general's roof. Day would fade soon, and evening would unfold. "Will you watch the fireflies with me?" Mitzko asked.

Chuo shook his head. "I don't think so. Your father needs some carpentry work done." He smiled. "I really shouldn't have gone off to the creek with you today."

"Of course, you should have!" Mitzko touched his arm. "And don't forget. You said you'd make me a top. You promised—"

"I'll make it."

Mitzko was very close to him. She could talk about anything to him, even death and bereavement. Anything except her parents' attitude about him—actually, her mother's. She caught snatches of Akira's and Komako's conversations, terminated as soon as they discovered she was within earshot. As children do, she pieced the snatches together and understood. Komako had accepted Chuo's presence, but never really wanted him there: Akira had imposed him on her. She was unfailingly proper, polite, even at times gracious. But no one could fool Chuo. Hidden by the willow, Mitzko had once overheard him say to Akira that he would leave. "Where could you go?" asked her father.

Chuo didn't answer.

"Don't be crazy," Akira continued. "I want you here, I won't allow you to go. Mitzko adores you. You're like a second father, and something more: a friend. And Komako does care for you. There's a stiffness in her nature, that's all. You're staying, Chuo. I don't ever again want to hear another word about leaving."

There was an uneasiness in the household, subtle but apparent enough for Mitzko to pick up. At supper, on the day she and Chuo had trekked halfway across the valley to the creek, Komako's tension was evident even in the way she served the food. Mitzko's distress with the situation persisted through her homework; when she went to bed, she couldn't fall asleep. Her parents were in the kitchen, as they often were at night. Inadvertently, their conversation drifted into her darkened room. "She spends entirely too much time with the man," Komako accused. "He has too great an influence on her."

"Aren't you exaggerating things?" Akira said.

"I am not exaggerating, Akira. I'm telling you what I see. What I know. You're too wrapped up in your work to observe what I do." Komako had abandoned her usual restraint; her voice trembled with righteous anger. "Why, she's more interested in roaming through the fields with him than in her schoolwork."

"I cannot send him away."

"I didn't ask you to send him away, Akira."

"But you're implying that I should."

"That's only in your mind."

"Then what shall I do?"

"Whatever you think proper, Akira."

There was silence. "I will speak to him," Akira said at length.

Mitzko knew that the bond between her father and Chuo was strong; it was rooted in what they had seen and suffered together. Nothing and nobody could ever break it. But Akira had his love for and duty towards his wife and daughter; he would have to discharge his obligation without wounding his friend. Chuo, in turn, would have to accept Akira's complaint graciously, so as not to offend the complainant. Mitzko imagined their talk. It would be like a duel between two fencers, neither of whom wants so much as to graze the opponent with his foil.

Mitzko never knew when her father's promised talk with Chuo took place, but she was certain it had. There was nothing said, but her relationship with Chuo changed. For one thing, it was difficult to locate him: he seemed never to be in the usual place at the usual time. She had to hunt for him, and most often came away disappointed. When she managed to find him, he never seemed to have any time. "Got to be going," he'd mutter. Or, "Your father needs me right away at the stables." Or else, "I'm up to my neck in work. I'm drowning." She had to ask him three times for the top he said he'd make. He spoke lamely, sometimes even shamefacedly. She listened dutifully; she told him she understood. Neither believed the other.

About six months after Chuo arrived, her father had bought a battered old wreck of a motorcycle. Working patiently, often at night past the time Mitzko went to sleep (at times, she'd heard the banging and filing from the toolshed, where the vehicle was kept), Chuo had repaired it. "It runs like new!" her father announced triumphantly, after a ride to the main gate and back. Akira took his wife and his daughter for rides, and Mitzko had ridden into town with Chuo on several occasions: that was before their relationship had altered.

Early one afternoon, Akira drove Komako into town on the motorcycle. Komako had clothes shopping to do; Akira needed some garden equipment. "We'll be back for supper," Komako shouted as they sped off. Mitzko watched them go, not without a measure of relief. After disturbed nights and endless rumination during school and homework hours, she had decided to confront Chuo. She was tired of excuses, weary of the inane games of hide-and-seek. She wanted to know what her father had said to him; she wanted to know why Chuo had agreed to his demands. What she really wanted was to know if her friend missed her companionship as much as she did his.

She began the search for him. He wasn't in the vegetable garden. The toolshed, with its smells of grease and turpentine, was empty. She walked all the way to the main gate to check the front lawn, where he sometimes mowed and raked: he wasn't there. There was no sign of him at the swimming pool, out of which he filtered the dirt. The stableboy, a gangling teenager with a shock of platinum hair and acned cheeks, hadn't seen him. "Not all day," he told her with a crooked smile, "and not yesterday either. He ain't been around. Maybe he died." Offended, Mitzko hurried out of the stable without thanking him or saying goodbye.

There was the general's garage, out behind the rear lawn, where on occasion Chuo tinkered with one or another of the cars. It was a remote possibility, but Mitzko walked over on the off chance that she might find him. The garage door was down, so nobody was inside. She retraced her steps. On Saturdays, she and Chuo had often gone off exploring together; because of their rift, perhaps he was wandering on his own. Frustrated and let down, she entered the house. About to go into her room, she heard a sound. That was it: the riddle was solved! He'd been hiding in his room all the time.

She meant to knock, but his door was open a crack and she couldn't help seeing in. He was sitting on the sofa bed, leaning forward, with a black, metallic object in his right hand. Almost indifferently, he raised the hand and touched the object to his right temple. For some seconds, he remained that way, then hand and object fell to his lap. Though she couldn't explain it, Mitzko felt sick. "Chuo?"

As if it were a foreign object—a machine part, perhaps—he turned his head. "Who's there?"

"Mitzko."

"Ah, Mitzko . . ."

She went in without being invited.

The room was always orderly and clean, but today it appeared immaculate to the point of being sterile, and there wasn't so much as a pin out of place. Chuo himself was groomed impeccably and dressed in his very best clothes. Mitzko was perplexed and, though once again she couldn't explain it, extremely ill at ease. "Were you planning to go somewhere?" she inquired.

He shook his head.

Then she saw the object on his lap clearly. "It's a gun," she said.

Her words seemed to snap him out of a trance. He stared at her; for the first time since she'd entered, recognition came into his eyes. He nodded. "Yes," he said slowly, "it's a gun. My service revolver." He held it in two hands and thoughtfully turned it over. "It needs a cleaning. I was going to clean it."

Mitzko was about to call him a liar, when her father's voice in the yard interrupted. "Chuo!" Akira shouted. "The cycle broke down at the first bend in the road. We had to walk back. Are you there, Chuo?"

Mitzko left the room.

Chapter 11

Ten days later, the dam burst.

Mitzko stepped lightly down from the school bus, passed through the main gate and walked slowly home, pausing to watch the pair of blue jays that seemed to accompany her. It was slightly after four; the sun was still well above the rooster vane; a slight breeze from the west stirred the leaves of the trees. As she approached her front yard, she saw that General Edwards was there, talking to her father. Invariably, Akira was summoned to the general's house when the need arose, but on rare occasions, Edwards came out back to see him.

Mitzko halted. General Edwards was something to see. Braided hat, crisp uniform, gold stars that trapped the sunlight on his shoulders. He had always frightened Mitzko: his exceptional height, powerful build and haughty demeanor intimidated her. Once, the first time she'd seen him, she looked for reassurance in his blue eyes; but they'd dismissed her with icy aloofness. She watched from a safe distance, one at which she wouldn't be noticed. Edwards was explaining something to her father, gesturing brusquely. Dwarfed by his employer, Akira listened.

Suddenly, Chuo stepped out of the toolshed. Though it was just a regular workday, he was dressed in his finest, in the very same clothes he'd worn on the Saturday Mitzko visited his room. His gait was steady, even determined, but he took small, mannikin-like steps. "General Edwards—" he called out in a voice that Mitzko didn't recognize.

The general's head turned stiffly towards the man he'd allowed to live with the Shiraishis, and to whom he now and then gave work on his estate. "Good day, Chuo," Edwards said. "What is it? Don't you see that I'm busy just now? I'll be with you in a moment."

Without a word, Chuo drew his service revolver from inside his shirt, pointed it at the general and pulled the trigger. The gun's report scattered the crows in the treetops; Chuo's high-pitched, screaming voice rose through their cawing: "This is for America! This is for what America did to me and my family!"

Before the stunned Akira could lunge forward and wrestle him to the ground, Chuo had fired again. The general's spotless shirtfront erupted with blood; his gold-braided hat fell forward over an eye; his hands reached high into air which could not support him. Heavily, his uniformed body buckled to earth.

Then Chuo, too, was on the ground, with Akira on top of him, crying: "What did you do? What did you do? My God, Chuo, what have you done?" The two men rolled over and over, dust rising from them like dirt from a carpet. Chuo offered no resistance, but Akira kept on pummeling and shaking him, as if by doing so he might compel the other to answer. "Oh, Chuo, what've you done?" he cried pathetically. Akira knew he was wasting his time. But he couldn't stop.

Mitzko wanted desperately to do something, but she didn't know what. Her thoughts raced like lightning, but her legs were limp: she felt they might give way. Then she caught sight of Komako. Her mother came out of the front door, pail in one hand and mop in the other. The pail dropped with a clang, spilling its water; the mop fell forward. Komako put her hands to her temples. Her mouth opened, but no sound emerged. Her mouth closed and then opened again: "Mitzko!" Mitzko obeyed. Mitzko ran. Her mother seized her by both hands and pulled her into the house. Holding her daughter tightly to her waist, Komako dialed the number of the general's house. "There's been an accident," she whispered hoarsely into the phone's mouthpiece. "The general has been hurt. Please hurry—"

"There's been a murder," Mitzko corrected through her chattering teeth.

But her mother didn't hear.

Chapter 12

Evening.

But for Mitzko, evening would never be the same again: Chuo had spoiled it for her. The ambulance had come and taken the general to the hospital. The police had arrived and taken Chuo to prison. Like one of the wheelbarrows her father used about the grounds, Mitzko's life had been overturned.

She was too dismayed to talk to anyone that night—even to herself. But as the days passed, she needed to ask questions. She and her parents were at the kitchen table for supper. But she couldn't get her food down. "Why did he do it?" she burst out.

Akira looked as if she'd slapped his face. He reddened. "Nobody knows the reason for what he did," he said, swallowing with difficulty. "Perhaps not Chuo himself."

"But surely, Father, you must have some idea—"

"Of what use are guesses?"

"What was in his mind?" persisted Mitzko.

Komako cleared her throat. "Enough of this talk. Please let your father eat his meal."

Mitzko saw that tears were in her eyes.

But the disclaimers or evasions or whatever they were didn't help. Mitzko daydreamed about the shooting at school, and had nightmares about it when she slept. None of her friends and nothing of nature comforted her. She struggled to keep her pain from exploding; she trusted no one in the world, not even her parents: she made a conscious decision to withdraw. Then, one evening, as she stood disconsolately by the toolshed, it came to her. She remembered the day she'd peeked through the crack in the doorway of his room and seen Chuo on the sofa bed with the muzzle of the service revolver at his temple. Instantly, she understood what had been in his mind on the afternoon he shot the general: death.

But the general did not die.

Chapter 13

Her father said: "This is for you."

She took the brown envelope from Akira's hand. "For me?" she said, glancing at the handwritten address. It was Chuo's scrawl, and she went directly into her room. The bed was made, her clothes were in place, the floor was swept; the shade was drawn full down over the window against the flood of sunlight that late afternoon would bring. She dumped her book bag onto the desk, and seated herself on the bed. For several moments, she sat with the letter in her hands, staring as if it had come from another planet. Then she ripped the envelope open. The letter read:

> *The 11th of April*
> *Dear Mitzko,*
>   *Of everything there is in the great world of freedom, I miss you most . . .*
>
>   *Your friend,*
>   *Chuo*

What Chuo had written her from prison touched her heart, at once lessening and increasing the pain. She saw him in her mind as she would remember him always: slight, solicitous, dignified, despondent. As well as she'd known him and as close as they'd become, there was a part of his nature that she'd never been able to approach, let alone fathom. The shots that felled the general had come from that abyss. His letter told her that he missed her, but didn't explain why he had gone away. It made her angry.

"Mitzko—"

"Yes, Mother. Come in—"

Komako looked apprehensive, almost afraid.

"I'm fine, Mother. You needn't worry."

Komako hesitated. "And Chuo? How is he?"

"In prison," said Mitzko bitterly.

After supper, perhaps because she'd received the letter, she approached her father. He was in the living room, in his armchair, with the day's newspaper in front of him, but he seemed only to stare at, rather than read it. Light from the standing lamp on his left fell across his face. He looked old, weary; for the first time in her life, Mitzko saw the frailty in him. She touched his arm. "Father—"

Without regret, he put the paper on his lap. "Sit here," he said, patting the arm of the chair.

If only it could be like old times—like the time before the shooting. But it couldn't. "Father," Mitzko said. "What bothered Chuo? I must understand."

Akira shook his head.

"Don't tell me I'm too young. Don't put me off—"

"It's not that," said Akira.

"Tell me about what you and he went through. In the army. In the war—"

There was a spot of blood on Akira's lip where he had bitten it. "Mitzko," he said slowly, "you know that we Japanese-Americans were held in internment camps during the war. We lost our homes and property, all that we'd worked for over the years. When your mother became pregnant with you, I enlisted. Chuo did a similar thing. We met in the army . . ."

"Chuo said he was married. That his wife died in child-birth—"

Akira nodded. "We were in Germany. I remember the day they gave him the terrible news. I thought it would kill him. But it didn't . . ."

"He said you helped him—"

Akira shrugged. "I was there when he needed someone. He was always there for me. That's the way it was with us . . ."

"And then—?"

There was a silence. The color drained from Akira's face; his skin looked like parchment. "And then . . ." He put a hand over his eyes. "And then," he murmured, as if from sleep, "we went on with the war. We advanced through Germany. Chuo and I were in the Five Hundred and Twenty-second Field Artillery Battalion. We . . . liberated . . . Dachau—"

"Dachau?"

Akira's eyes clouded. "Dachau . . . was a concentration camp—"

"You mean, like the internment camps we were in?"

Akira shook his head.

"Then what?"

"I can't tell you," he said in a broken voice. "No one will ever make you understand. I was there . . . and I'll never understand . . ." His body heaved. Burying his face in his hands, he began to sob.

"What's the matter?" said Komako, coming in from the kitchen.

Mitzko held her father. Komako sat on the other arm of the chair and embraced Akira as well. Then the two women wept. They wept for the man. But the man wept apart from them.

Chapter 14

Through the years, Mitzko had seen the boy. But always from afar. And only infrequently. He seemed to be on the grounds only occasionally, mostly during summers. She asked her father.

"He's General Edwards's son," said Akira.

"Why does he dress in those funny clothes?"

"They're not funny clothes, they're his uniform. He goes to a military academy. He comes home on vacations."

Once, Mitzko had seen him ride out of the stable yard on a horse. He had on a high hat with a black visor that made him look severe. His uniform was slate-gray, with a navy blue stripe running down the pants; the high-necked jacket was braided with blue and had gold buttons. The horse—her father told her it was a mare, and that it'd been given to the boy as a birthday gift by the general—was white. The rider looked splendid, like a knight or an angel. But he looked unreal. He looked remote. Beyond her world.

The first time they'd met was by the main gate. She'd been chasing a butterfly—not to catch it, but to observe where it landed and watch it. It alighted on the mane of the stone statue of a lion, which she'd named "the gentle garden lion." From behind the hedge, the boy burst out. He was in his uniform, and he had a sword. He halted. Something pulled her towards him. He unsheathed the sword. "Oh, please, Mr. Soldier," she pleaded, not for an instant believing that he meant her harm, "don't kill me—" He seemed appalled at her words. "Hurt you, Fair Lady?" he stammered. "All I want is to protect you."

A lock of hair, dislodged by his leap from the bushes, lay on his forehead; it glinted like a thread of spun gold. His blue eyes could be hard, she sensed, but their expression was soft; the same went for his lips. To Mitzko, the boy—with legs planted apart and sword held aloft—was like one of those heavenly creatures which spring from fiery clouds and fly down to earth: her teacher in school had called them seraphs. Mitzko was moved. She wanted to kiss him, but she felt shame and fear; someone might see them. So, instead of kissing him, she turned and ran. He called after her. But she didn't stop until she reached the toolshed. Then she looked. He was still there, by the stone lion, the sunlight prancing over the blade of his upright sword. She could make him out clearly, even to the blue-braided buttonholes of his uniform jacket. Yet the distance between the two of them seemed immense.

Another time, she was in the vegetable garden, helping Komako pull carrots from the earth. Towards noon, her mother said: "I must see to what's cooking on the stove. Keep working, Mitzko. I'll be back—" Not long after she'd gone, the boy appeared. He was dressed in uniform shirt and trousers, but no jacket or military cap. The shirt was open at his neck; his hair was tousled. "The string on my kite snapped," he said breathlessly, "and the kite sailed over this way. Did you see it come down?"

She shook her head.

He smiled, seeming to lose interest in the kite. "May I have a carrot?"

She handed him one. "There's a faucet over there. You can wash it off."

He nodded. When he came back, chewing, he said:

60

"What's your name?" His eyes were bluer than the sky above him; again, the hardness was held in check.

"My name is Mitzko," she said.

"Then I shall call you . . . Mitzi!"

She dug her knees into the earth. "What's your name?"

"Garrett. Garrett Wilson Edwards." He bit into his carrot. "Wilson was my grandfather's name. He was a colonel. My father's a general." He stared down at her. "Your hair is so black," he said: "Blacker than crow feathers—"

She was amused.

"And your eyes are green . . ."

She laughed. "How green?"

He considered. "Greener than—"

There was a noise from the house. Both of them looked over to where Komako exited the front door. "Good-bye, Mitzi," said the boy. "Good-bye for now . . ."

"What about your kite?"

"Who needs it?"

From the beginning, she'd felt at ease with him. In his presence, she seemed more keenly aware of herself; he gave her the odd feeling that she had secret, unsuspected powers. She was drawn to him. But they met haphazardly, rarely—only for brief intervals. Generally, she saw him from far away. He appeared alone, or with other friends, also uniformed. They walked together, or played baseball or volleyball or touch football or tennis on the courts; they rode in a noisy, animated group from the stable out of the estate and into the valley. His friends had no meaning for her; they were beside the point. She was interested solely in him.

Once, during the summer, there was a party. His friends came in dress uniforms, bedecked with braid and ribbons. The young ladies wore fancy frocks, pink and powder-blue

61

and apricot. Colored bulbs, balloons, and lanterns festooned the trees, hedges and shrubs of the front yard, all the way from the main gate to the portico of the house; the razor-shaven sward of lawn shimmered in the light. In addition to the regular staff of servants, waiters had been hired: they bore silver trays of food and drink. The guests met and moved off; they ate and drank and chose partners for dancing. They gestured and chattered and laughed—all with decorum; here and there, always in shadow, couples kissed, more for effect than with purpose.

Akira and Komako had been pressed into service for the occasion. It was the year before Chuo came to stay with them, so Mitzko was alone. The noise from the party was a blur, like the drone of insects. But when she thought of him (she meant Garrett, but she almost never said his name, even to herself), the sounds suddenly intruded; she could no longer ignore them, and left the house. By the trunk of a cypress, in deep shadow, she halted. Like a play in the theater, the party presented itself to her eyes. Over the grass and under the portico, the cadets and their dates seemed in perpetual motion. The band's music rose up, perhaps to the stars. Now, framed by the front doorway, the general appeared. His silver-gray hair was cropped, the cast iron of his face unsoftened by the festivity. In full-dress uniform, with white belt and sword, he stepped forward; his wife, gowned in mint-green, was on his arm. To Mitzko, they looked like a king and queen.

But where was their son? What young lady had he invited to be his date? What color was her frock? Was her hair blond or chestnut or red? Certainly, it wasn't black, like the feathers of crows! Mitzko searched the crowd, but couldn't pick him out. The guests hid him among them, protected him from her. She shrank back against the tree. Why had she ever

62

come? What had she hoped for? It was ridiculous, absurd! He belonged to a world that could never be hers. She had reached its outer limit; she could go no further.

Gingerly, as if fearing rejection, she put her cheek to the tree trunk. The bark was coarse, parchment-like. She found no comfort in its touch, simply her way back to reality. In her mind, the cypress urged her to leave at once and return to the little house behind the big one. But she didn't stir. She watched as three white-suited trumpeters rose to their feet on the bandstand and sounded a salute. A second and then a third flourish rang out. The crowd hushed. Wearing white caps, tar-black dresses and over them frilly white aprons, two of the general's staff of servants marched forward, wheeling before them a wagon with an enormous birthday cake on it. The spotlights went out; the candles on the cake blazed; the guests applauded. "Happy birthday!" they called out. "Happy birthday!" And then, led by the jubilant bandleader, they sang it.

Mitzko saw it all through tears she did not at first realize were there. How had they come to her eyes? What right had she to them? Why should she have been invited to the party? What ghost of a claim did she have on the young man in whose honor the party was being given? The cypress seemed to rebuke her. Instantly, she rushed away, stumbling in the darkness onto the familiar path that led home.

Her parents wouldn't be back for hours. She undressed and went straight to bed. Surprisingly, sleep came just as soon as her head touched the pillow. She dreamed she was picking carrots in the garden. The noise of hooves rapping the earth startled her. She looked up. On his white mare, Garrett was charging forward. His face was set and dark—almost a perfect replica of his father's; his eyes seemed to spark. She rose as the mare reared, flailing the air with her legs. "What's the matter with you?" she called to the rider. "You promised to protect me! Don't you remember?"

But instead of his sword, Garrett had a riding crop in hand.

"You promised—"

He raised the whip to strike her.

"Mitzko . . . Mitzko—"

Her mother, weary-eyed in black dress and white apron, bent over her. "Are you all right?"

Mitzko nodded. "I'm all right."

"You screamed—"

"Just a dream, Mother."

Komako kissed her daughter's forehead. "Then go back to sleep." But Mitzko couldn't. Garrett was waiting for her there with a whip.

Chapter 15

Summer was coming to an end. Four months had gone by since Mitzko had received the letter from Chuo, but she hadn't written back. She'd tried—shut herself in her room at her desk—again and again, but failed to write an answer. The pain and bafflement he'd caused seemed an impenetrable barrier. She thought of him often, at times obsessively. Worse still, she dreamed of him. The same dream, given a detail here or there, over and over. He was in the room they'd made over for him on his arrival, hunched over on the sofa bed, staring blankly into space. He had his service revolver in his hands. "It's a forty-five," he told her. "It'll blow a hole as big as a barn door in a man. I took it when I got out of the army and kept it." He held it to eye level and sighted down the blue-black barrel. "Thought it might come in handy one day—"

"Put it away," she said to him. "Get rid of it. It won't do you any good."

A scowl came onto his face. He half-turned and pointed the gun at her. Loud as a thunderclap in the silence of the room, the safety catch clicked from on to off. She realized that she might die, but somehow she wasn't frightened. What frightened her was the knowledge that he'd fire. At that point, she always woke up, so she never knew for certain.

September arrived. In a couple of weeks, she'd be back in school. New classes. New teachers. Essentially the same circle of acquaintances, most of them Japanese-Americans ("our kind," as Komako and, less often, Akira, put it), a few

65

of them Native Americans. No real friends—that is, nobody who even came close to being to her what Chuo had been. One who wanted to be close, who pursued her shamelessly. Toge was his name. Tall, lean, black-haired and black-eyed. Stubborn and intense. Born, as she'd been, in America. The mere thought of Toge—of his glittering eyes and hands ever-eager to touch—made her anxious. She had always to be on the alert with him, always on the defensive. Gladly, she'd have signed an armistice: but Toge demanded nothing less than unconditional surrender.

On the last, free Friday before the school bus came to pick her up, she left the estate for a walk. Since the shooting, she'd never really ventured out; the loss of Chuo's company had all but drained the countryside of its appeal. But today, something drew her. She didn't intend going as far as the creek—it was too late in the day for that—but she was prepared to wander for a number of hours. She'd completed her household chores—she'd even cooked dinner while Komako ironed the laundry—and her weeding in the vegetable garden. The air was fresh and inviting; the sky was a depthless blue, with small white clouds in it that looked like bathers on their backs. Her urge to ramble was strong.

When the outer stone fence of the estate could no longer be seen, she felt relieved. This was another world, one that seemed limitless and accepting. She felt free of the past, unconcerned with the future. She could breathe, dream, yearn for nothing she could name; she could yield graciously to the trance of nature; without embarrassment, she could enjoy her naked self. The path, near the spot where she and Chuo had discovered the remarkable anthill, forked: she chose the westward extension that pointed towards the citrus groves.

Between the branches, gray-silver cobwebs shimmered; from their coverts came the whining of cicadas; above, in the blueness, some of the clouds had unraveled, as if stretching lazy limbs. It was good to be there, out in the countryside again. Mitzko saw that separating herself from the world of birds and dragonflies for so long had been a self-inflicted, too-cruel punishment for a sin she hadn't committed. She glanced down, saw the red earth of the path meet her feet, and felt welcome.

All at once, she became aware that the rhythm of her feet was being overwhelmed by another rhythm. She turned, saw the white mare advancing at a gallop, and stopped where she was. Within minutes, as she watched their progress, horse and rider reached her side. "So far from home?" said Garrett, reining in the mare.

Mitzko shrugged and looked about her. "This . . . is also home."

He followed her gaze as it roved the valley. She studied his face: as remembered, it was poised precariously between softness and steel. He was out of uniform—the first time she'd ever seen him so—in jeans, a navy blue T-shirt, and sneakers. Idly, she wondered what it would be like to get closer to those eyes, to feel the touch of his lips. The surprising intimacy of her questions didn't seem to bother her.

"Do you ride?" he asked.

"Once or twice. When I was small, my father took me to the pony rides at the fair outside of town."

He smiled with her. His eyes were clear, his features relaxed. "Want to ride with me?" he said casually.

"Sure."

"That's great!"

"What's great?"

"That you didn't hesitate," he said.

She said nothing. He leaned over and gave her his hand. She jumped and at the same time felt herself lifted. Now, as he pulled her towards him, she knew what it was like to see his eyes at closer range. There were still his lips.

"Are you okay?"

Behind him, on the warm, broad back of the mare, she nodded her head vigorously: "Yes."

"Put your arms around my waist."

She did.

"Hold tight!"

They seemed to fly. The wind rushed at them; the earth drummed with the mare's hooves; all the way to the hills, the valley blazed around them. But to Mitzko, it wasn't the scenery that counted, wasn't that they seemed to skim over the ground: it was the touch of his torso, ribs, back. That was what mattered. Holding his body made her feel safe physically, but vulnerable in another way. She was aware that the experience would change her, that there'd be no going back.

"Still okay?" he shouted.

"Fine!" she shouted in return.

"Like it?"

"I love it!"

They rode as far as the creek—it seemed to take no time at all. At a bend, where the water was shallow and trailed limpidly over smoothened stones, they forded. Then they headed to the east, almost to the outskirts of the town— Mitzko caught sight of the silver town hall dome, half-obscured by poplars—and on around what seemed endless, repetitive citrus groves and finally back towards where they'd come from. Swathed in scarlet and gold bunting, the sun was beginning to set as they traversed the last stretch of open field before the estate came into view over the rise. Garrett tugged at the reins. "Want to sit and talk for a while?"

"Sure."

"Still no hesitation?"

"None. Why would I hesitate?"

He didn't answer. Twisting his body, he helped her off the mare and then dismounted himself. He draped the reins over the mare's neck, and let her go; the horse moved away, sniffed at the ground, and stood quietly. Garret was close to Mitzko, facing her, with arms folded loosely across his chest. He stared at her. "You're a woman," he said.

She was silent.

"A beautiful woman—"

"Whatever that's supposed to mean . . ."

He frowned. "Your hair—"

"What about it?"

"It's so incredibly black—"

"Like crow feathers."

"You remember?"

"Why not? It wasn't so terribly long ago."

"You were a child then. So was I. And now I'm off to college in a couple of weeks. To West Point"—he snapped his fingers—"just like that!"

"You can't rein in life . . . like you can a horse."

"No," he said, with a tight, dry smile that could have hidden pain. He gestured. "Shall we sit?"

They sat together on a large tree trunk, from which the bark had all but peeled. Her shoulder touched his. He was stiff—she could feel it. And his face had darkened: she'd glimpsed the tenseness of his features as they seated themselves. The gold and red in the west were rapidly crumbling; the sky, as if mourning for the lost sun, was turning ashen. Soon it would be evening: there would stars—and fireflies. But before that, something would happen between them. She sensed it. He had put the something off—and she'd allowed him to—but now it was fated to come. There was no place to hide, no way to escape. She almost regretted that she'd come with him.

He fixed his eyes on the ground. After a time, he murmured: "My father . . ."

Since the moment they'd met that afternoon, the shooting was what they had avoided. Her heart pounded against her rib cage with such force that she feared he'd feel it, and moved away. He appeared not to have noticed. "There's good news," he said slowly. "Today is a great day . . ." He drew a deep breath. "This is my father's final session at the rehab center. He'll be home for good—"

"Then he's well?'

Garrett sighed. "He's paralyzed from his right hip down. He'll have to depend on a wheelchair to get around—"

"Have you seen him?"

Garrett shook his head. "No. My mother called from the center to give me the news."

Mitzko saw the first star: its light was more painful than soothing. She wanted to speak, but felt overwhelmed by her emotions.

Garrett broke the silence. "Who is Chuo?" he asked in a tight voice.

She didn't hear—or comprehend. "What?"

"Who is Chuo? The man who shot my father."

"A friend of my dad's. They were in the war together."

"In the army? The U.S. Army?"

She nodded. "Yes. In the Five Hundred and Twenty-second Field Artillery Battalion. They fought all across Europe. They liberated Dachau."

"Dachau?"

"Yes. The concentration camp . . ." Mitzko swallowed the lump in her throat. "Do you know what a concentration camp is?"

"Vaguely. I've heard of them . . ."

"I didn't know what they were. I thought they were like the

internment camps Japanese-Americans were imprisoned in during the war. My father had to explain. But—"

"But what?"

"But he said I'd never understand. No matter what he told me. No matter how many times he explained. He said that no one who hadn't actually been there and seen Dachau could even begin . . . to understand—"

Then she wept. It was the last thing in the world she'd expected to do in his presence. But there she was, sobbing. It came upon her like a sudden cloudburst—she hadn't time even to hide her face from him. Stricken and ashamed, she turned away, trying to stifle the sobs. Her body shook uncontrollably. Better to keep balance, she hunched over.

Then his hands grasped her shoulders: she felt them without seeing them. His hands lifted her. Up she went. Gently, his hands turned her around. Around she moved. At some measureless distance were strange, flashing blurs. She couldn't decide: were they stars . . . or fireflies . . . or were they his eyes? She wept, and he brushed the tears from her cheeks.

It took Mitzko time to realize that he was doing it with his lips.

Chapter 16

Komako and Akira had heard the good news about the general from one of the servants in the big house. Mitzko received it from them as if for the first time. It was not her habit to hide things from her parents, but she had her own life, her private thoughts and secret feelings. She felt that Komako and Akira wanted it that way, but it wouldn't have mattered had they not, like parents of some of her acquaintances at school. Mitzko was her own person: the right to reveal only that which she wished to reveal was sacred to her. She did not tell her mother and father where she'd been that afternoon— or with whom. She had too much to say to herself before saying anything to them.

Though it was no special or festive occasion, Komako spread a cloth over the table and asked her daughter to lay out the good dishware and utensils. Akira and Mitzko seated themselves in their places, but Komako did not serve. Instead, she turned the kitchen light off, brought over a candle in a polished silver holder, and set it down between the water pitcher and the breadbasket. "What is this for?" asked Akira.

"The general's coming home," said Komako. "Perhaps one day Chuo will as well . . ." She touched a match to the wick of the candle and bowed her head. "Let me offer thanks," she said.

Husband and daughter were silent as she murmured her prayer. Then she served the food, and the three ate; it wasn't by any means joyous, but it was less somber a meal than those which had followed the shooting. After supper, Mitzko helped her mother clear the table and do the dishes. "I'm tired," said Komako, when they'd finished. "I'm going to lie down and rest for a while. Tell your father I'll see him later." She kissed her daughter's cheek.

Akira wasn't in the living room. The daily newspaper lay unopened on his armchair; nearby, on a little end table, were his glasses. Mitzko went out. There was a full moon in the sky and the yard was silver-white in its glow, as if someone had poured mercury over it. She had a clear view of the big house: the chimneys and turrets and rooster weather vane were sharp silhouettes. Garrett's bedroom was on the second floor, on the extreme left—he'd told her that. One of its rear windows faced the yard she stood in. She found the window at once. It was dark, the panes touched faintly by quills of moonlight, but she stared at it nevertheless.

The touch of Akira's hand on her shoulder jarred her. At afternoon's end, other fingers had been there and she feared—although she realized it was absurd—that her father might somehow know. As unobtrusively as possible, she pulled away. "Father, I was looking for you—"

"I came out for a breath of air."

Mitzko regarded him: lean, slightly stooped, his nearly white hair brightened to snow by the moon. Life had wrung him like a rag, but what Chuo'd done had twisted and aged him. "Father, when did we come here?"

"Here, to the general's?"

"Yes."

"After the war. When you were just a toddler."

"How did you get the position?"

"I answered an advertisement in the paper. The general hired me. He wasn't a general then, he was a colonel." Akira sighed. "There were many applicants for the job, but he picked me . . ."

"Did he know you?"

"No. To him, I was just one of many. But something drew him to me—I can't say what." Akira fell silent, then he said: "But I knew who he was . . ."

"How?"

"I recognized him. Immediately—there could be no mistake. He was the same officer who brought the notice of eviction and internment to your mother and me. Major Edwards. I can still see the cars driving into our yard. I can still hear his voice."

"Did you ever tell him, Father?"

"No."

"Why not?"

"What for? What would I have gained?"

Mitzko's voice trembled: "Perhaps . . . your self-esteem."

Akira took her hand. It was ice-cold. "I never lost that," he said softly. For a split second, he saw in Mitzko's face the face of her geisha-grandmother, the face in the photograph his uncle had given him as a child. "She, too, means to protect me," he whispered to himself.

"Did you ever tell Chuo," said Mitzko, "that Edwards— the general—seized your property and put you and Mother in a prison camp . . . ?"

"It wasn't Edwards personally. It was America. The government."

"But he was the soldier who served America, the one who carried out the order, wasn't he?"

"He was—yes."

"And you told that to Chuo?"

"I did."

"Why?"

Akira did not reply. He stood without moving, staring into the night. To Mitzko, he suddenly looked frail, like a reed that the wind might at any moment snap in two. She came closer and touched his arm. "Father—why did you tell Chuo about General Edwards?"

"Out of my own bitterness, perhaps. I told him, not knowing what it would bring. Does anyone know what his words will bring?" Akira shrugged. "But why does it matter? What happened happened. It's done with."

Mitzko saw that he shivered.

"I'm chilly," he said. "I think I'll go in. Are you coming?"

"No."

"Taking a walk?"

"Yes, Father."

Her cheeks burned. She'd told him that she was going for a walk. But she hadn't told him with whom.

Chapter 17

She saw Garrett every night.

She'd started school on Monday, so the days were lost. Afternoons were for chores, evenings for homework. When she finished these, she was free. Akira was involved in the installation of a new irrigation system on the estate; he was more tired than usual. Settled back in his armchair, mechanically turning the pages of the newspaper, he dozed off. Komako sat curled up on the sofa and crocheted, or read one of the novels that Mitzko brought home from the library. They seemed to pay scant heed to their daughter's departures. But on Thursday, Komako suddenly looked up from her book. "Going out again?"

Mitzko was at the door. "I'm late, Mother."

She hurried across the yard. Unlikely as it was, she didn't want Komako calling after her. And she didn't want to be late, to waste a single moment of their time. He would leave the estate before they had a proper chance to be together. After their first encounter, in the evening, she'd gone to her room and located West Point in the big atlas. Putting her finger on the exact spot somehow seemed to reduce the distance.

The stable was their meeting place, even if they didn't ride. She increased her pace, hoping to be early. But he was already there, looking serious as usual, extending hands to her. She took them and pressed them, but they didn't kiss: that would come later. They left the estate through a little-used side gate in the stone wall and walked south, in the direction of the river from which Chuo had taken his catches of fish. In many places, the terrain was rocky and uncertain; he steadied her. As on every one of their outings, they spoke almost without stop.

Essentially, she told him a story of loneliness. Close to her parents, but bent on separating from them. Close to Chuo, but he had been abruptly taken from her—or removed himself, however one saw it. Many acquaintances, with whom she could chat for an hour or go to the movies or the library in town, but no real friends. No one with whom to share her deepest self. She told him about that self. And about the force of nature in her life.

He spoke of his early childhood on the army bases where his father had been stationed; of summer vacations in France and Spain and Switzerland; of his years as a cadet at the military academy. Of sports and contests; of competition and conflict. He told her about loneliness, as well. Alienation from his father. "I couldn't touch the man with a twenty-foot pole if I were fifteen feet away!" Distance from his mother. "Buddies" and "comrades-in-arms." But no true friends, friends he could count on to understand his inner life. His career plotted for him down to the tiniest detail, as if on a military map.

"What about girlfriends?" she asked.

"I've dated."

"And the girl at the party?"

"Party? What party?"

"The big birthday party on the front lawn."

"That was almost a year ago!"

"But what about the girl? Your date. I didn't see her, but is—was there anything between the two of you?"

"Oh, you mean Elizabeth . . ." He laughed—his first of the evening. "She's the only daughter of a major general. My father's a brigadier general. It was obligatory."

"How far does the 'obligation' go?"

"Nowhere."

She trusted him. "I was there."

"Where? At the party?"

"I was watching from the sidelines. I hid behind a tree. At one point I cried. It was—childish."

"I'm sorry," he said, stroking her hair. "You won't cry again, if I can help it."

They didn't go as far as the river, only to a poplar that had fallen across the path, then they turned back. As they walked, he asked: "And you? Have you gone out?"

"No," she said, "you're the first." She thought: "And the last."

But she didn't say it.

At the stable, with the muted, shifting sounds of the animals in their ears, they embraced and kissed. The first ride began it; their kisses sealed it. She was certain of her feelings for him. From now on, they would lead her, and she would follow. There was no other way.

When they broke away from each other to part, she said: "We'd best skip tomorrow night . . ."

"Not meet tomorrow? But why? I've only a week left before I go."

She was uneasy. "My mother's—curious."

"So? What does that mean?"

Lightly, she ran her fingers over the fine down on his cheek. "Garrett, please let me handle this in my own way."

"All right. But Saturday—"

"Yes, we'll meet on Saturday."

"Maybe you can come earlier. In the afternoon. I'll wait for you at the fallen tree."

"I'll try."

"Sorry. Not good enough—"

"I'll be there, Garrett."

Chapter 18

Komako touched her husband's shoulder. Akira didn't stir, so she had to shake him. He wakened with a groan. "I dreamed of Chuo," he murmured thickly. "It was terrible. He hanged himself in his cell."

"It was only a dream," Komako said. "I must talk to you about something real."

Akira turned himself over so that he could see her. She was sitting up, her back braced against the headboard. Her face, whitened by the moonlight streaming in through the window, was expressionless, but her eyes glittered restlessly. "I haven't been able to sleep," she said.

"Are you ill? What's wrong?"

"It's Mitzko. Something's going on. She disappears from the house every night."

"Every night?"

"Every one this week, so far."

"But where does she go?"

Komako shrugged.

"Perhaps she's with friends. Has a social life at last. Haven't we wanted that?"

Komako shook her head; she put a moon-silvered hand to her cheek. "No, Akira, that's not it. A girl like Mitzko doesn't suddenly acquire a circle of friends. Become a social butterfly overnight. It isn't in her nature."

"Then what?"

Komako stared at her husband. "There's an attachment,

Akira. She is attached to one person. She's seeing someone."

Akira propped himself up on an elbow. "That Toge boy," he said. "The tall, skinny young man who was over here a couple of times this summer. What's the name of his family —?" He considered. "You know, they live just north of town. The father drives a truck. Their name escapes me right now . . ."

Komako gestured. "No, it's not that Toge young fellow. Mitzko barely tolerated his presence—she couldn't wait for him to leave. It's someone else."

"Who? Somebody from town? From school?"

"Someone she cares for, Akira. Mitzko doesn't open up easily. But when she does, it's serious."

"But who? Tell me what you think."

Komako didn't reply; she seemed deep in thought. Her husband knew her well. She could have spoken, but wouldn't commit herself. To say out loud what she surmised might be false, even dangerous. Akira wouldn't pry, wouldn't prod her. He'd wait. Let her take her own good time. Better to wait than to intrude, to pressure. The two of them had always respected each other's need for individual resolution: that was one of the basic principles of their marriage.

His gaze shifted round to the shimmering white square of the window. He seemed to see Mitzko's face there, made up of swirling moonbeams. Had she changed? How was she different? When had he and Mitzko really talked? When had he last questioned her about herself? About her hopes and dreams? Her future? A feeling of bitter regret came over him. The truth was that he hadn't noticed for longer than he cared to know, that he'd been too preoccupied and self-absorbed to find out what was happening in her world. He'd been supervisor and provider—not a real father. Life always moved on. Without your knowing it, a person could metamorphose before your very eyes: one day, he won't hurt a fly; the next, he tries to kill someone.

Tired as he was, he lay awake, staring at the window, waiting for his wife. After a time, he turned to glance over at her. She saw his distress, his weariness. "Good night, dearest Akira," she said, leaning forward and kissing his forehead. "We'll talk about this again in the morning. Go back to sleep now . . ."

But he couldn't.

Chapter 19

Fumiko, who for a number of years had pursued and failed, but nevertheless come closer than anyone else in class to winning Mitzko's friendship, proposed that they spend lunchtime together. Grateful for what would be a diversion from her thoughts, Mitzko agreed. Fumiko, a short, heavy, unpopular girl who wore what against her cramped features seemed overlarge glasses, had been prepared for rejection: she was unexpectedly delighted. "Let's go over to Mason's," she suggested.

During free periods, the seniors were permitted to leave school grounds, so the two left the yard and crossed the street to the drugstore with, as its fitfully lit neon sign proclaimed, "The Best Soda Fountain in Town." Fumiko chattered; Mitzko half-listened. Ironically, her companion's high-pitched voice, struggling with its own intensity, made her less anxious. Since their lunch period was an early one, they readily found two stools in the rear. "I dumped my sandwich in the bathroom first thing this morning," Fumiko confided. "I'm going to have a sundae instead. Double scoops of vanilla fudge and chocolate chip—and a double order of whipped cream! How about you?"

"I'm having a Coke," said Mitzko.

She was drinking it, half-attending to Fumiko's diatribe about the chemistry teacher, when she glanced up and saw Garrett coming through the doorway. His eyes were directly on her; it was obvious that he'd been watching the school yard and had followed her. She put the Coke down.

Fumiko's spoon hung in the air. "Is something wrong, Mitzko?"

In several swift strides, he was at Mitzko's side and then up on the stool beside her. "I couldn't wait to see you," he said, almost with shyness. "I just cannot picture myself wasting a whole day."

She wanted to answer, but no words came out.

"You're not angry with me, are you?"

She shook her head.

He slid off the stool. "Come on, Mitzi—"

"Come where?"

"I've got the jeep; we'll go for a ride."

She followed him towards the door. Behind her, she heard Fumiko's high-pitched call, but didn't turn to acknowledge it. "We can't really drive far, Garrett—I've got to be back at school in half an hour for my next class."

"Not necessarily . . ."

They were out on the sidewalk. He pointed. "The jeep's just down the street," he said, taking her hand.

"Mitzko—"

At first glance, she failed to recognize him, but then she saw that it was Toge. Accompanied by several of his cronies—boys whom Fumiko called toughies—he barred the way. She sensed his hostility, saw that he was staring savagely at her hand in Garrett's. "I'm in a hurry now," she said quickly. "I don't have time to talk."

"In a hurry for what?"

Garrett bristled. "Who is this guy, Mitzi?"

"No one, Garrett. Just someone in my class—"

"What does he want?"

"Nothing, really." Mitzko forced a smile. "Toge, please let us pass—"

Instead, Toge lunged forward and grabbed her other

hand; Mitzko struggled to free it, but Toge tightened his grip.

"Stop it, Toge! You're hurting me!"

"Let go," said Garrett.

Toge's guffaw was echoed by his friends.

"Let go, I said. I'm not going to tell you again—"

"Make me."

"Get out of the way," Garrett ordered. He yanked Mitzko back just as Toge swung. Garrett ducked, weaved and counterpunched; blood spurted from Toge's burst lips. One of Toge's companions rushed forward. Garret sidestepped, and shoved him to the pavement. The next friend tried to jump Garrett, but Garrett twisted neatly aside and smashed the fellow's nose with a jab. Now, Toge, leaking blood onto his shirt, his face contorted with pain and rage, came on again. Disdainful, even amused, Garrett eyed him with cold composure.

"You bastard," choked Toge, "I'll kill you."

Garrett danced, bobbed, weaved, waited for the right range and instant, kept himself in constant motion.

"When I catch you, I'll kill you. I swear it."

Garrett's left hook caught Toge's jaw and this time broke teeth. He watched as Toge sank on his knees to the sidewalk, and then, fists thrust out, turned to the third friend. "And you, what about you, huh?" He crouched, bobbed, jabbed. "Well, where are you? I'm waiting—"

But the third friend shrank away.

"Toge! Enough! For heaven's sake—"

Mitzko's cry made Garrett wheel about. Once more, Toge was on his feet. He could barely keep his balance, wavered this way and that, like some gigantic insect about to expire. "I—kill—you—" he muttered hoarsely, just about able to force the syllables from his battered mouth.

Garrett cocked an arm.

"Garrett, don't—"

"He deserves it, Mitzi—"

"Garrett, don't do it! I beg you—"

Mitzko shut her eyes. When she opened them, Toge was sprawled full-length on the sidewalk; two of his friends bent over him. Standing to the right, Garrett watched them, his fists at the ready.

Chapter 20

They drove halfway across the valley to the river.

They'd driven without exchanging a word, and now they sat side by side on a lichen-covered boulder, silently watching the water flow. Garrett held her hand, but Mitzko didn't return his pressure. "Is something bothering you?" he asked.

She didn't reply. "It's okay to tell me. I'm a big boy, Mitzi . . ."

She turned. "Did you knock Toge down again, Garrett?"

"You mean—for the third time?"

"Yes."

"What do you think, Mitzi?"

"I don't know."

"You really don't know?"

Mitzko shook her head. "I begged you not to strike him again. Then I shut my eyes. I didn't see what happened."

Garrett patted her hand. "Don't fret, Mitzi. I never touched him the third time. Twice was enough—he collapsed on his own."

Mitzko stared at him. "Garrett, did you like it?"

"Like what?"

"Hitting him. Hitting Toge."

"I had to do it, Mitzi. You know that."

"I know that. But did you like it? Did it give you a thrill?"

Garrett reflected. "I like that I can do it well," he said. He considered again. "And I have to confess: doing it well . . . does thrill me—"

86

"Did it make a difference that Toge's Japanese?"

"I'm sorry—what exactly are you saying?"

"Americans don't like 'Nips.' Did hitting a 'Nip' give you . . . special satisfaction?"

"That's rubbish, Mitzi! I hit him because he was hurting you. Because he attacked me. That's all. I didn't particularly give a damn what he was—black, yellow, red or white! Does that answer your question?"

"Someone once said that, in the identical situation, the Americans wouldn't hesitate to use the atom bomb on the Japanese, but that they'd never drop it on the Germans. Because the Japanese are 'Nips.' And the Germans are white men . . . Aryans—"

"Who told you . . . such a thing?"

Mitzko stared at the swift, dark pull of the current, in places undisturbed, in others ripped like silk by the rocks. "Chuo," she said softly.

He turned her face towards his. "Mitzi. I care for you . . . because you're you. That's it. End of story."

She sank against his chest, glad to surrender. He was a warrior, and that in itself wasn't bad. It all depended on when and whom he fought—and why. She felt safe with him—and aroused. Enveloped in the sounds of the water and the birds, they kissed. Then they left the boulder and walked for a time along the riverbank. Mitzko glanced at her watch. "We have to go. The bus gets me home around three on Friday."

They went back to the jeep and pulled out. On the road, Garrett said: "Has your mother said anything about us yet?"

"No."

"She will, you know."

"I know."

"What'll you say?"

Mitzko shrugged.

"Will you tell her the truth?"

"What is the truth?"

"That we're going out; that we care for each other . . ."

"I can stall, Garrett. Be evasive. You're leaving next week anyway."

"I'll be back, Mitzi."

"So I can worry about it then . . ."

"Mitzi—"

"Garrett—I've already told you: it's my problem."

He didn't contradict her. They were nearing home. "See you tomorrow," he said. "By the fallen tree. Around four—?"

She shook her head. "It won't work. Better make it at night. After supper, as usual. About eight."

"Okay. If that's the way it has to be . . ."

He let her off at the main gate and sped away on the road that led to the side entrance of the estate, where the garages were located. She stood where she was, lost in thought, her book bag over one shoulder, until the sound of the jeep's engine had faded; then, slowly, she made her way down the path past the big house she had never set foot in. Shading her eyes from the sun, she saw her mother at work in the garden.

"Mom," she called out.

Komako stopped hoeing. Silhouetted black against the brightness of the sun in the west, she was a strange figure, almost alien, a little forlorn—like a scarecrow. As Mitzko came closer, Komako edged out onto the flagstone path, and leaned on her hoe. "You're late."

"A little." Mitzko reddened. "The bus—" The rest of the words wouldn't come out.

Komako's eyes fixed themselves on her daughter's flushed face; they were eyes that expressed warmth, but chose not to ignore the cold truth they saw. Komako's lips parted as if to speak, but instead she permitted only silence to flow. There was a moment of dumb, stark communication between the two women on the path; each had a clear sense of the words that the other refrained from uttering. A lizard scurried out of the garden; from the stables came the neighing of horses waiting to be fed; above, in the flawless sky, a flock of raucous crows raced by.

Their cries seemed to rouse Komako. She stirred her sandaled feet. "Freedom is wonderful," she said. "It's intoxicating. But, like wine, it has limits . . ."

"Sorry, Mother—I don't quite follow."

Despite her wish for control, Komako's voice trembled: "Stay in your own world, Mitzko. You aren't free to go elsewhere."

Mitzko's cheeks burned; she averted her face to hide the brimming tears in her eyes. "I'm going in now, Mother," she mumbled, unleashing the book bag's strap. "I've lots of homework for the weekend." And she hurried off. As she entered the house, she sighed with relief; she was rid of her mother's strained, subversive voice. That much was true. But what about her mother's warning?

Chapter 21

Saturday: a day that would scar Mitzko's memory forever.

She was up early—a little past six—in time to see the cautious light of dawn nibble at the window. Her homework, including the assignments Fumiko had relayed on the phone, was finished by nine; her bath was over by nine-thirty; the breakfast and household chores were all completed by noon. That left the unfinished weeding in the vegetable garden, and some tidying up in the estate's hothouse that Akira had the previous evening asked her to do.

The day was cloudy and gray; haze shrouded much of the valley. It suited her mood. Even gardening, which she had loved and shared with her mother since childhood, did not dispel her depression. She worked rapidly, quickly, mechanically, with little pleasure or appetite. She and Komako had pointedly avoided each other since they'd met the afternoon before, and spoken only when necessary. The problem was simple and terrible: her mother knew about Garrett and disapproved. There was nothing that she, Mitzko, could say or do to change her mind. And there was no way for Komako to dissuade her from seeing him. The two had reached an impasse. Over all the years of love and understanding between them, a deadly shadow had fallen. Everything was imperiled.

Mitzko heard footsteps and looked up. Akira had come out of the toolshed. "Finished with the weeding already?" he asked.

"Almost . . ."

"I saw you start." Akira glanced at his watch. "That must be record time. You didn't cheat, did you?"

"I never cheat in the garden."

Akira smiled. "Or anywhere else."

Mitzko was silent. What about her father? Did he know about Garrett? She knew that Komako never troubled her husband until all other means were exhausted, until there was no choice. She was protective of her mate, as, in all fairness, she was of her daughter. But there had to be a difference in the protectiveness. One remained for life with a spouse, while one released one's offspring. She studied her father's tanned, worn face, with its kind eyes and almost savage furrows. Had his wife mentioned anything? Alerted him? Komako had observed her daughter's behavior closely and at length. She had managed to decipher the truth, but had she told it to Akira?

Mitzko didn't think so. She would have sensed that he knew. He might have held his tongue, but she would have seen it in his eyes. What would his attitude be when he did know? Would he feel as Komako did? Her parents were so close, so aligned, so attuned: their views of life almost always matched. Yet they were individuals, truly their own persons. It was difficult to gauge his reaction. He might assent—or he might object. She feared that she might lose her mother; she didn't want to lose her father as well.

Nervously, she prodded the loose earth with the hoe. Before she spoke, she weighed her words. At length, she said: "Tell me, Father . . . what is our world?"

Akira was puzzled. "I don't understand, Mitzko. What do you mean?"

"I mean, Father, what world does our family live in? Do we live in the American world? Or is there another world we live in: an old world—one I've never seen or known, but can't seem to escape?"

Akira's eyes clouded. "Ah," he murmured, "the old world. It was so long ago. I was just a child then; I scarcely remember . . ." He spread his hands. "I have no ties whatsoever to that world; I never did."

"Then you—we—are in the American world?"

Akira shook his head. "My daughter, I believe the truth is that we are part of neither world. We do not belong to the old one; we haven't been admitted to the new one—and never shall be . . ."

"Then we are nowhere?"

Akira's voice was low, almost musical: "Earth is our mother."

"What is that supposed to mean?"

With feather-light fingers, Akira touched his daughter's cheek. "We live on the land, and the land nourishes us."

"Father—we're hired help. We're servants!"

Akira shook his head. "No, we only seem to be servants. But our earth mother frees us. Places us beyond the reach of any world, old or new. But why . . . this serious conversation?"

Mitzko was silent. He had pushed her into a corner. There was nothing to say without telling him the secret his wife hadn't revealed—as yet. "Another time," she said.

"I'm in no hurry, Mitzko."

"No, Father—I'd like to finish my work. We'll talk another time."

Akira shrugged. "So be it . . ."

She watched him go. At the turn of the path, he looked back. "Don't forget the hothouse," he called out.

"I won't."

She had not much work left in the garden, but she remained there a long time. Too long, because she still had the hothouse to clean up. With a start, she hoed the final row and hurried over. As she moved about, setting the place in order, she considered what her father had told her. It was perplexing, but in some ways it seemed to make sense. She, herself, had no connection to the world of her ancestors. Nor did she feel American; she simply lived in America. The earth that Akira spoke of with such reverence was not "American" earth: it was simply earth. Was it enough to sustain her, as it did her parents? She didn't know for certain, but she reckoned it wasn't. She needed more; perhaps what Garrett offered—or professed to offer. Precisely what that was, though, she couldn't tell.

The hothouse was done, "spic and span," as Chuo had liked to say after a thorough cleaning job. She dusted off her clothes and stepped from the shelter of glass into naked daylight. To her right, was the flower nursery; ahead of her was the big house, with the late afternoon sun draped carelessly over it like a robe. Out of a rear door came a number of servants, one or two of whom Mitzko vaguely recognized; then came several men in army uniforms—noncommissioned officers, she thought. Something was going on in the house, not one of whose thresholds she'd ever crossed. She remembered Garrett's birthday party, touching the bark of the tree, weeping. Despite her resolve, Komako's warning stirred in her mind: "Stay in your own world!"

Mitzko shivered. The mansion, the estate, their tenants and their guests: all were alien to her. The past and future of America: barred to her. Komako said so; Akira concurred. It might be so now, but had it always to be so? For a time, she observed the servants and the soldiers—they talked, laughed, smoked, gestured expansively with their hands—then, slowly, she went round to the right where she had a clear view of Garrett's second-story room. She imagined him there: he was lying on his back in bed, or sitting at his desk. She imagined he was thinking of her, wishing that it already was eight o'clock and they were embracing by the fallen tree. She tried to get a glimpse of him, but the sunlight imprisoned in the windowpanes blinded her. Nevertheless, she continued to gaze upwards. What was really on his mind, in his heart? She could not see the future. Couldn't divine whether he truly meant or was able to bring her into the world that her parents swore was eternally out of reach. Standing there, she lost all track of time. A light in a window at the front end of the house informed her abruptly that the afternoon was at an end.

No one was home when she arrived. That was odd. She called her mother's name. No answer. She felt relieved; the relief made her feel guilty. She decided to shower, and got into her robe. The front door banged. It was Akira. "The hothouse is all cleaned up?" he asked.

"It is."

Akira unfastened a button of his shirt. "Don't shower yet," he said. "I need to wash up and change. There's a reception over in the big house tonight, and I've been pressed into service. Your mother's already there . . ." He undid a second button. "Some major general or other's coming . . ." Smelling of dirt and sweat, he brushed past his daughter.

While Mitzko waited in her room, he used the bathroom and then proceeded to the large bedroom to change. "Hey there! Want to see how I look?" he called from the hallway.

"What's that?"

"Come over here, Mitzko—see how I look!"

She sat on the edge of her bed, head held in her hands. "Like a lackey," she muttered bitterly, too low for him to hear.

Chapter 22

The ship's clock on the mantelpiece chimed seven, and she was off. Earlier, through her bedroom window, she'd seen a half-moon in the sky, but now it was covered over by cloud. She crossed the yard, started up the path, but promptly halted. Ahead, at the main gate, she saw the swirl of activity. In the glare of floodlights, a column of cars, limousines and military vehicles drew up and discharged the passengers. Officers in glittering dress uniforms, women wearing gowns and wraps, men in tuxedos stepped out onto the front walk and, ushered on by house servants, entered the estate. The carefree chatter and bubbling laughter of the guests reached Mitzko's ears; she even—or so she fancied—got whiffs of their perfume and cologne.

Her route would have to be altered, so she turned and headed for a side gate. The detour would take longer—it was a good thing she'd left the house at seven. Nevertheless, she walked more quickly. As she exited the estate, she glanced back. Light seemed to blaze from every window of the big house: it looked like a cruise ship riding at anchor. Strains of waltz music drifted lazily into the darkness. Mitzko hurried on. She was anxious to be with Garrett. Eager to follow the compass that had directed her since the first afternoon they'd been together. No matter where it led. Even, she determined, if it were to take her from the world that Komako had admonished her to remain in.

A few moments of walking, and it all faded: the house, the

merry guests, the music. The night took her over. She found the trail at once, and followed it easily. It was the way to the river; Chuo and she had walked it countless times. Despite the detour, she made the trek in plenty of time. Her watch said exactly seven forty-three. Garrett and she always sat together on the fallen tree; she didn't want to sit on it alone, so she stood and waited.

Alone. Essentially, as she'd told Garrett, she'd been alone all her life. But she'd come to accept the fact, had adapted. Until Garrett. He had broken the seal she'd set; it could never be replaced. At will, the lid of her vulnerability could be lifted. Anticipating his arrival, she glanced at her watch. Six minutes to eight. He was invariably early; perhaps the reception for the major general at his house had somehow delayed him.

Over her head, in the branches of the scrub pines, something rustled. A bird, maybe an owl. Chuo had never tired of identifying birds for her; she'd sometimes wondered where he'd gotten his considerable store of knowledge from, and then remembered that once, long ago, he'd had a house, his own land, a beloved wife and an unborn child. Once, before—. She tried to keep Chuo out of her mind, but he seemed always to be there, as if he had some valid claim on her memory. Often, she imagined what it was like for him in prison. She knew him. And feared that, like some charging human battery, he must be storing up hatred.

Again, she looked down. Four minutes past eight. But it was impossible! Garrett had never been late. In the darkness, the luminous numerals of her watch danced, wriggled. She brought her wrist close to her face. No, she'd seen correctly. Now, it was five after eight. Garrett had to be on his way—almost there. She strained to hear him on the path, but heard nothing. Only the bird sounds from above, and from a distance, in the direction of the river, the dull, orchestrated croaking of frogs.

She was uneasy. Something had happened. Something had befallen Garrett, or—? She didn't finish the thought. The music and lights and merrymaking entered her mind, but she didn't want to connect them to him. It was eight-fifteen. She hesitated, and then took several steps down the trail in the direction of home. She stood perfectly still. Listened. Heard nothing. No footsteps. No outburst of greeting. Nothing at all.

A twig snapped. Then another and another. Footsteps! Her heart raced. "Garrett!" she cried out.

"No, not Garrett."

The sky had cleared; the light of the half-moon drained whitely through the tree branches, making it bright enough for her to see. "Toge! What are you doing here?"

"Following you, Mitzko."

"You'd better leave. Garrett's on his way. He'll be here any minute . . ."

Toge half-turned. "Hiroki and I are ready for him . . ."

Several steps behind him, a hulking, slope-shouldered fellow—Mitzko recognized him as the one Garrett had shoved to the sidewalk—brandished a baseball bat.

"Toge—this is crazy! Go away—"

Instead, he caught her by the wrists. "This time . . . you won't escape—"

His face, badly bruised and swollen, was very close. She was frightened by his eyes. He looked possessed, out of touch with his self-restraint. She had the eerie feeling that he was a total stranger, that she'd never seen him before.

"Kiss me—"

She turned her head. "Toge . . . please . . . stop—"

"Kiss me, Mitzko—"

She struggled, but he was far stronger. His breath spurted over her hair, her neck. She tried to break his hold, but his fingers were like handcuffs. "I won't . . . kiss you—"

"I'll make you—"

She wanted to cry, but something didn't let her. To twist her face back to him, Toge had to release one of her wrists; with the freed hand, she slapped him. "You . . . won't . . . make me—"

"The bastard—you kiss him! You'll kiss me—"

Wildly, without effect, she kept slapping him.

"Hiroki, you ass! Get over here and help me—"

"Let—go—of—the—girl."

The voice was contained, but seemed to ring out like thunder. Hiroki, who had started forward, stopped in his tracks; Toge froze. All eyes turned to the right, where the voice had come from. Framed by trees was the small figure of a man. Not standing erectly, yet not in a crouch: the posture of an animal set to spring. The man held out one hand stiffly. In the hand was a knife, its blade licked white by sympathetic moonlight. He jabbed the blade into air—as easily as he would have dipped it in flesh. "I'll count to three," he said in his even, imperious tone. "And if you two vermin aren't gone—"

There was no need to finish. Toge dropped Mitzko's wrist; he ran after Hiroki, who had bolted down the path. Shivering, Mitzko faced the little, lean, half-crouching man with the knife. Apparition? Or—? Her knees were weak. She seemed to hear the blood drumming through her body. Parting dry lips, she whispered hoarsely: "Chuo . . ."

He didn't stir. Didn't move a muscle. "My . . . dearest . . . Mitzko . . ." he managed to say.

And then he wept.

Chapter 23

"Except for Dachau, this is the first time I've cried," he said, "since I found out that my wife was dead . . ."

They were down by the river, not far from the spot where she and Garrett had sat on the rock. Mitzko was seated on a tree stump; Chuo squatted. It was still difficult for her to believe that he was there, that she was talking to him; she could not shake the uncanny feeling that she was in a dream.

"That day will always be with me," Chuo said. "It was November. Very cold. Snow had been falling for several hours. We were well behind the front line, resting. It was a Thursday. I was in the tent I shared with your father; he was off somewhere—I don't remember where. I'd left the flap open—deliberately, so I could watch the snowflakes . . ." He paused; the rushing of the river filled the silence.

Mitzko wasn't sure that he'd continue. "Go on," she said softly. Her words seemed to rouse him from reverie.

". . . I was thinking of my wife . . . thinking of the child inside her . . . thinking of the time we'd be together: just thinking . . . and watching the white flakes come down . . ." Chuo lifted a hand; it looked fragile, like a child's. ". . . Suddenly, there were pants, army boots; they . . . blocked my view. The officer called my name out. It was eerie: the sound of my own name frightened me. Something told me: 'Don't go.' I crawled through the flap. Stood . . . and the officer—he was our company commander—gave me the news. As he said the words, he spat snow from his tongue. I listened . . . heard him . . . said nothing . . . showed no emotion . . . didn't let him see a solitary tear." He looked at her. "Do you understand?"

"I . . . understand."

". . . That night, I wept. Your father held me. The snow was still falling. 'When we leave,' I told him, 'I stay right here. Let the snow bury me.' He held me like a baby. Said he wouldn't leave me. At dawn, we pulled out. He helped me with my gear. We rode towards the front line. 'I hate myself,' I told him. 'I want to be dead, and I go on with living.' He said nothing. But his eyes . . . held me to life. Do you understand?"

"I do."

". . . After the war, when we were demobilized, your father said to me: 'Where will you go? Come and live with us.' I refused. 'I'm not fit to live with anyone,' I told him, 'I'm poison.' He argued, tried to persuade me. But I wouldn't be swayed. I chose to be alone. To hover, with minimal contact, somewhere on the periphery of humanity . . ." Chuo's voice dropped, and Mitzko had to lean forward to catch it through the noise of the water. ". . . Alone, with my dreams of my wife . . . and my nightmares of Dachau . . ."

"What finally made you come to us?"

Chuo was silent. He might have answered, but from the highway, which was about a quarter of a mile to the east, came the faint but insistent sound of a siren. Chuo's head turned. His body stiffened. He was no longer the man she knew, but the one she didn't know: the man with the gun and the knife, the man who—though in the sudden happiness of seeing him again she'd brushed it aside—had run away from jail. "Chuo—"

He did not turn to her.

"The police are looking for you—"

100

Effortlessly, in silence, he rose. "What else would you expect them to do?"

She hesitated, but only for an instant. "Chuo, turn yourself in."

"What's that?"

"Go back, Chuo."

"Chuo never goes back."

"But they'll find you, Chuo—" Her voice quavered: "They'll do you harm. They'll—" She didn't finish.

He came close to her. She could see that he'd aged, and also that he'd hardened. He was tight-lipped, gaunt-cheeked; his eyes had the look of a man who has witnessed the forbidden. In that single instant of moonlit revelation, she knew that she could never recover the old Chuo, that she could only deal with the new one. She groped desperately in her mind for a way.

But he spoke first: "You're a woman now, Mitzko."

"Yes . . ."

"Help me."

"Chuo—"

"Don't try to control me. Help me."

"What do you want?"

"Clothes—I need to remove this prison suit." He placed his hands on his shirt. "And I need food. I haven't eaten in—a while."

"Then you mean to keep running?"

"Never mind what I mean. Will you bring me the clothing and food?"

She didn't reply. If she sought guidance, she could not find it in the hoots of an owl, the rasp of the river on the rocks, the rustle of leaves in a slight breeze; all spoke an unknown language. The answer was only inside her. Nowhere else.

"Mitzko, I'm waiting."

"I'll help."

"Good." He reached out a hand and touched her cheek, lightly, lovingly, as in days of old. "I'll wait in the cave. Remember where it is?"

The cave was downstream, about a hundred yards. The two of them had often feasted on fish there; he'd caught the fish in the river, she'd gathered the twigs and branches for the fire. "I remember," she said sadly.

"Good." He turned and started downstream. "Hurry," he called over his shoulder.

She went as quickly as she could.

Chapter 24

Her parents were still at work in the big house—she was in luck. She went at once to Chuo's old room, but found the door locked. Then she remembered: out of respect for his comrade (and, though he never spoke of it, perhaps in the belief that Chuo would one day return), Akira had shut the room up. Initially, after Chuo's arrest, the police had come to search and ransack the room; Akira had subsequently restored order. She had no idea where he'd put the key, and there was no time to look. It meant that she'd have to take her father's clothes, but they had to be old ones, ones that he might believe he'd already discarded. Such garments would be found hanging in the toolshed.

So she went first into the kitchen to get the food. She could take what she wished, but had to be careful not to take too much. Komako was a frugal and meticulous housekeeper who kept track of everything. Into an old cloth napkin, Mitzko put hard cheese, sausage, several cans of sardines and beans, raw carrots, walnuts, and a bar of chocolate; she added two cans of evaporated milk and a small, cheap can opener. In the bread box, there was a half-loaf of rye; she would tell her mother that it had been moldy and she'd thrown it out. When all was packed, she carefully folded the ends of the napkin together and knotted them.

The toolshed was locked, but she knew just where to find the key: up on a nail to the right of the door frame. She entered, pulling the door shut behind her. There was no need to switch on the light; she knew every square inch of the place by heart. She took a worn pair of pants, one of several falling-apart jackets, and an ancient, cast-off cap that had been lying in a corner ever since she could remember. She made the clothing into a roll, which she tied with a cracked leather belt. With a hand on the doorknob, she hesitated. Was there anything else? This was her final chance. She thought hard. Anything? There was.

At the rear of the shed stood a tall cabinet in which her father housed tools, irrigation parts, nails and screws and the like. She bent, fumbled along the bottom shelf, and at length closed her fingers over the object she wanted. Before she lifted the roll and bundle to leave, she opened her hand. A nickel-plated compass, whose luminous dial glowed at her in the dark, lay in her palm. Some weeks after Chuo first came, he'd given it to her. "You already have a compass inside you," he'd said with a smile. "This one is for outside." When he shot the general and was taken to prison, she'd transferred it from her room to the shed. In the first rush of bitterness and anger, she had wanted to throw it away. But somehow, she couldn't. Now, she'd give it back to him. It would be of help in the outside world, but only he could deal with the compass inside him.

Around the corner of the shed, she stopped abruptly. Down at the entrance of the estate were the flashing red lights of squad cars. She knew they'd come to look for Chuo, that she had to get out of sight. Within seconds, she had dashed across the open yard and ducked into the stable. Sanctuary here would be short-lived; the police would comb the grounds and buildings, search everywhere. She had to disappear quickly. But how? Anxiously, she paced back and forth in front of the stalls. There wasn't time for anxiety. She had to make a decision and act. Suddenly, she found herself at the white mare's stall. Garrett's horse. She'd ridden all over the valley with Garrett, but never on her own. He'd given her one lesson, and though he had promised others, no more had occurred. Wraith-like in the dim light of a single bulb above the feed bin, the mare stretched her neck; hesitantly, Mitzko touched the silky muzzle.

If there was a chance, the mare was it. Mitzko might ride out the rear entrance, cut through the orchards, and reach the river path before the police had spread across the estate. At once, she set down her parcels on a bale of straw. Garrett had shown her how to fasten saddle and bridle; it was a matter of finding the right ones and then remembering how. It mightn't be easy, but she had no other choice. She looked around. All of the riding gear was hung at the far end of the stable. She believed she could recall exactly where the mare's tack was kept.

"So here you are!"

She whirled.

"Mitzko! I've been looking high and low! I was going to saddle up the mare and scout around—" Garrett spread out his arms to embrace her.

But she stepped back. "Saddle the mare," she ordered.

Garrett stared at her. "You were going to do it yourself— that's why . . . you're here . . . in the stable. Am I right?"

"Garrett—please—hurry!"

As he cinched the saddle in place and fitted on the bridle, he said: "I was late escaping from that damn reception! By the time I got to the tree, you were gone. I'm really sorry—"

"Never mind that now. Just hurry—"

Garrett led the mare from the stable and mounted; Mitzko shifted the roll and bundle so she could take his hand. As she swung up behind him, he asked: "What are those?"

She ignored the question. "Ride out the back gate," she said, "and cut through the groves to the river path. I want to get there as fast as we can. Please, Garrett, do as I ask."

Without a word, he obeyed her. But she knew that he was disturbed. They didn't hide things from each other, one of the chief strengths of their relationship. Later on, when he got back to the estate and learned that the police were scouring the area for a fugitive, he'd know why she had the parcels and to whom she was taking them. But she couldn't tell him now. He might try to dissuade or prevent her—or even to take Chuo. She had chosen a course; there was no turning back. Nor could she know where the course would lead.

The mare flew. The distance from the rear gate to the road that traversed the groves was short; soon, they were riding down a corridor through the trees. She was silent as was Garrett. He was tense; her encircling arm felt the tautness in his body. After they reached their destination and he'd asked the inevitable questions, they would part from each other—in silence and in tension. It would be the first real crisis between them. Somehow, it would have to be resolved. She didn't know how. She was afraid. Even the hooves of the mare beating buoyantly on the earth couldn't comfort her.

Beyond the last grove was an open field; where the field ended, the path to the river began. Garrett slowed the horse, reined her in. They were motionless. "We're here," he said. "What now?"

Without answering, she dismounted.

"What's this all about?"

She looked up at him. His jaw was set; his eyes demanded a reply. Mechanically, he wound the reins around his knuckles. She held tightly to her parcels. "I have to go on now, Garrett. Alone."

"Go where?"

She shook her head.

106

"Mitzko—tell me where you're going."

"I can't, Garrett."

His eyes were dark. Impatiently, with a savage energy, he unwound the reins. And yet he was cold—like some drop-forged tool. "Can't or won't," he said. "It comes to the same damn thing."

"Trust me, Garrett."

He was silent.

It pained her to look at him; there was nothing more she could say. No way to explain. She turned and started down the path.

"Mitzko—"

She kept going. There was a moment of stillness, then the mare's retreating hoofbeats broke it.

As Mitzko approached the cave, a cricket sang: solitary, shrill, steadfast in sadness. She parted the bushes that screened the entrance, and stooped inside. It took time for her eyes to adjust to the darkness, and then she made him out: he was sitting cross-legged on the dirt floor at the rear. He didn't move, but she knew he wasn't asleep; he looked like a stone idol in some Far Eastern temple. Pebbles and small rocks popped under her feet as she went forward. Though there was no need, she spoke his name: "Chuo . . ."

"You came . . ."

"You knew I would."

He nodded. "I knew," he said, "but you didn't. You entertained your doubts, but in the end . . . you honored my certainty . . ."

Mitzko put the roll of clothing down and then the bundle of food. "I brought what I could."

"I'm grateful."

She extended a hand. "And here's something else—"

He reached out and took the compass. For a moment,

there was silence. Then, looking up, he said gently, in a tone that brought all the free, happy days they'd had together back. "I remember . . ."

"Do you remember what you said when you gave it to me? About the 'outside compass' and the 'inner one'?"

"Yes. I do."

"I say the same thing to you, Chuo. The compass I returned will help outside. But that's all. You must use your own, inner one . . ." She steadied her voice. "Chuo, they're looking for you. You heard the sirens before . . . the police are all over the estate . . . they'll comb the valley. Chuo, they're armed with guns, they'll bring dogs. Stop running, Chuo—"

He did not respond.

"Turn back, Chuo," she pleaded. "Before it's too late—"

"Early? Late?" He shrugged. "I don't consider them anymore."

"The general didn't die; in fact, he's getting well. He'll be out of the hospital. You may be pardoned one day—who knows?"

His laugh, harsh and bitter, filled the cave—but only for an instant. "Do you think I recognize their right to pursue me?" he said disdainfully. "I'm not the criminal; I don't need their pardon. It is I who will never forgive them for murdering my wife and my child. Edwards is the guilty one!"

His eyes clouded. "In April of 1945, I entered Dachau. A young girl, perhaps your age—a living skeleton—fell on her knees before me. 'Kill me,' she said. 'Get it over with.' I wept. 'We're American soldiers,' I said. 'We came to free you.' And then I thought: 'My own people are in American camps, but I cannot free them—' "

He stared at her. "Your father and I wandered among the skeletons in a daze. He gave one of the inmates some K rations. The man vomited, fell to the ground. He hadn't eaten for so long that he couldn't digest the food. He was liberated at last—but he died . . ."

Chuo shook his head. "Those inmates . . . those people . . . those almost-corpses: why had they suffered so, suffered beyond all description? Because they were Jews. Just as we—my little family, my friends, my people—had been robbed of our possessions and shut in camps only because we were Japanese. General Edwards and his kind were the ones who actively made our prisons and tacitly declared that the Germans could torture and annihilate the Jews . . ."

His voice altered. He stopped speaking of Dachau, its gas chambers and crematoria. Now, he spoke of the time he had lived with his wife in their own house on their own land, before all had been taken from them. Of how his wife had looked, smiled, spoken, walked; of her gentle spirit, her caring ways. He had never discussed this period with Mitzko; she tried to follow, but couldn't really concentrate, let alone retain what he told her. His voice overwhelmed her. It was charged with pain and anger; she found it hard to tell which was the dominant emotion.

Then he was silent. Just a man's empty body in a cave. Now Mitzko knew exactly what was inside him, what preoccupied his mind, ruled his heart. She remembered a picture in a book she'd read as a child: duck hunters on the shore of a lake. Guns at the ready, they crouched behind the screen that hid them from their unsuspecting prey. It was that way with Chuo. He showed one man to the world, another waited behind the blind. Sorrow—the sorrow of loss she felt she couldn't prevent—swept over her.

There was everything and nothing to say. She thought she heard the sound of the river, but she knew that she was deceived: the river was too far away.

Chuo rose. "Little Mitzko . . ." he murmured.

"I know . . . it's time for us to go. This is good-bye . . ."

"We'll meet again—"

She was silent.

"Little daughter . . ."

But Mitzko was already running from the cave.

Chapter 25

The following Saturday, Garrett was gone.

During the week, he'd made no attempt to contact or meet her. Early on, without believing that he'd appear, she had waited at their regular meeting places: the toolshed, the stable, even by the fallen tree. Time dragged by and confirmed the bitter fact that he would not appear; she realized that the waiting was more a forlorn gesture than anything else. The bitter truth was that their rupture was bound to be inevitable. She had known as much when he left her at the river path with her bundles. It was clear that he'd ride back and encounter the police and discover that Chuo had fled prison, and deduce that the clothing and food were for the fugitive. Had Garrett gone to the police and told them what he had learned? She was certain that he hadn't, that it was not in his nature.

She had expected the loss, but not resigned herself to it. On Friday night, the last before he left for West Point, she'd stood in the dark and gazed at the big house, up at the window she knew was his. It was lit, and remained so until nearly midnight. She'd wanted to get a glimpse of him. But he never showed himself. Around eleven, someone lowered the shade. A woman. It was done in a flash, so Mitzko saw almost nothing. But she saw that it was a young woman. Perhaps the daughter of the major general. Perhaps someone else. Someone Garrett had never mentioned to her. Someone from a past that Mitzko had never touched.

It didn't matter. She and Garrett were through. She had

elected to do what she did; he had chosen to react as he saw fit. Komako was right: she belonged in one world, even if she didn't properly know what that world was; he belonged in another. Still, she'd stood looking up at the window. Had longed to see him one more time before he left. A curious longing! What was the use? He had come into her life; she had allowed it. For some months, they'd moved towards each other. Ultimate purpose didn't matter: the point was that they'd come closer. Suddenly, a wedge had split them apart. What of it? Nothing between them had been signed or sealed. Then nothing was really lost. Surely, it was logical.

That night, she slept fitfully. Ugly dreams kept her twisting and turning. Sometimes, the fleeing Chuo was trapped by the police and gunned down in cold blood, despite the fact that he'd thrown away his weapons and lifted his hands in surrender; sometimes, he burst out of ambush and shot policemen to death. In one dream, the clothes she'd given him in shreds, Chuo took refuge in the stable. He was in the white mare's stall; the horse reared back. Mitzko tried to warn him, but Garrett covered her mouth with his hand, and the mare kicked in Chuo's skull. When Garrett freed her mouth, she screamed: "Why? Tell me why?"

She wakened in a cold sweat. The clock said it was just past five; ribbons of daylight filtered in at the window. She had no desire to risk sleep again: she was relieved to be up. Noiselessly, she got dressed and left the house. The valley was buried in mist. Quickly, she walked down the path to the main gate, then she hid herself behind the cypress tree that had sheltered her once before. Twenty minutes or so went by; then the silence was broken by the sound of the opening front door of the general's house. Two voices seemed to collide: Garrett's and the voice of a woman—Mitzko presumed it to be his mother's.

Beyond the outer fence, a car came crawling along the road, the beams from its headlights crumpled by whiteness. Mitzko heard the house door close, and then Garrett's footsteps. She knew them to the last detail, their impetuous yet controlled rhythm. Opposite the gate, the car braked; Garrett called out. Someone's name—probably the driver's. There was an answering greeting; it, too, was garbled. Mitzko shifted her position, and strained to see. But Garrett was no more than a grayish wraith, a blur. A car door squealed, luggage thudded onto the floor, the door slammed shut. Mitzko stepped out from behind the trunk of the tree. The car engine flared. She ran forward, determined to shout, "Good-bye!" She reached the fence in time to see the fading red scars of the taillights.

Chapter 26

More than all else, Mitzko was numb.

She functioned well, performed responsibly, did what was expected of her, made no complaints. Komako had no fault to find in the way she did her chores at home; if anything, her teachers noticed a more meticulous approach to her schoolwork. She was up promptly at six, and went to bed exactly at ten, filling her waking hours with her tasks and her obligations. It seemed the only way for her. Garrett had departed without a word, in anger and undoubtedly in disillusionment; Chuo was a fugitive from the law. Mitzko chose to bury her pain and her fear in the numbing monotony of daily routine.

Between mother and daughter, the tension had eased. Komako never mentioned Garrett by name, never repeated her warning. There was no need. The tempter was gone; the danger had passed. Komako sensed that the parting between Mitzko and the general's son had been traumatic—a sudden rupture, rather than some romantic pledge to the future. She knew that Mitzko had been hurt. But Komako felt that a minor wound now was infinitely better than a major disaster later. Mitzko was injured, but, thank heaven, she had not been devastated! To alleviate the pain, Komako tried to get closer to her daughter.

One Saturday, she said: "Mitzko, we haven't been shopping together in ages. Father told me that he's driving into town this afternoon—how about coming along?"

"I don't think so, Mother."

114

"You really need a new blouse, Mitzko—the pink one's all worn out. Father will be involved in his own business. We'll be alone, just the two of us—"

"Too much homework, Mother. Thanks, anyway." Mitzko forced a smile. "Some other time, maybe . . ."

On a Wednesday, when she'd finished her usual round of work early, Komako proposed that she teach her daughter to cook a new dish. She put on an apron—one that Mitzko had sewn for her a year or so ago—and got all the necessary ingredients ready and arranged all the pots and pans on the stove. Then she hurried to Mitzko's room. "It's an unusual curry recipe," she said with enthusiasm that wasn't insincere. "I found it in a magazine. It sounds wonderful! Shall we give it a try?"

Mitzko shook her head. "I have an exam tomorrow morning. Physics. My worst subject—" She squeezed a note of promise into her voice: "Next week, there'll be less pressure. Thank you for asking me, Mother."

Mitzko knew what Komako intended. But her mother's good intentions couldn't help her. Pain was a powerful enemy. It could defeat a mother's love. It could crack the mind. Break the heart. Pain was a cunning adversary: it could erode the protective coating of numbness. As the days and weeks went by, her protection wore away. It was her nature; little by little, she would test the level of pain that she could manage. Garrett, especially, was on her mind. He'd be home from West Point for Christmas, only several weeks distant. They wouldn't see each other, of course; would have nothing to do with each other. But it didn't matter. She knew herself: the fact that he was there would pervade her life.

As superficial as it was, Mitzko began once again to avoid her mother's company. Komako's attempts to draw closer made her uneasy. Confiding in someone else, Mitzko believed, was worthwhile. But it took a certain strength to do so; she seemed to lack the strength, or the will. She was more relaxed with Akira. He made little or no emotional demands. He never tried to comfort or to "save" her; he seemed willing to accept her as she was. When she spoke, he did not care much what she said; he gave her the feeling that it was enough for her to be near him. She knew that he wanted nothing from her, but sensed that he needed her. Though he never talked of it, her father was also in pain. She saw it in his eyes. It was pain that he would not bring to his daughter, could not bring to his wife.

Chuo. His escape from prison had shaken Akira to the core. The police and then the state troopers and then the FBI had come; they'd searched the estate with fine-tooth combs; they'd questioned Akira. He had nothing to tell them; they believed he was concealing something. He endured the grillings well: it was the rank suspicion, the very idea of the questioning that so disturbed him. They interrogated Komako as well; for her it was unpleasant, but not critical. She had no positive emotional investment in Chuo. She had accepted the fact that he would live with them solely out of regard for her husband; despite her resolve, her feelings for their guest had cooled. Eventually, because of Mitzko's close relationship with him, they had soured. The shooting of the general had shocked her, and it had also justified her disapproval.

Akira was well aware of how Komako felt. Chuo was one of the rare issues on which husband and wife disagreed. The escape distressed him, left him quite alone. He became preoccupied with Chuo's fate. After supper, he scoured the daily paper and intensively pursued the radio news for reports on the hunt for the fugitive. There were rumors of alleged sightings, stories about his supposed whereabouts, but they came inevitably to nothing. Komako's prediction was uncharacter-istically grim. "He's a fool for running," she told her hus-band. "In the end, they'll find him and kill him."

Disconsolately, Akira looked up from his newspaper. He shook his head. "No, they won't. He'll kill himself first."

Mitzko, who was not in her room but happened to be in the hallway, overheard. She did not agree with either of her par-ents. In her heart, she believed something entirely different: the general, completely recovered, would come home; Chuo, realizing his folly, would turn himself in; the authorities, un-derstanding his misguided intentions and somehow in touch with the pain that had motivated his deed, would grant him pardon; and the escapee would be free to return to them. She could not entertain the thought of it ending any other way.

A phantom Chuo remained at large, bound for the myste-rious destination he'd chosen. Christmas drew near; there were only several weeks to go. As the days went by, Mitzko's painstakingly fashioned numbness faded. To cut the edge of the pain and keep her balance, she went out on walks into the countryside. Some days, they were "Chuo walks"; other days, they were "Garrett walks." The old sites and scenes, which she'd abandoned for so long, gave her bittersweet pleasure. She spent hours on these excursions, lost in memory—as if the happiness of the past could somehow anesthetize the harshness and uncertainty of the present.

There were two weeks to go until Christmas. And then one. On Friday afternoon, Mitzko came home from a walk that had taken her to the river and back. Visibly uncomfort-able, Komako greeted her at the front door. "You have a vis-itor," she told her daughter.

Mitzko froze. How was it possible? Garrett had never once come to her house; never, in more than a passing, civil saluta-tion, met either of her parents. He would never intrude: never drop in without an express invitation. Or would he? She studied her mother's face; Komako's features were composed, but her eyes were clouded with an anxious light. But how could Garrett be there? He was scheduled to arrive home on the twenty-fourth, the day before Christmas. Ages ago, he'd told her that—and she had never forgotten it.

"Aren't you coming in?" Komako said.

Sitting on the pink sofa in the living room was Toge. When Mitzko entered, he rose stiffly, as if someone had yanked him up on a string. He was dressed in an obviously new blue suit and wore a starched white shirt and floral-patterned tie. His face had been scrubbed; his glossy black hair was slicked back; with both hands, he held tightly to a bouquet of flowers wrapped neatly in silver paper. "These are for you," he said, offering them.

Mitzko stared at him in disbelief. At once comic and pathetic, he reminded her of a character in one of the films she saw occasionally with Fumiko at the movie theater in town.

"Here," he said again, "these are for you."

Mitzko took the bouquet from him, and her mother accepted it from her.

"It's so thoughtful of you," smiled Komako, already on her way out of the room. "They're lovely. I'll put them in water."

Toge sat on the sofa again; Mitzko seated herself on a chair to the right. She was at a loss. She had no idea what he was doing there or wanted, or of what she should talk. "Thank you very much for the flowers," she told him after an awkward silence.

Then it was quiet again. Uncertainly, she watched him. His face was expressionless, but his hands, placed cumbrously on his knees, trembled. He saw that she was looking at him and cleared his throat. "Mitzko," he said in a sudden, almost violent spurt of voice, "I—I'm sorry—" And he went on to tell her at length, and in what she felt was unnecessary detail, about his behavior on the sidewalk near the ice cream parlor and on the path to the river and how he was ashamed of and regretted it. "I didn't mean to hurt you," he told her. "I don't know what got into me. I'm sorry. I apologize—"

As he spoke, his thin face contorted; his gestures were irregular and disjointed: he looked grotesquely abject, foolish, like a clown struggling to play Hamlet. She could only pity him.

"Toge, I understand . . ." she ventured lamely.

He wasn't through. "It will never happen again, Mitzko. I promise you. I swear it. I want you to forgive me, Mitzko; I want us to be good friends"—he swallowed—"to go out together—"

She could appreciate the effort he was making; she allowed him to satisfy himself. But it left her empty. When at last he finished, there was again silence. Then, steeling herself, she said: "Toge—"

Ramrod-straight, he sat waiting. He was all attention—heaven only knew what he expected to hear. "Yes, Mitzko—"

She leaned forward. "The man—"

"What man?"

"That night, Toge. The man in the woods. On the path to the river. Remember?"

Toge paled. "What about him?"

Mitzko looked around to make certain that her mother hadn't returned to the living room. "You haven't told anyone about seeing him," she said in a lowered voice, "have you?"

"Told . . . whom?"

"The po—anyone at all—"

He shook his head. "It's none of my affair," he said. "I don't want to be involved."

Mitzko heard the shuffle of her mother's deliberate footsteps; she signed with a finger set to her lips for Toge to be silent.

"I've prepared tea," Komako announced. She beckoned to the visitor. "Come, Toge—drink with us."

In the kitchen, the table was set daintily, with the fine dishware and cloth placemats and napkins; in the center, arranged meticulously in a porcelain vase, were the flowers that Toge had brought.

It took some forty minutes for the three of them to drink the tea and eat the sugar-coated cookies which Komako had baked the night before. The time, passed in small talk, clumsy gestures and artificial smiles, seemed unending to Mitzko. Eventually, it was over. Thanking his hostess and her daughter profusely, Toge rose. But at the door, as the guest was about to depart, Komako held him in a web of maddening chitchat. Mitzko squirmed. Finally, to her enormous relief, Toge was gone.

Over the sink, as she washed the cups and saucers that Mitzko would dry and put away on the shelf above the counter, Komako said: "Toge is so respectful and well-groomed. He's a fine young man, is he not?"

Mitzko nodded. "I'm sure he is."

Her mother carefully wiped her hands on her apron; she said not another word on the subject.

But Mitzko knew exactly what she thought.

Chapter 27

In the Edwards family tradition, the big tree always went up on the front lawn four days before Christmas. This year, it was Wednesday. The truck bearing the spruce came up the road to the estate just after eight in the morning. Workmen climbed down; they were joined by members of the household staff and handymen, including Akira. The supervisor shouted instructions through a megaphone; his voice echoed over the sward back from the façade of the house. The truck had a winch: block and tackle rattled; ropes strained. Green and majestic and two stories high, the tree lifted and rose and speared straight up at the sky. Hammers banged the wooden stand firmly into place; ladders were raised; cartons were untied and flapped open. Directed by a senior member of the household staff, the routine yet engrossing ritual of decoration commenced. As she'd done every year since coming to the estate with her parents, Mitzko was there to watch. She reckoned that it would be safe enough: Garrett wasn't scheduled to arrive until Saturday.

As usual, she stood to one side, "in the wings," she put it to herself. She watched the process appreciatively, with aesthetic interest. But Christmas had no religious meaning for her. She was close to her father in that respect: the two were unconnected to any formal, organized faith. Like Akira, Mitzko respected her mother's right to pray. However, she doubted that Komako's prayers helped anyone but the woman who offered them. Praying lightened Komako's load;

121

lessened her pain; on occasion, it supplied the fuel for her spirit to soar.

Going up on the lawn, the great spruce—which the Edwardses always designated the "outside tree," as distinguished from the smaller but not an iota less regal tree which was installed inside the house on the twenty-fourth—had seemed resistant, a captive but unsurrendering giant. Now, as the multicolored bulbs and baubles and silver tinsel fluff draped its branches like chains, the spruce looked beaten and cowed and, despite all the finery, desolate. Mitzko questioned her decision to come out and watch. Maybe her break with Garrett had influenced her, or maybe she was older and saw life differently, but the Samson-like tree made her sad.

The men collected their gear and left. The truck rolled away. Shrill-voiced and gesticulating, the senior servant spelled out his last directions. Feet scurried up the rungs of the ladders. Ornaments passed from hand to hand. Emptied, the cartons were closed and sealed. But for the star to crown it, the tree was done. The director stepped back and turned. Three figures came slowly across the lawn. On the right, dressed in severe black, was the chief housekeeper; on the left, wearing a pristine white uniform and cap, was a nurse; between them, clad in a fuchsia dress with matching scarf, walked General Edwards's wife (never, for an instant, did Mitzko think of her as "Garrett's mother.") In her arms, like a precious infant, Mrs. Edwards bore the glittering gold star.

Reverentially, the servant who had managed the entire process took the star from her and passed it to the head handyman, Carlos. Though it wasn't at all necessary, two subordinates held a ladder steady, and Carlos ascended. In the sight of all, he fixed the star precisely into place. For a moment, he remained to admire what he'd done, then he came down. On the ground, someone plugged the cord into the socket of an extension line. The tree was finished. Ready to dominate the lawn and, one might think, the world. But it would not be lit now. That would wait until nightfall when, according to another Edwards custom, one of the family members would switch it on from the house.

So the spectacle was over. The tools were collected; the empty cartons were packed in careful order onto a waiting wagon and removed to storage; down to the smallest particle, the litter was cleared away. Slowly, turning now and then to make certain that nothing had been overlooked, the servants and workmen, including Akira, trooped off. As was the case every year, Mitzko watched them go, then it was time for her to leave. Yet she remained in her place. She had a clear sense of something extraordinary in the air. The strange presence of a nurse, as well as the fact that Mrs. Edwards and the housekeeper didn't return to the house, clearly meant that something would happen.

Sedately, the three ladies moved to the front gate. Once there, the housekeeper checked her watch and turned to speak to her mistress. A hand at her scarf, Mrs. Edwards nodded—just a slight movement of her head, like that of a fuchsia-petalled flower in the wind. Moments later, as the women stood in silence, Mitzko heard the sound of a car. Beyond the fence, a private ambulance appeared and slid smoothly to a halt. Both driver and attendant got out. They rolled a side door open and carefully lowered the wheelchair with the man in it to the ground. Responsively, the housekeeper opened the gate. As the ambulance driver withdrew, the attendant pushed the chair onto the main walk.

Mrs. Edwards leaned down and kissed her husband's forehead. Gray-faced and unsmiling, the general acknowledged her greeting by lifting a hand. His body was covered to the waist by a plaid blanket; his upper torso was clothed in a

brand-new, beribboned uniform jacket. Smiling profession-
ally, the attendant departed, and the nurse took control of the
chair. Mrs. Edwards marched ahead at the general's side; the
housekeeper fell back and walked alongside the nurse. No
one spoke or broke the steady, procession-like rhythm of the
trek over the slate flagstones of the pathway.

As the party came abreast of the ornamented green tower
of the tree, General Edwards looked up. At his wife's prompt
signal, the nurse halted the chair. For an instant, Mitzko believed that the granite of the convalescent's face might soften.
But she was wrong. Stiffly, without emotion, the general
touched the fingertips of his right hand to the peak of his
gold-worked officer's hat. Then he broke the salute smartly
and dropped his hand. Nothing more. The party went on and
entered the house. In the stillness of the morning, the closing
of the front door rang out like a gunshot.

She promised herself. Pledged it. Swore over and over that
she wouldn't do it. She was resolved. Determined. Yet she
was uncertain of her strength to carry out her decision. She
yearned for confirmation from her mother, support from her
father. But neither of her parents was privy to the pain—or
the all but irresistible pull. Throughout the day, she was
tense; by the time it was dark, she was beside herself. Komako
asked her several times what was wrong; even Akira eyed her
strangely. She couldn't wait for supper to be over. When her
chores were finished, she went directly to her room and
locked the door.

It was impossible to read or write. All she could do was
think, and her line of thought led inexorably to pain. She sat
in darkness. Somehow, the hours passed and it was time to go
to bed. She didn't believe she'd fall asleep, but suddenly
dropped off. Over and over, she bobbed awake from an ocean
of formless, frightening dreams. Before dawn, she left the

bed. At her window, she stared blankly out as day emerged from chaos. What harm, she asked for the thousandth time, would it be for her to see Garrett arrive? But what good would it do? Suddenly, she abandoned the window and collected her scattered clothing.

Quickly, she dressed. Left her unmade bed and the silent house. Hurried to her place by the cypress. Waited for the taxi that would bring him to announce itself on the road. Glanced at her watch and saw that six had come. Knew that the taxi had just departed from the train station at the edge of town on its ten-minute ride to the estate. Began the final stretch of waiting. Then—only a moment or two before she was due to catch the sound of the cab's engine fumbling around the bend—quit the tree and ran frantically back down the path to her house. Heard, as she reached for the door-knob, the sound of the taxi's brakes at the main gate.

Chapter 28

Komako was in the kitchen. A ring of blue flame burned under the teakettle; finely diced vegetables lay in neat heaps on the counter. Mitzko had hoped to slip by, but her mother, cutting knife in hand, turned. "Been walking already?" she asked.

"Yes, Mother."

"So early?"

"I couldn't sleep."

The two stared not at each other, but at the barrier between them. There were questions Komako would not ask, just as there were answers Mitzko wouldn't give. Mother and daughter were warily silent; each of them preferred no word to the wrong word. Dressed in new overalls, Akira appeared in the hallway. "Good morning, Mitzko," he called out. "Want to drive into town with us? We're leaving after breakfast."

Mitzko shook her head.

She was grateful when her parents rode off in the pickup. Being alone and doing her chores helped her to balance. She felt that the crisis had passed. She had survived Garrett's arrival; she would endure his stay. There was nothing between the two of them. That was a fact of life: she could accept it. Briskly, she finished what she had to do inside the house and went out into the yard. It was just past ten. She placed the basket of laundry on the ground and began hanging out the clothes. From the branches of the willow came the perky chatter of the birds. She fixed two clothespins to one of Akira's shirts and stooped over the basket for another item.

Above her, a passing crow cried out stridently. But it wasn't the cawing that made her glance up. It was another sound. Footsteps. Terribly familiar footsteps.

She saw before all else the uniform. Blue-gray cloth cut razor-sharp, buttons running severely up the tunic's front, broad-striped trousers: not the outfit of a high school cadet, yet not that of a soldier either. Slowly, as if she were likely to upset some delicate balance, she rose. There was no need to brush back any of the clothing; his head and shoulders were visible over the lines. He was hatless, and his hair was rumpled; his high-necked collar was open at the throat. Strangely calm—like a sailor in the eye of a storm—she stared at him. "Garrett—"

"Hello, Mitzko."

"I knew you were back. But I didn't expect to see you."

He shrugged. "Here I am."

"We should talk, Garrett."

"Yes, we should."

"As soon as we can."

He nodded. "Tonight. It's Christmas Eve—there'll be a gathering in the house. I'll meet you later on. Say, midnight—"

"Where?"

The expression in his eyes flickered desperately between control and surrender. But his voice was even, almost casual. "At the stable," he said.

"All right."

They didn't want to make small talk; what they really had to say had to wait until their meeting. Still, they didn't want to part; even the silence between them was valuable. Divided by clothesline, they stood and felt the growing tension of desire. Each became aware of how much he or she wanted to touch the other. But they restrained themselves: in his or her

127

own way, each had long ago learned that without discipline he or she could obtain no such thing as freedom.

It was difficult for him to speak. "At midnight, then," he said finally.

"Yes."

She watched him go. His stride was measured, graceful, resolute. One could see that he carried his lineage with him proudly, but that it was also a burden to him. It occurred to her that he was like a man who suffers a wound in battle: the man may be proud of the wound, but then doubtful about the battle. She watched him take leave of their yard—the "enemy territory" into which he had dared to intrude—and step onto the gray flagstones of the path. For the first time since she'd known him, she saw his tragic streak. He knew that he had his father's nature in him, and wanted fiercely to desert it for another, unfamiliar realm. He wasn't at all sure he could do it, but he was certain that she could show him the way. That mutual knowledge was an essential part of what drew and bound them to each other.

He reached the crosswalk to the big house and turned, then the hibiscus hedge hid him from view. For some moments, she stared at the last spot he'd been and now was not. The retina of her heart was branded with him. Forever—no matter what else happened. At length, she turned around and bent over to the basket. She selected one of her mother's nightgowns, lifted it, and shook it out. Pinning it to a line, she again thought of him. Of his sudden return: solemn, brave, agonized. Begging silently for the help he knew would be given him. She stooped and pulled out a pair of Akira's pants. "In healing another," she thought as she straightened up, "one can heal one's self . . ."

It was a good thought. A true thought. But somehow it filled her with fear.

Chapter 29

They rode east out the back entrance, veering away from the road that cut through the orchards. Garrett urged the mare forward; Mitzko held him firmly about his waist. To the right, she spotted the great spruce on the estate's front lawn. Ablaze in a rainbow haze of light, it was no more than several hundred yards from them—and yet it seemed to be infinitely remote, like some glittering galaxy in deepest space. She wanted to say, "Look at the tree, Garrett!" But she said nothing. She hesitated to break the silence. In the stable, she'd found him waiting; the mare was saddled and ready to go. He had mounted and helped her get into place behind him. But they hadn't spoken. It wasn't time yet. They would know when it was.

She closed her eyes. Abandoned herself to the motion, to the beating of hooves, to the feel of Garrett's back and ribs. In the stable, thick with the smell of hay and horses which she'd missed for so long, they didn't embrace either. An unspoken taboo kept them apart. Aside from his hand grasping hers and lifting her, there'd been no physical contact between them. But now it was different. Suddenly, it was different. Beyond the shadow of a doubt, she knew that before the night had ended, they'd be together as man and woman. She hadn't planned it, considered it, even given it a thought. Now she was certain. His body had told hers. His mouth had been silent. But his body had revealed the secret. She hadn't spoken a word. But her body had confirmed that it would be so.

She had passed over the usual adolescent stages of fumbling towards the other gender. Skipped the familiar kissing and caressing and fondling, the clumsy, tentative touching and exploring and groping. She had missed out—by nature or choice, or more likely by the two combined—on what she'd heard discussed and boasted about in the locker room of the gymnasium, or furtively whispered and giggled over in the corridors and cafeteria and playground at school, or smirked lasciviously at in the corner ice cream parlor. She had avoided or eluded or escaped what a roiled-up Fumiko, engaged in unburdening herself, had from time to time confided about sexual exploits and misadventures. "He undid my bra," Fumiko told her, "and put his hands on my tits. Then he massaged my nipples with his fingers." Or, "He slid his hand up my thigh, and tried to get it into my panties. I was very hot— but I wouldn't let him. That's going too far, don't you think?" Mitzko had no answer. She always listened patiently and with attention. But she refrained from comment or criticism. She was a friend. Not a counselor. Or a judge.

Once, after a richly detailed description of a sexual encounter with a classmate, Fumiko asked Mitzko if she masturbated.

Mitzko shook her head.

Fumiko laughed. "I do it all time," she admitted. "I think about being with boys I like, and I make myself come. It's great! Why don't you try it and see?"

Mitzko shrugged.

"I'll show you how if you want—"

"No, thanks."

She wasn't a prude. Or what the girls at school called "frigid" or "angel" or "saint" or "Goody Two-shoes." Something else was at stake. It was simple: what the rest of them did simply didn't suit her. She knew the anatomy of sex, was familiar with the mechanics. Occasionally, she had sensual dreams and indulged in erotic fantasies. But they were vague, insubstantial, uncompelling. They were amorphous clouds that blew in and readily dispersed. Prurient stories and practices didn't arouse her. Haphazard, casual male advances didn't interest her. She felt—she knew—that sex was a profound part of the world, of her. But no one called her to it. Until Garrett . . .

They rode on until they reached the creek, and then followed the bank to the north. At once, Mitzko knew where they were going. About a mile up ahead, was a little hollow, screened in by a thick growth of shrubs and trees. A lush layer of grass covered the earth, fed by the water of the creek which at that point fanned out to form a shallow pool. They'd been there before—on their first night-ride. Both she and Garrett had been taken by the beauty and privacy of the place. "We've discovered our secret hideout," he said. "It's lovely."

"It's more than that," she told him. "It's—the Garden of Eden."

"Not quite," he laughed. "But close."

The mare gave her all to Garrett. By the time they arrived, she was trembling with the effort and sheeted with sweat. As Mitzko looked on, Garrett walked the horse slowly to and fro until she'd cooled, led her to the creek to drink, brought her back up the slope and tethered her to a tree. That done, he turned and took Mitzko's hand. Leading the way, he helped her squeeze through the foliage. The branches of the last bush snapped back. The two of them were enclosed. He put his arms around her waist; she threw hers about his neck. They sank to the grass. It was time . . .

His body covered hers. She felt his heaviness, yet he was light. He seemed to be sleeping, yet she knew he was awake.

She sprawled there on the bed of grass, her legs still parted, her womanhood still grazing his manhood. As she stared past the curve of his cheek upwards, it seemed to her that all the host of lights from the Christmas tree on the lawn had, purified of their colors, risen like bubbles through space and embedded themselves in the firmament. Her eyes swept the unruffled, black expanse of sky. The vast distances were cancelled; the sense of hopeless isolation was gone; the stars were intimate and close. She felt content, replete, at peace. Like the heavens, she was radiant. Even the remote awareness that it wouldn't last could not blemish the perfection of the moment . . .

Chapter 30

They sat side by side on a flat rock, their shoulders touching. Except for the faint plashing of the brook, as its current entered and took leave of the pool, there was silence. When he picked up her hand and retained it in his, the tension returned. It was time to talk. And they knew it. Mitzko faced him. "You stopped seeing me," she said, "because of what I did the night before you left—that was the reason, wasn't it?"

"It was."

"And you still disagree with what I did?"

He stared at her. "Why did you do it, Mitzi?"

"Because I had to. He would have done the same for me."

Garrett shook his head. "You'd never pick up a pistol and shoot anyone, Mitzi."

She shrugged. "I don't know that. And you don't know for certain, either. Given the proper set of circumstances, I might very well shoot someone. Even kill him."

He looked away.

She didn't know whether he believed her or not; or whether what she'd said might drive him away, but she felt she had no option except the truth. "Why didn't you report the incident to the police, Garrett?" she asked him. "Why did you keep silent?"

"I couldn't tell the police, Mitzi . . ." His voice fell. "I was bitterly opposed to what you did. I still am. But I could never report you."

"Garrett, why didn't you say good-bye to me before you went away? Why didn't you write?"

"Because I never intended seeing you again."

"What made you change your mind then?"

He put his hand on her cheek. "My heart . . ."

"And when exactly did you decide to see me?"

"This morning. As soon as I got out of the taxi. It took me several hours to work up the nerve."

"A brave warrior like you?"

He smiled thinly. "Come on, Mitzi," he said. "You know as well as I that the hardest battle of all is a human relation . . ."

He had stayed through the truth. They could kiss. And relax again.

"Tell me about school," she said softly.

He told her that he loved—no, adored—school. That he led his entire class in grade-points; that he'd won a medal in rifle marksmanship; that he'd qualified for the fencing and boxing teams; that he fully expected to be chosen for the freshman football squad. "I'm going to go up in rank like a meteor," he told her with a fierce enthusiasm. "One day, I'll be the top cadet officer. The chief." He squeezed her hand. "I made myself that promise—and you know I never break promises!"

"So you're happy, Garrett."

"I'm really very happy," he said, looking off into the darkness again. "But—" He broke off.

"But what?"

He didn't reply; his body stiffened; he hunched forward. "I don't know how to describe it . . . how to approach it even—" Slowly, deliberately, as if he were moving the muscles to be sure they still worked, he shrugged. "Something's missing. Despite it all. I can't explain . . ."

"Try, Garrett—"

His eyes met hers. "I thought we might find whatever's

134

missing together, Mitzi. At least . . . we could look for it together—"

Suddenly, she had a clear and penetrating glimpse of the other part of him. She saw his softness, his generosity, his unspoiled innocence. In an instant, she beheld the gladiator who had willingly, believing now that all the world was not an arena of combat, flung away his lethal weapons and become instead a yearning, groping—even openly bewildered—boyman who, in embracing her, had dared to make himself vulnerable. So it was evident to her: he could leave his father if he chose to. But the struggle to choose was awesome. She knew that—and was moved.

"Are you crying?" he asked her.

"No."

"But you are, Mitzi! I can see the tears—"

"I'm—it's—" She had to search for the word. "Happiness—" she just managed to say. She said no more.

"And you," he said, breaking into her thoughts. "What are your plans? What'll you do when you graduate?"

"I'm going to State College."

"To study what?"

"I've decided to become a physical therapist," she told him. "I want to heal . . ."

"Yes," he nodded, "that suits you."

"I was born for healing, Garrett. How lucky for me to know it!"

On their slow ride back, she told him that she loved him. And was told that he loved her in return . . .

In the stable, the white mare pawed the straw and munched the double ration of oats Garrett had given her. Garrett held Mitzko in silence and then the two parted. Only when Mitzko was up on her front steps did she think to look at her watch. It said ten past five.

She entered the house quickly and bolted the door. Halfway along the hall, an instinct made her turn. In the foyer stood Komako, the thin light of dawn filtered over her like frost. Her hair had tumbled free and was in utter disarray; the hem of her nightgown reached down to her bare feet. To her startled daughter, she looked like a wraith forever condemned to wander the earth without rest . . .

Chapter 31

With a hand that shook visibly, Akira held the newspaper out like a banner.

Almost with disdain, Komako turned away; either she'd already read it, or she wasn't interested in looking at what her husband displayed. Mitzko saw the expression of consternation on her father's face and at once took the paper from him. Akira was sitting in his armchair; Mitzko moved more into the light of his reading lamp. She bent forward.

On the front page, in the right-hand corner of the bottom section, was what was obviously a prison photograph of Chuo; beside it ran a three-column article whose bold-faced headline read:

WANTED FUGITIVE SIGHTED
NORTH OF SAN FRANCISCO;
ONCE MORE ELUDES POLICE DRAGNET

Keeping the paper steady with effort, she read an account of how Chuo had been recognized by inhabitants of a small town just to the north of San Francisco and pursued. The police gained ground and closed in, hoping to recapture him; there ensued what the author of the article called "an exchange of gunfire," but Chuo managed to get away "without so much as a scratch." The writer described him as an "escaped criminal," who had been serving time in a maximum-security state penitentiary for the "attempted murder" of a prominent citizen; Chuo was "heavily armed," "desperate" and "extremely dangerous." The article concluded with a notice that a reward of $5,000 had been posted by the authorities for "information leading directly to the apprehension and arrest of the escapee." Readers were invited to phone or send what they knew or imagined they knew to the newspaper, with total assurance that all disclosures would be received and reviewed in the "strictest of confidence."

Mitzko finished reading and glanced once again at the photograph, in which Chuo looked bleak and pathetic, like an ageing orphan.

Akira remained in his chair, but he was highly-agitated. "Chuo will die," he murmured hoarsely.

"He's a damn fool," said Komako bitterly. "If he doesn't turn himself in, he's bound to die."

Akira stared at her. "You don't understand, Komako, do you?" he said slowly. "You don't understand at all: Chuo wants to die."

Mitzko threw the paper down and went to her room.

Komako followed and knocked at her daughter's door. "Mitzko—let me in. I want to speak to you. Mitzko—"

"Please, Mother—just go away and leave me alone."

Garrett was going back to West Point the next morning; they'd made plans to meet that night by the fallen tree at ten. During the week, they'd managed to get together only twice because there had been much coming and going on the estate, and he had been involved in what he cryptically called "family affairs." He sensed her uneasiness and tried to allay it. "Dad's home from the hospital, as you know," he told her. "And this is a special time. So it's more difficult for me to disappear from the house."

"I see," she said.

He shook his head. "No, you don't," he told her. "You

138

don't see at all. But I want you to understand: I have obligations. He—Dad—makes certain that I keep them strictly."

"How strictly?"

"As strictly as he deems proper."

"And what about your feelings?"

"I—" he began, but didn't finish.

"He gives the orders and you obey them—is that it?"

"That's not a fair description! I owe him—"

"And yourself? What do you owe to yourself? And to me?"

"Let's not quarrel. Please, Mitzi. We have so little time . . ."

She saw his dilemma. He was with her now, but he was going back. He would pass through his father's ancient gate and return to the mock-fortress, the pseudo-battlefield. He would don armor and buckler, raise up sword and shield. He would box, fence, play football, shoot out a squirrel's eye at a hundred yards; ascend the slippery rungs of the hierarchical ladder until he stood bellowing alone at the top; pull the best grades in the academy's long history; fancy-dress and drill himself dizzy to triumph and glory. Tenderness and compassion would be folded and tucked crisply away for a rainy day; softness and reticence would go securely under lock and key. If the command were issued from on high, he would lay down his life. "For my flag," he'd gasp out with his last living breath. But it wouldn't be true. He would die just for the idea of flag. She was sorry for him. But more sorry for the both of them. For what they had. And might have.

She was at the fallen tree first—always a bad omen. But he wasn't late by much. Breathing hard, he arrived at a full trot. "Sorry," he sputtered. "Didn't mean to be late."

"The major general and his daughter?" she asked. But she got the line off lightly.

He was amused. "Not exactly," he said. "Two brigadier

139

generals and a chicken colonel." He smiled. "The colonel's a relative of the commandant at West Point . . ."

"I understand."

"Well, I should hope so."

Hand in hand, they walked slowly through the woods to the river. The bank was clear of trees and sloped down. A full moon was in the sky; its light swirled in soft tatters on the water. They stood and watched for a while. "I used to come down here when I was a kid and fish," said Garrett. "It was one of my favorite spots."

Instinctively, she wanted to tell him about her excursions to the river with Chuo, but had to restrain herself. Instead, she said: "I've always loved the river." Then she drew him up the path to the right.

"Where to?" he asked.

"You'll see."

They walked for several hundred yards to the cave. Parting the brush that screened the entrance, she asked: "Ever been here before?"

He shook his head.

They entered and held each other and made love. She gave and took fully, without effort. Lovemaking was natural for her: it left her with both repletion and hunger she'd never experienced before. Then she lay in his arms and let herself drift. He had to rouse her and say it was time to go. "If we must . . ." she murmured dreamily.

"We must, Mitzi."

They walked back in silence. When they were out of the woods, and the big house—made to look like a medieval castle by moonlight—swam into view, she said: "You can write to me care of Fumiko, my friend." She handed him a neatly folded slip of paper. "She lives just outside of town. Here's the address . . ."

"So," he said, taking the slip from her and pocketing it, "we're quite the same after all."

"What do you mean?"

"You have to keep things secret . . . because you're also subject to your parents' wishes. Right?"

"No, Garrett, you're wrong. I make my own choices. Always. Without interference. My parents express their opinions, but I decide for myself." Her smile was pained. "I just make every effort not to hurt them. There's a difference in our positions—I hope you understand it."

He didn't address the point, so she had no way of knowing whether he understood or not. He was abstracted, almost, she felt, indifferent to her. From his point of view, it was understandable. He was on the verge of leaving. Already, the other world called. When he embraced her and told her that he loved her, she trusted him. Believed in the power of his words. But she wasn't a fool: she did not in the least underestimate the power of the other world.

"I'll write," he told her, "care of Fumiko . . ." He patted his pocket. "I have the address."

"When will we see each other again?"

"Spring vacation." He kissed her for the last time. "Take care, Mitzi . . ."

Before she went to bed, Komako always saw to it that the house was in complete order. In her quick, determined, graceful fashion, she moved from room to room, tidying things up. Akira and Mitzko often teased her about it. "Nobody's awake to see," they told her, "so why bother?" But Komako paid no attention. Making certain that before she slept all was spic-and-span and in its appointed place was a fetish with her. As did prayer, orderliness comforted and sustained her. She believed that as God had established order from chaos, so were human beings obliged to follow suit.

As she passed through the front door, Mitzko saw at once that the house was in disarray. Akira's hat had fallen from a hook in the foyer and hadn't been rehung; his shoes were where he'd left them when he traded them for slippers. In the kitchen, there were teacups and spoons out on the table; a dish towel lay rumpled over the sink faucet. The kettle sat on the counter; the door to the pantry was open. She went into the living room. The standing lamp by her father's armchair was still on; open pages of his newspaper were scattered across the floor. On an end table stood Komako's sewing kit; its lid hadn't even been replaced. Mitzko was more amazed than taken aback. For the first time in her memory, her mother had gone to bed without straightening up. What did it mean? As she went about ungrudgingly doing the job herself, Mitzko considered the question. By the time she put the last cup in the cupboard, she was certain of the answer. Komako hadn't remained awake to say anything to her daughter; she'd let the household disorder speak for her. It meant that Komako knew precisely with whom her daughter was spending her time, and that she was profoundly concerned and unhappy about it. But the statement didn't change matters. It was a total failure. It could neither intimidate Mitzko nor in the least shake her confidence. When the toll of conscience sounded out, it was—just as she'd said to Garrett—her own bell that Mitzko harkened to. Always, Komako was free to counsel, advise, contradict, admonish or rebuke: never had she the right or the power to control.

Mitzko lay in bed without sleeping. Her window shade was up; the moonlight laved the floor of the room with mercury. Garrett would leave in the morning; she had no desire to stand at a distance—like a spectator in a stadium—and watch him depart. She pictured the taxi arriving and him stooping to get in, then the cab turning and disappearing around the bend. From that point on, the two of them would live parallel lives. At Easter time, they'd meet again. But what did that mean? When, if ever, would the separated lines of their lives converge? They loved each other: that was established. But what did love without union signify? Love without the single road down which they'd walk together? Would such a time ever come? She wondered . . .

Before her heavy-lidded eyes, the silvered floor turned to moon-paved stones. Where the stone ended, the main gate of the estate swung open. Through it, at furious speed, came the wheelchair. She wanted to run, but held her ground. The chair, its wheels spitting silver fire, rushed at her. In it, frozen as a chess piece, sat the general. He had one arm upraised. Did he brandish a cane or a sword? She couldn't tell. When, inches short of her, the chair screeched to a halt, she saw that it was a broomstick.

The general caught her amused look. "Don't be fooled," he cautioned. "The stick's just a warning! There are real weapons at my command: machine guns, mortars, bombs— anything I need!"

She tested some bedrock faith, some inveterate stubbornness. They were firmly in place, she was calm. "Why must we be adversaries?" she asked. "After all, aren't we both interested in Garrett?"

"Oh, but we're not adversaries, dear girl," the general corrected. "We're enemies. You see, you're interested in my son's weakness. I am concerned with his strength."

"So . . . we can never reach accord?"

The general's laugh was bitter. "Armistice is for the feeble; the strong man has his way." The broomstick, propped against one of the chair's wheels, had turned into a cavalry saber in a gold-and-silver–wrought scabbard; it lay comfortably across his rug-bound knees, and as he spoke, his fingers grazed it. "What you have to say, my girl, is of no importance. Your kind is gossamer; mine is steel. My folk control the world; yours hop to attention—or detention, as the case may be. Oh, you may fancy you've won a skirmish or even a battle, but you've already lost the war—" He lifted a hand. "Poor dear, you never even had a chance. Not, so to speak, a Chinaman's chance—"

Then, before she could reply, the wheelchair spun around and raced away. As it receded, she saw that it was no longer a chair but a taxi, the taillights gleaming back like uncompromising eyes. But whose? The general's? Her mother's? Garrett's? Or her own?

Chapter 32

The days moved ahead. Sometimes, they crept by her like a milk-train, making every local stop; sometimes, they roared down the track like an express. She perceived their motion, was uncertain of the destination. But she didn't preoccupy herself with ultimate goals; she lived in the present. Kept herself busy. Her schoolwork went exceptionally well, better than ever. She was up for awards in biology and math; she played varsity volleyball and sang in the senior choir. Two days a week, after classes were over, she volunteered her services in the town's old-age home; on Wednesdays, she worked in the school library.

Male admirers—foremost among them, Toge—pursued her: she rebuffed them all. Female classmates sought out her company: she remained aloof. She was polite, tactful, impeccably civil—but always guarded. Only to Fumiko did she speak at any length, or engage in any measure whatsoever of serious conversation. And even when she was at comparative ease with Fumiko, she retained the wariness; her deepest self remained inaccessible. That didn't bother Fumiko. She never conceived of a quid pro quo relationship; she was only too happy to confide her most intimate secrets to Mitzko. Even the fact that she was pregnant. "Will he stand by you?" Mitzko questioned.

"Will who stand by me?"

"Why, the father of the child, of course."

Fumiko shrugged. "I don't know who he is."

Several weeks later, she said to Mitzko: "It's okay. I'm not really pregnant."

"What do you mean?"

"I made a mistake."

But Mitzko was sure that she'd had an abortion.

It was Fumiko who faithfully brought her the letters from Garrett. She handed them over cheerfully, though Mitzko never satisfied the messenger's keenly aroused curiosity. The first week following Garrett's departure, there were three letters; two letters arrived each week after that; one came during the fourth. None was long. Most were sketchy, and centered for the most part on the writer's schedule of studies, duties, and accomplishments. All ended with the word "love."

In February, two-thirds of the month had gone by before a letter was delivered by Fumiko to her friend. It consisted of only several, hastily scrawled lines describing how busy and under what pressures Garrett had been. It ended, however, by telling Mitzko how much he missed her and how greatly he looked forward to seeing her at the Easter break. The word "love" was written in large letters and underlined.

"Who's this guy that writes to you from West Point?" Fumiko wanted to know.

"A friend," said Mitzko.

"Must be a good friend, eh?"

Mitzko made no comment.

"Where'd you meet him?"

"Around . . ."

Fumiko shifted her textbooks from one arm to the other. "Want to tell me a little bit about him?"

"No."

Fumiko looked genuinely disappointed. "Why not?"

"There's nothing to tell."

"That's not true!" exclaimed Fumiko with a frown.

But it was. Mitzko had nothing to tell Fumiko. Or anyone else. Garrett was an exclusive province, a private preoccupation. Their relationship was a world unto itself. Secret. Intense. Unfinished. When the time was ripe to let others know about the universe of love that she had discovered, she would. But only she—and she alone—had the power to decide when. Mitzko wrote back. She always mailed the letters herself from the post office in town. She wrote to Garrett about school. About her grades and interests and extracurricular activities and plans. Told him that all of the preparations for State College had been completed; her outstanding record during her senior year in high school had earned her a partial scholarship. Explained that she was proceeding on two tracks simultaneously: training her mind for the theoretical side of physical therapy, and building up her body to do the work. "I'm certain of my purpose," she wrote, "and sure of my abilities. I've made up my mind to become a superb physical therapist and work in a hospital. We're very much alike in that respect, dearest Garrett: when we make up our minds to do something, we succeed . . ."

About her home life, she wrote: "Things seem balanced— at least, for the time being. As always, Father's busy with work. On the estate, and around our place. If there's nothing much to do, he invents it. At night, he goes methodically through his newspaper and occasionally reads a book; lately, he's taken to making entries in what for years now he's called his 'personal encyclopedia.' I've never had even a glimpse of what's in it, nor to the best of my knowledge has anyone else in the world, including my mother . . .

"As things stand, my mother doesn't bother me, doesn't probe or pry. Since you went back to school and I'm essentially at home, in my room, every night, she seems to be more or less at ease. I'm sure that the future troubles her, but the truth is that the future disturbs us all. Mother can register dissatisfaction in the various ways she knows how; she can voice her opposition, but she can and will never command me to do her bidding . . .

"Both my parents, I feel, are apprehensive about my leaving for college in the fall. They certainly want me to go, but clearly sense an impending void; in many ways, I'll feel the same void. It's not to be helped, it's only natural. My chance to leave home has—as did yours—at last arrived, and I fully intend to take it. At this point, September seems a good way off, but it'll be here before we know it."

She signed all of her letters, "with deepest love, Mitzko." Love that was truly felt and meant, but not entirely understood—if ever it could be. Mitzko had already come to the conclusion that love was, like all of the most profound and important things in life, essentially a mystery. Time and growth helped to define it. And part of its charm was the endless search to understand it . . .

Garrett was slated to come home late in April. Mitzko knew the exact date and day of the week and train schedule down to the precise minute; this time, she planned to surprise him at the station in town. She'd have the joy of greeting him on his arrival and of sharing the cab ride to the estate; the taxi could drop her off just before it reached the last bend in the road. As the days flew, her excitement grew. She waited impatiently for word. But, from the middle of March on, she received no mail from him. She wrote several letters asking if all was well and sent them express. Nothing came in return. She became restless, and entertained the notion of telephoning him. But every time she decided to act, she resisted the impulse. Then, at the start of April, a letter finally arrived. Fidgeting and fussing, Fumiko handed it over. "That West Point guy again," she muttered.

Mitzko turned the envelope over, but didn't open it; she always read Garrett's letters alone, in private.

"I thought you two were finished," said Fumiko.

"Why would you think that?"

"Well, I mean, the guy hasn't written anything to you in months."

"In weeks," corrected Mitzko, at once angry with herself for responding.

"Whatever," said Fumiko.

At home, in her room, Mitzko slit the envelope with an opener. Inside was a brief, almost brusque note informing her that Garrett was not coming home for Easter. He gave neither reason nor explanation. There was nothing but the blunt statement and the usual sign-off, "with love." She was bewildered and dismayed. At once, she wrote to ask him about the sudden change of plans. What had happened? Was he ill and hiding it? Would he remain at school for the break to catch up on work? Was he being punished for some infraction? Would he travel elsewhere? Or what? He owed her an answer. She demanded it.

There was no reply. Then, in mid-April, something happened in the Edwards household. All activity seemed suddenly to grind to a halt. To a greater or lesser extent, Mitzko was aware of the Edwards family: peripheral but always there. Mrs. Edwards, regally attired and aloof-looking, could occasionally be seen riding—with friends or alone; her mount was a coal-black gelding; often, she visited the gardens or sat in the gazebo on the side lawn, sipping coffee; sometimes, she lounged at the pool. The general himself was taken regularly every morning by his nurse on a sweeping circumnavigation of the estate: Akira liked to say that one could set his watch by the measured progress of the wheelchair; there were frequent guests at the big house; and, of course, a never-ending series of parties and festivities.

But all of this ceased. Only a servant or two, looking unsupervised and rather lost, could now and then be glimpsed poking around on some errand of no particular urgency. Mitzko was puzzled and went to Akira to ask. "They're gone," he told her.

"Gone? What are you talking about? Where to?"

"The general and his wife have gone off on a trip. Just the other day, Carlos mentioned it to me. It's their anniversary and they're taking a cruise. He told me where they were going, but it slipped my mind. Somewhere up the coast, I think he said . . ."

"I see."

Akira was oblivious to his daughter's pain. "I believe that their son is coming from West Point to join them," he rambled on, fumbling with a length of rope he was trying to untangle. "Why do you ask?"

Mitzko averted her eyes. "No special reason. It's so quiet around here—I just wondered what was happening . . ."

Akira grunted and untied his rope.

To cope with what she had learned that afternoon, Mitzko buried herself in books. She had become adept at studying. She was strongly motivated and highly disciplined; when she studied, nothing could harm or disturb her. Biology, anatomy, physiology; medical textbooks dealing with the brain and the spine. After school was over, she trekked to the town library for books and then carried them home in shopping bags. On occasion, Fumiko accompanied her. "What're you going to do with so many books?" she asked.

"Read them, of course. What else?"

"But so many! And some are actual textbooks! Do you want to be a doctor or something?"

"I want to be good at what I do."

And she wanted to stave off the loneliness and desolation that shadowed her steps. Wanted to escape her mother's warning. Wanted to flee from what she'd always known might happen. So she studied to free her mind, and did chores and jogged for miles and exercised to build up physical stamina. One day, as she came back from a run that had taken her all the way to the creek, Akira spotted her. "Training for the Olympics?" he teased.

"For my own personal Olympics," she said.

And was able to smile.

Close to the end of the Easter vacation, she got a letter. Fumiko rode all the way from town on her bike to give it to Mitzko. "From that jerk at West Point!" she exclaimed, braking savagely and offering the letter over the handlebars. She favored Mitzko with what she believed to be a lascivious wink. "I bet it's a steamy one!"

Mitzko turned the envelope over. It was heavy—Garrett had apparently written at length—and was postmarked San Francisco.

"Go on, Mitzko—open it up . . ."

Mitzko stared at her.

"Come on, relax. For once, give us a break—"

Mitzko did nothing of the sort. Instead, she thanked Fumiko, said good-bye and went into the house. In her room, she tore the letter to shreds without reading a word. What Garrett had to say no longer interested her. What he had done—or failed to do—was all that mattered.

She got through the vacation safely and went back to school. If she'd worked hard before, she redoubled her efforts. Teachers couldn't find sufficient praise: her fervor, diligence, thoroughness, superb standard of performance in every area. She became a model for emulation. She had been wounded to the core, but she had not allowed the injury to become fatal. What had bound her to Garrett could be buried; what had hurt her could be overcome. She'd found a way out, and she followed the signposts . . .

Toward the close of May, as the two of them exited the lunchroom, Fumiko said: "I guess I'm not your private mailman anymore, am I?"

"I guess not."

"Sorry about that," said Fumiko. She smiled thinly. "I kind of got used to it, you know. I actually liked it. It was as if I was helping you to—" She didn't finish.

Mitzko was touched by the other's empathy. Despite Fumiko's promiscuity and pretenses at worldliness, there was something astonishingly naive and good-natured about her. Mitzko took her friend's hand, which she rarely—if ever—did. "I'm sorry too," she said, unable to keep the huskiness from her voice. "But there's nothing to do about it."

"Are you sure, Mitzko?"

"Quite sure."

During the first week in June, they were in the library together; Fumiko had insisted on helping Mitzko carry home the newest books she'd chosen. Out on the broad stone steps of the building, they paused to adjust the distribution of the load. "Listen," said Fumiko, her eyes lighting up with sudden inspiration, "what are you planning to do this summer?"

"To study. Keep myself in shape. Maybe I'll learn to really play tennis. And I'll generally get myself ready for college in the fall. Why do you ask?"

"How'd you like to come with me?"

"Come where?"

"To summer camp. About a hundred miles south. I got a job there. I'm going to be a counselor; I signed up a few days ago. They need more people. How about it?"

"I don't know . . ."

152

"It'll be great! Especially for you! Kids to supervise. Lots of swimming, boating and tennis—all the sports! And when the kids go to sleep, you can read and study all you want. What do you say?"

"It sounds reasonable. It's a possibility . . ."

"And the two of us could be together! For two whole months! After all, when we graduate, we'll be parting—won't we?"

The idea appealed to Mitzko. She could keep up both mental and physical regimens. And find stimulation in her contact with the campers. And enjoy the freshness of Fumiko's company. And—last but not least—avoid Garrett's return to the estate. At night, in bed, she gave the matter serious consideration. Before she dropped off to sleep, she'd made up her mind: she would go.

She informed Fumiko the next day at school. After their last class, Fumiko excitedly took her to the camp official. Mitzko was interviewed, and subsequently signed the contract. That night, as the three of them were at the kitchen table eating dessert, she told her parents. Akira kept eating. Komako put her spoon on her plate. "But you're leaving for college in the fall. Why do you want to go away for the summer?"

"It's a fine opportunity, Mother. I'll work with kids, meet some new people, take advantage of all the camp facilities. And I'll make some extra money, besides . . ."

Komako frowned, and looked to her husband. "What do you say?"

Akira wiped his mouth with his napkin; he rose from the table in silence. As he turned to go into the living room, he replied quietly: "I have nothing to say. Nothing at all."

"Really, Mitzko," persisted Komako, "think it through in earnest before you make your decision—"

"Mother, I've already made it."

153

★ ★ ★ ★ ★

Her parents were at the graduation. Akira wore the only suit he owned—it was black and he used it primarily for funerals; Komako was dressed in a two-piece blue dress and had on a hat with a feather. Mitzko was seated in one of the front rows; she turned and saw them. They looked diminutive and frail, like two sparrows, but she knew their strength. They were committed to each other; they were entwined in each other's lives until death; and they loved her sincerely, as her own person. She half-raised a hand in greeting; they smiled in return. She felt secure, exhilarated, resilient, able to cope with loss.

A trumpet flourish rang out. The school principal asked the audience to rise. The national anthem was sung, the audience was seated, the inevitable series of speeches began. They were formulaic, delivered with stiff, unavoidable eloquence, but the graduates listened with not insincere respect. Then the award winners were called to the stage; Mitzko was last in line. She walked with poised, measured steps, oblivious to the applause, conscious of what she'd managed to achieve. The praise of strangers meant little or nothing to her; it was only outward recognition, the plaudits of the unknowing and uncaring. To Mitzko, it was only the inward applause—the hardest of all to come by—that counted. "Congratulations," smiled the assistant principal, pressing her hand and steering her toward the lectern. "Congratulations, dear," echoed the principal, passing the award certificates to her and gesturing towards the exit from the dais.

As soon as she was seated again, the band played "Pomp and Circumstance," and the file of graduates in caps and gowns marched up to receive their diplomas. When the roll call was completed, the band struck up a recessional; one of the priests from the town rose to solemnly intone a concluding prayer; a trumpet finale sounded, and the ceremony was over. The auditorium became a sea of milling, jostling parents and offspring. Mitzko moved slowly out of her row. She was wearing a canary-yellow dress that Komako had designed and sewn by hand for her. In the aisle, classmates crowded around, eager to convey their appreciation. The girls tried to hug her; the boys attempted to kiss her cheeks. She resisted them all: a polite handshake, more formal than not, was what she offered—no more.

Except for Fumiko, who was genuinely moved, and whose embrace she allowed. "I'm so proud of your prizes," Fumiko exclaimed. "And you look so pretty! Like an orchid—"

"Orchids are purple," Mitzko laughed. "Or white . . ."

"It doesn't matter," contested Fumiko. "You still look like one!"

As Mitzko pushed through the crowd towards her parents, a hand caught her arm. It was Toge. He looked splendid in a brown, double-breasted suit and scarlet tie—like a candy bar, Mitzko thought as he grinned at her.

"Congratulations on your awards," he exclaimed.

"Thank you, Toge."

"This is for you," he said nervously, bringing out a lone, long-stemmed red rose wrapped in silver paper from behind his back and giving it to her.

She took it. "It's beautiful, Toge."

He was flustered. "So are you . . ." he murmured.

It was obvious that he wanted to say more, but she didn't permit it. "I have to go," she said with a smile. "My folks are waiting for me . . ."

They were. In the foyer, Akira stood with his hands at his sides, looking uncomfortable and attempting to hide it; Komako fussed with her hat. When they caught sight of their daughter, they smiled broadly. Akira embraced her; he mumbled something, but Mitzko couldn't catch what he said. Komako kissed both her cheeks. "We're very proud of you, dearest Mitzko," she said with emotion. Going home, the three of them were squeezed into the cab of the pickup. They traveled in silence; no one seemed able or willing to break it. Akira concentrated on the driving; Komako scrutinized her beautifully manicured nails; Mitzko gazed out the window: all of them thought of the future. And all of them knew that while the road—bending and twisting as it did—would finally bring them to the estate and their snug, safe domicile, the future would take them they knew not where . . .

Chapter 33

Toge had asked her to the prom—that was expected. But two other boys from her class had unexpectedly asked her as well: Robert Eakins, the big, blond captain of the varsity football team; and the small-statured, gentle-mannered boy who'd won the literature award, Edmund Wilcox. Mitzko summarily turned down all three. Fumiko, who was going to the dance with someone whom she unabashedly called "the horniest guy in the class," couldn't understand. "What do you have against proms?" she asked Mitzko with annoyance.

"Not a thing. Proms are just fine."

"Then why did you refuse those guys?"

"That's the point, Fumiko: none of those boys is of particular interest to me."

"Tell me, Mitzko, who does interest you?"

"We won't get into that . . ."

They didn't. The prom came and went. The corsages were tucked away in dresser drawers; the photographs were pasted into albums. Fumiko told Mitzko that after the dance, she and her date had gone to a popular bar for drinks and then had the "best sex ever" in his car, but that she'd been "much too drunk to remember it in the morning." Mitzko tried to keep a straight face, but ended up laughing. Then Fumiko burst into laughter as well. "I feel so close to you," she said to Mitzko, "like a sister. I'm very glad that we're going away together." Mitzko squeezed her friend's plump hand. "So am I," she said softly.

Then the time to depart for camp arrived. Mitzko said good-bye to Komako in the house. Akira drove her to the bus station, where Fumiko, sitting astride a heap of shopping bags and valises, awaited her. Akira patted his daughter's shoulder awkwardly. "Take care," he said. "And write to us—"

"I will," said Mitzko. "Be sure to write back."

Without his being aware of it, she watched him through the plate glass of the door as he went towards the pickup. The other day, he'd mentioned to her in passing that the general's son wouldn't be home for the summer, that "the boy was in a special program." If Akira knew anything about what had gone on between Garrett and her, he never showed it. He was a man of great reserve, dignity and respect for another's sensitivities; he thrived on responsibility and devotion. She was very much like him . . .

The camp was set in rolling, wooded hills. Two sides of its perimeter fronted a large lake. There were hiking trails and nature paths, and a river that was easily navigable by canoe. Mitzko was impressed by the surroundings, and with the array of sports and recreational facilities. Fumiko was excited by the staff of male counselors. "How do you know?" Mitzko asked her as they unpacked. "You've only just gotten here; you didn't really meet anyone yet."

"I got a good look at them," Fumiko replied, stuffing bras and panties into a cubbyhole. "That's enough for me! I can't wait to try them out!"

About a week later, after everything had been readied, the campers themselves arrived. Mitzko and Fumiko were in charge of a group of intermediate girls, ranging in age from ten to twelve. Fumiko tolerated them well enough; perhaps she even liked some of them. She did her duty by them—but no more. And they knew it. It was different with Mitzko. She was drawn to the girls; she had feeling for their pain; she wanted to share life and experience with them; she even hoped to inspire joy. The girls perceived Fumiko's indifference and business-like attitude; they sensed clearly Mitzko's eagerness to give of herself. They were civil to Fumiko, correct: they stayed at a distance. But, seeking what many parents and peers failed to offer, they pushed their defenses aside and dared to come close to Mitzko.

Only now did Mitzko realize what camp really meant. The girls were the point. The reason she was there. In the very first days of her stay, she knew what direction her career would take. "I've decided to do physical therapy with kids," she told Fumiko as they walked towards the dining hall for supper. "I'm going into pediatric neuromuscular work."

"That's nice," said Fumiko. She nudged her companion. "That guy over there—the one with the crew-cut and U of M sweatshirt—see him?"

"What about him?"

"His name's Bob Berry; he comes from Duluth. He's in charge of the waterfront. You should see him in swimming trunks—he's built like a stallion—" She ran a hand over her hair. "I keep wondering what it'd be like to—" She didn't finish, more, Mitzko felt, to silently savor her fantasy than to spare her companion the explicit details.

Mitzko wasn't angry. She was used to Fumiko's erotic speculations and the thousand-and-one-night tales of her sexual exploits; she heard them more with sadness than amusement. But she accepted Fumiko the way she was, and would never have considered trying to effect a change. That would be utterly impossible, like chipping away at a granite mountain with a toothpick for a tool. Fumiko followed her own path, slipping out of the tent-topped bungalow at night for the tryst she'd scheduled by day. Mitzko remained on her cot, reading her books by flashlight while the campers slept. As always, Mitzko organized her time strictly. The camp wakened to the reveille bugle at six-thirty; she was up at five-thirty. She read religiously for an hour before going through the day's schedule; she read again during the rest hour in the afternoon. Free time in the evening was devoted to tennis. The tennis counselor was teaching her. She had observed him instructing her girls, and on an impulse asked him if he'd help her. His response was spirited, unhesitating: "I'd be glad to. When do we start?"

They started that evening. "We have very limited time," he told her, glancing at his watch, "so please pay attention. Concentrate. Make every lesson count." He promptly showed her how to grip the racket, how to position her body and her feet, how to hit the ball.

They met at dusk by the recreation hall promptly at the start of free time and went to the courts, preferring silence to small talk as they walked. After he'd been teaching her for a couple of weeks, she said: "You know, I think I'm imposing—I'd be only too happy to pay you for the lessons . . ."

"I'll be the judge of who's imposing on me," he countered. "Let's just drop all the crap about paying me . . ."

She liked his serious attitude, his intensity, his obvious proficiency. She felt at ease with him, able to learn, able to enjoy the learning. She wasn't afraid to question or to err; she could readily immerse herself in the game. "Like this?" she called, rushing the net for a forehand.

"Keep that elbow stiff—" he shouted back. "Follow through now—that's the way—" Watching her stroke the ball, he missed his return. "Hey! That was sweet! Great shot!"

She flushed. He wasn't playing anywhere near his best,

but she was playing very well. He never flattered her; when he complimented her, he meant it. Her enthusiasm grew. She invested more energy in her play, concentrated more intensely. She worked on her serve, practiced her backhand, improved her control and placement. "You're really good," he told her one evening after they took leave of the courts and, drying their sweaty faces and arms with fresh towels, headed slowly up the hill towards the center of camp. "You're a natural . . ." He wiped his neck. "I bet that if you'd started playing earlier—when you were a kid—you'd be a pro by now—"

"I didn't start earlier."

His name was Rusty Dansworth. Like Bob Berry, the waterfront counselor, he was a senior at the University of Michigan. Rusty was a pre-med student, and number one man on the tennis team. He'd come to California with Berry for the summer, he told her, "to get away from it all." When the camp season ended, the two of them planned to buy an old jalopy and drive back to the Midwest. He was slightly more than medium height, had red hair and freckles, and a lithe, wiry build—not, she realized with a start one day, unlike Akira's. She liked Rusty. His openness. Generosity. His balance and patience. She also realized that she liked it when he touched her.

To teach her tennis, he had to touch her. But she didn't have to like it. Yet there could be no denying that it pleased her. Maybe it was more than pleasing; she couldn't say. He had never been anything more than professional, never expressed physical attraction. And yet—? When people were drawn to each other sexually, it was hard, if not impossible, to split desire into his and hers. Desire was mutual, indivisible. She wondered if there was anything sexual between Rusty and herself. She didn't know. And didn't care to find out. She wanted to learn how to excel at tennis—no more and no less.

She found an unexpected release in the game, and decided to devote more time to it. So she set her alarm for five and skipped reading in the morning. Instead, she dressed quickly and hurried down the hill to the courts for practice against the boards. Dew was still on the grass, the lake glittered silver-gray through the trees, the sun was just up. Aside from the kitchen staff, the camp was asleep. She was all alone. The green surface of the court gleamed. She crouched slightly, planted her feet apart. Her body was at her command, her timing exact. She kept her eyes on the ball as it sailed towards her, and stroked it. Moved it, drove it, smashed it. Smoothly always, with the motion of a keel cutting into water. It satisfied her, gave her the feeling of control.

One morning, someone called her name. Off-balance, she turned and nearly fell. It was Rusty. He had a racket in hand and a towel draped around his neck. "What are you doing down here?" she said.

"I could ask you the same question."

"What I'm doing is obvious; I think you need to explain."

He ignored her remark. "Doesn't it bore you to hit the ball at the wall that way?"

She nodded. "A bit."

"How about a partner?"

"You're on!"

They began playing every morning. Some days later, he proposed that they play at night, after taps was sounded. "The courts are lit," he told her. "We should take advantage of the fact."

She declined: "I need to read and study. I've already given up my mornings, you know."

"Oh, come on—take a break," he insisted. "That's what summer's all about!" He spread his arms. "Look at me—I'm as free as a bird! Haven't cracked a single book since June!"

They compromised. She agreed to play Mondays and Thursdays when the campers went to sleep, providing that Fumiko would cover for her. Fumiko said she would. "Bob can come to visit me in the bunk . . ." She stared at Mitzko curiously. "I don't . . . believe it . . ."

"Believe what?"

"That it's finally happened . . . that you've got a boyfriend . . ." She clapped her hands with child-like joy. "At last . . . a sexy body isn't being wasted anymore . . ."

"Rusty and I play tennis. That's all."

"Is that so?"

"That's the truth. He taught me how. Now, we play."

Fumiko giggled. "I bet he did teach you how . . ."

"We play tennis. You imagine the rest."

"Really? Well, I've seen the way he looks at you, and the way you look at him. It's as plain as day. You can't fool me. I know."

The conversation disturbed Mitzko. Was it Fumiko's prurient imagination, which uncovered sex in every nook and cranny, every glance and gesture, at work? Or was it the truth? Could other people sense and see what Mitzko had deliberately elected to ignore? She took to watching Rusty whenever they were together. "Why do you look at me that way?" he asked her.

"What are you talking about? What way?"

He hesitated, then he said: "Never mind—it's not important . . ."

On a Wednesday night, Fumiko stumbled into the bunk a little past eleven; she sat down heavily on her cot. Mitzko looked up from the textbook on her pillow. "What're you doing back here so early?"

Fumiko sighed. "Bob and I just wore each other out. That man is something else. I'm absolutely dead; I'm going to turn

163

in . . ." Grunting, she hoisted her sweatshirt over her head. "See you in the morning . . ."

"Sleep tight!"

Just after midnight, there was a tapping at the screen. Mitzko lifted her flashlight and directed the beam. It was Rusty, with a half-shy, half-determined look on his face. "Did I wake you?"

"I was studying."

"I know: for an exam you don't have to take."

Mitzko laughed. "Life's my exam . . ."

Shielding his eyes, Rusty shrugged. "Come down to the lake with me, Mitzko."

"Now?"

"Best time. Nobody else is there. We'll just sit and look at the water. There's a breeze. And the moon's out . . ."

"Listen, it's very nice of you to offer, Rusty, but—"

"Oh, come on, Mitzko, give yourself a chance! Take a breather . . . relax a little. The book will keep. I promise you."

She stared at him. He looked earnest, eager, frustrated. Part of her wanted to send him on his way, but somehow she couldn't. She glanced at the clock on the cabinet by her cot: the luminous dial said a quarter past twelve. For some time now, her concentration had been waning. Maybe it was opportune to stop reading; maybe a bit of relaxation by the lake wouldn't hurt. The night would certainly be beautiful. And Rusty was always good company. "Okay," she said, "I'll be right out."

She switched off the flashlight, and got into her sneakers. Draping a light sweater over her shoulders, she made her way down the aisle between the two rows of sleeping girls and went out. One of the steps of the wooden stairs creaked, the same one that invariably announced the return of an exhausted Fumiko. Rusty waited at the bottom. He was wearing white dress shorts and his varsity sweater. "Hi, it's real good to see you," he said softly, unable to conceal his excitement. "Hi."

They walked in silence down to the water almost the way they did when they went to play tennis. Only it was different. Tennis wasn't the common denominator. They were. To her consternation, Mitzko found that she felt anything but serene. There was a vague but certain tension between them. She couldn't put her finger on what it was. They had strayed considerably past the dock and raft and waterfront facilities, when Rusty abruptly stopped and gestured: "Is this spot okay?"

"It's fine."

They seated themselves. Far across the moon-dappled lake, the intensely dark blur of a spruce forest marked the opposite shore. Rusty poked the ground and came up with a flat stone; he leaned backwards and then pitched forward as he scaled it neatly over the surface of the water. They heard the final, hollow plunk but couldn't discern where it had gone down. Out of the corner of an eye, Mitzko observed him. On the tennis courts, he was giving, gracious, poised. Now, he seemed unstable, needy. It became evident to her that he wanted something. But that did not entirely surprise her. Toge and others had wanted something. What disturbed her was the fact—which she realized she'd worked diligently to suppress—that perhaps she wanted something as well. Even the use of the word "perhaps" was an evasion. She had to face the truth: he attracted her. Suddenly, Rusty got to his feet and began walking; he stopped at the edge of the lake and looked back at her. Stared back at her brazenly, with open desire. She averted her eyes.

Gazing out at the needles of moonlight on the waves, she wondered. What was so terrible about being attracted to

Rusty? What was wrong with it? No one had a claim on her, least of all Garrett. It was understood that she and Garrett had parted, cut their ties. Then why did he come to mind? How did he manage to poison her heart, to render her paralyzed? Why did she feel the force of a bond she believed severed for good? She owed Garrett nothing; she owed herself everything. Then why did she feel guilty? How did a phantom from the past have more power over her than a living man in the present? Why wasn't she an available woman, permitted choice and conjugality, free to do as she wished?

"Mitzko—"

She looked around.

"Mitzko, come swim with me—"

His clothing was scattered over the shore; where he'd tossed them, his sneakers lay like white stones. He was standing ankle-deep in the water, naked. He had a graceful, muscular, beautiful body. The moon had turned it to a statue. But she knew it was flesh: warm, hungry, male flesh waiting to meet her own female hunger. Her face burned. Without hesitating, she rose.

"Come on, Mitzko!" he called. "Take off your things and swim with me!" He held out his arms to her.

Drawing her sweater about her shaking shoulders, she turned and hurried away. From behind her, the waves lapping dully at the shore seemed to mock her steps as she ran . . .

The misaligned stair creaked under her feet; the screen door of the bunkhouse squealed on its hinges. Quickly, she closed it behind her.

"Mitzko?" murmured Fumiko's sleepy voice. "Is that you?"

"It's me . . . it's just me, Fumiko . . ."

"Where were you?"

"I went out for a breath of air . . ."

There was a pause. "You went walking at three in the morning?"

"Fumiko—hush! You'll wake the girls—"

Fumiko lowered her voice. "Nonsense," she said. "You never went for any innocent walk. Not at this hour of the night. You must have been with that tennis pro of yours. You know what I think? I think that you were doing it with him, that's what!"

"I wasn't, Fumiko."

"Then you damn well should have been!" Fumiko laughed. "Try it sometime, Mitzko. Believe me, it'll do you a world of good!"

Mitzko was seated on her cot in the corner; she had removed her clothing and was slipping into a nightshirt. She didn't answer.

Fumiko sighed audibly. "I just don't understand you, Mitzko . . ."

"That's all right, Fumiko. As long as I understand myself . . ."

But Fumiko was already snoring.

Chapter 34

Mitzko wrote to her parents regularly. Told them that she was doing well—very well. That she enjoyed being with Fumiko. That she was making new friends. Progressing at tennis. Wrote that she loved working with her girls. "My campers seem to advance, develop, mature. It's wonderful seeing the changes in their personalities, the improvements in their skills: we've gotten very close—the lot of them and I. On visiting day, I had the opportunity to meet their parents and, in some cases, their siblings. Many of the girls in my group are, I believe, freer here with me than with their own families. It seems odd, but it's so. There are few things in this world more subtle, insidious or corrosive than the alienation of children from parents . . ."

Komako replied religiously to every letter she wrote. Beneath her mother's formal salutations, casual observations and surface comments, Mitzko understood the deep pain of inevitable parting, and grief over the loss of former intimacy and confidence. That there was enduring love between mother and daughter was never for an instant in doubt, but the delicate balance of their relationship had shifted radically—and it would never be the same again.

The entire summer long, Akira wrote to her only once. It was, however, a lengthy, discursive letter telling her that it made him very happy to know that she was doing well. He went on to say that he was occupied with his "usual chores" and a number of extra ones as well. The general and his wife had returned from their "excursion" and were intent on fixing up the estate. Both General and Mrs. Edwards looked "tanned and fit." The general looked rested, and somehow "satisfied," though Akira wasn't sure that was the proper word to describe him. As the general pursued his daily rounds, he spoke with surprising animation to his nurse, and exhibited "enthusiasm" that hadn't been in evidence since the time of what Akira circumspectly called his "accident." Their son had not come back with them after the cruise; he was enrolled, as Akira learned, in a "special, advanced course" at the academy.

The letter also made an unexpected and puzzling reference to Akira's secret journal, the "Encyclopedia of the Soul" that Mitzko knew was in constant progress over the years, but had never once so much as glimpsed. "I work at it every day without fail," Akira wrote. "The reason is simple: it keeps me afloat. In its pages, I note down what I do not say aloud, and there is much satisfaction in it. I also attempt to write what I am not able to say, and though I seldom succeed, I obtain a measure of satisfaction in trying. Lastly, I make an effort to record what cannot ever be said; of course, I'm doomed from inception to failure—but even that has meaning for me . . ." He concluded the section with the words: "In essence, I try to understand the world and man's place in it. But everything essential remains a mystery . . ."

Then, abruptly, Akira closed with a single sentence: "There is still no news of Chuo."

With that sentence repeating itself in her mind, Mitzko folded the letter and tucked it safely away.

She had stopped playing tennis with Rusty. Nor would she consent to spend time with or even see him. He made repeated attempts to approach and speak with her, but she avoided him at every turn. Of course, the evasion couldn't last: camp was too small and contained for that. One night, after a gala performance of *The Mikado* by the seniors, he crowded her into a corner outside of the recreation hall. "I've got to go," she told him with mixed annoyance and urgency. "The girls will be getting ready for bed; I always say good night to them."

"Fumiko can look after the girls," he countered. "I spoke to her about it before the show, and she said she would. So you don't have an excuse—"

She stared at him. "Rusty, it's pointless," she said curtly.

"What are you talking about? What's pointless—?" He was visibly agitated. "Are you married? Engaged? Do you have a boyfriend hidden away somewhere? Are you uneasy about being a Japanese-American? Do you have some reprehensible disease? Which is it!?"

"It's none of those things."

He struck his fist into the palm of his other hand. "Damn it, then what the hell is going on!? What's wrong?"

"Nothing's wrong, Rusty. You just aren't listening to me. There won't be anything between us—that's all."

"You don't like me? Is that it?"

She shook her head. "I like you well enough, Rusty. You're a nice guy. A real nice guy . . ."

"But—?"

"But there's no future for us."

"How can you say that? You don't know. No one knows the future."

"It's pointless, Rusty. I already told you. How many times must I repeat it?"

He glowered at her. His body was taut, crouched—almost as if he were engaged in some life-and-death tennis match.

"Please, Rusty. Let me by . . ."

She had to find a replacement for tennis, something to

offset her tension. It was riflery. She passed the rifle range one day—it suddenly aroused interest. She stopped in to ask. The counselor in charge was a very tall, heavyset, slightly balding fellow in his late twenties. He was called Big Ed, and hailed from somewhere down south. Big Ed was affable, easygoing, popular with both campers and staff; he liked coming to camp every summer to "be with the kids—and be a kid again." In his late teens and early twenties, he'd been a Marine. She asked him outright if he'd coach her. "Sure," he said amiably, spitting out a watermelon seed, "why the heck not?"

She went to the range several times a week and was an apt pupil; when she made up her mind, she learned quickly. Locking the rifle into the armpit so that it was ramrod-stiff; setting the target on the blade of the sight like an apple on a lollipop stick; squeezing the trigger so that one scarcely discerned the point of no return: and then, blat! The shot was off. She knew she was in the ring. Knew it—and was right. A trim, tight grouping within the circle, with three of the shots breaking the bull's-eye. Big Ed congratulated her. "You're a natural," said her coach. "You're the best these ol' eyes have seen in many a year!" When she unslung the rifle and rose, he patted her shoulder. "If you continue to shoot when you get back home," he drawled, "you're gonna win some competitions and take some medals . . ."

"Really?"

"For sure, honey," he laughed.

For some inexplicable reason, she kept all of her target sheets. Filed them neatly and in strict order on the shelf above her cot with all of her letters from home. A few days before camp ended, it dawned on her that it had something to do with Garrett. But what? Why, as much and as often as she might consciously deny it, was he still a factor in the equation of her life? She'd spoken the truth to Rusty. Garrett was not her husband. Or fiancé. Or boyfriend. Then what was he? Why did he remain with her? What power had he over her? Why did she let him?

For Fumiko, parting from the girls was a matter of course. For Mitzko, it was painful. They crowded around her, kissed her, hugged her with all of their strength. They all said they'd write to her and made her promise she'd answer; some said they'd invite her to their homes in all sorts of faraway cities. Most probably, Mitzko knew, she'd never see any of them again. The cars swerved into the parking lot, rolling dust up into the sky; out stepped the parents, waving and shouting and rushing forward. There were the last, prolonged good-byes, the inevitable tears. Then the joy—and apprehension—of reunion. And then the campers were gone. The last car pulled bumpily out of the lot. For evaluation sessions and to shut things down, the counselors would stay on for a few days. Then the place would be a ghost camp.

Fumiko had a date with Bob Berry in the dining hall and ran off to meet him. Mitzko headed slowly back to the bunk-house to retrieve a book she'd borrowed from one of the kitchen staff. On a transverse path, by the infirmary, she caught sight of Rusty. He was dressed in immaculate white—shirt, ducks, suede shoes—and a blue blazer with polished brass buttons. Set rakishly aslant over his mop of red hair was a new white golfer's cap. He looked trim, pressed, snappy—like a mannikin magically escaped from a trendy men's shop. Totally engrossed in a spirited, tête-à-tête conversation with one of the female senior counselors, he didn't notice her. The counselor and he were so close that they might have been em-bracing: her smile was intimate and inviting; he looked bright and eager. Mitzko felt as much connection to him as she would have to a passing bird or leaf.

Chapter 35

Akira enjoyed Mitzko's being at home, but he knew it was for the briefest time and so kept aloof. To his daughter, who saw him after a period of absence, he seemed both balanced and at risk—like a man on a tightrope without a net beneath him. Komako, to the contrary, was exuberant and welcoming; she acted as if Mitzko had come home for good. She demonstrated her affection in a thousand little ways, she fussed and pampered, she courted her daughter's company. Instinctively, Mitzko sensed that a good part of her mother's attitude derived from Komako's knowledge of her daughter's break with the general's son, Garrett. Though the subject had never once been discussed openly, Komako had shrewdly put the pieces together. She hadn't a single concrete detail in her possession; nevertheless, she had figured everything out. Mitzko was convinced that her mother knew exactly what had happened. Komako had predicted failure and disappointment, and they had come to pass.

Three days before Mitzko's departure, they got the news about Chuo. This time, it was Akira who knew it first. Komako was in the kitchen; Mitzko was in her room, sorting out the books and clothing she wanted to take with her. Both heard Akira's howl from the living room, where he'd been listening to the radio. Gray as ash, he clutched the arms of his chair. "What's wrong?" said Komako, bending over him. But he couldn't speak. Komako turned. "Bring a glass of cold water, Mitzko . . ." But he couldn't drink. He could only cover his face with his hands and moan.

Akira had heard a bulletin. Later on, when the full news program was broadcast, they learned the complete details of what had happened. Early that morning, Chuo had broken into a large private home some 200 miles northeast of San Francisco and forced the inhabitants—a young couple and their infant son—to leave. The authorities had been contacted immediately. Local police, state troopers and FBI agents surrounded the place. Chuo proclaimed that the land was his, that it had been unjustly seized by the U.S. government, that he demanded its return. The authorities ordered him to surrender. The impasse lasted about three hours. Then the law officers issued an ultimatum. Chuo had fifteen minutes to decide: either he could give himself up—or they'd come in to get him. At precisely the tick of the fifteenth minute, the house burst into flame. It burned to the ground with Chuo inside.

Akira remained in his chair, while the women wept, trying vainly to comfort themselves and him. The radio kept on playing, as if a different news program, with different news contradicting what they'd heard, might come on. Then Komako, grim-faced and dry-eyed, shut it off. "I told you it would end this way," she said bitterly. With a convulsive shake of her shoulders, she walked out of the room.

Mitzko knelt at her father's side. She held his hand; his fingers were stiff and lifeless—like scabs. Her weeping, too, had ceased. All her life, she would cry silently inside, but that was another story. She concentrated on rousing Akira from his coma. "Dad," she pleaded, "it's almost midnight. Please— have something to drink. Mother's made a pot of fresh tea. Let me bring you a cup—"

He stared at her blindly.

"Dad . . . I'm speaking to you. Please answer me—"

Still without seeing her, he parted his dry lips. "Chuo dreamed Dachau," he said in a hollow voice. "Only he was awake . . ."

Chapter 36

On the night before Mitzko left for school, she went to bed early. But just past three, she wakened and—unable to fall back to sleep—got up to make herself tea. At the entrance to the living room, she stopped and peered in. "Dad—"

She saw him in his armchair, somehow folded in on himself, like an insect about to give up the last spark of animation. His lamp, the radio, his pipe in the ashtray: all were there. But they looked different, grim, like objects placed at the tomb of a dead man. She hesitated, then approached. He seemed not to notice her presence; when she touched his forearm, the flesh was cold. "Dad—" she said softly, wanting but not daring to bend and kiss his cheek. "Are you all right?"

Without looking up at her, he said: "I dreamed of my mother . . ."

She knew he wanted to speak, not talk but speak, and she knew he wanted her—though he'd scarcely acknowledged that she was there—to listen. Quickly, she moved to the sofa and seated herself opposite him. Between them, with faint starlight sifting its way in through the lace curtains, was the window—and rimless shadows.

He continued: "My mother came to me from the moon, her eternal abode. I happened to be staring at the moon—whether I was man or child, I don't really know—and suddenly, on rungs of darkness, she drifted down. I was terrified, exultant, speechless. She was all in shining white: hairpiece, eyelashes, face makeup, fingernails; she wore a full-length white robe tied round with a white sash and white sandals dotted with pearls. How radiant was she! How exquisite! She had brought with her person the cold, pacific, cruel, pristine-ancient beauty of the moon! 'Oh, Mother,' I cried out. 'It's been so long . . . so very long . . .'

" 'Has it?' she said in her thin, flute voice. 'I don't re-member. I didn't keep track. I'm so careless about time . . .'

"I was adamant: 'But why did you cut me off? Why did you give me away? Why did you harbor me in your womb . . . and then banish me? Tell me, Mother! Tell me the truth I've a right to. The painful truth at last!'

"She shrugged. 'That's all past,' she said. 'The dead are the past; the past is for them, not the living . . .'

" 'But I must know—'

" 'Nobody knows . . .'

" '—so that I'll finally be free—'

" 'Nobody's free . . .'

" 'And why are you dressed in white? The color of purity, when you aren't pure; the color of innocence, when you're not innocent—why? At least tell me that, Mother—'

" 'I wear white because I mourn.'

" 'Mourning robes are black, Mother.'

" 'Mine are the mourning robes of birth, so I wear white.'

" 'Whom do you mourn, Mother?'

" 'My only son . . .'

" 'You mourn your son!? How can that be? I'm not dead! See, I'm alive, Mother.'

"At once, she extended her arms. In her upraised hands lay a small pillow of silk. On the pillow, was the hara-kiri knife. 'This is for you,' she said sadly. And, proffering the pillow, she wept.

"But the weeping was hollow, without tears or tone . . ."

Then Akira was silent.

For a long time, Mitzko remained silent as well. Then she rose. She had considered what she wanted to tell him. "Father," she said, "I—if you wish, I—"

Sensing what was about to come, Akira cut her off. "No," he murmured, the spirit returning in some measure to his voice. "I don't want that; neither does your mother. You'll go to school as planned. You must go. Your life is yours: take it—"

Unable to sleep, she lay in bed and awaited the first, familiar strains of dawn at her window. Thoughts of childhood, of how her parents had raised her, drifted through her mind. She reviewed her life until the point of her relationship with Garrett—at that juncture, her mind skipped ahead. The mechanism was protective; she had scrupulously trained herself to employ it. With the first light, she arose and washed up and dressed. Before leaving the room, she placed her packed suitcases by the door. The hour was at hand: with her parents' blessings, she was ready to be on her way.

In her robe, Komako was already in the kitchen; breakfast had been prepared; the kettle was on the stove and hissing. Akira, in overalls and work boots, joined them at the table. "I'll pray now," said Komako. Mitzko and Akira also bowed their heads as Komako prayed silently. When the meal was finished, Akira said: "Carlos will drive you to the station. I arranged it with him yesterday." Outside the house, by the old willow tree, Komako embraced her daughter, and Mitzko heard the two insuppressible words that her mother whispered: "My baby . . ."

Sunlight sparkled on the dew; in the vegetable garden, a slight breeze stirred the sleeves of the scarecrow's jacket; beneath the kitchen windows, flowers that Komako and Mitzko had planted showed radiant faces. Akira picked up one of the two suitcases and walked along the paths with Mitzko to a

178

side entrance where the pickup waited. He took his daughter in his arms: she felt his strength—and weakness. Without a word, he released her and walked away. She watched him go until, from the cab of the truck, Carlos called: "It's getting late. We'd best be on our way . . ."

She didn't look back at the estate. It was behind her now: the great, slate-roofed mansion; the lawns and gardens; the paths and walkways and trails; the gazebos and pool and stable—and the little house in which she'd grown to womanhood. Her past was behind her; her mother and father had taught her to look to the future. Often, she tried to imagine what the future would be like. There was always a piece missing in the picture. No matter how she turned things, there was always a void: Garrett. He was missing. No other could replace him. She wished it were different, but it seemed there was nothing she could do to change matters.

At the station, Carlos helped her out and put her suitcases down. "Your parents are very proud of you," he said huskily. "So am I. I wish you the best . . ." The two shook hands and he got back into the truck and drove off. The pickup slowed and rounded a corner. She was on her own . . .

Chapter 37

Mitzko's roommate was a tall, big-boned girl from St. Louis. Her full name was Alexis—everyone called her Lexi—Quentin Atherton; she was an art history major with a special interest in the French Impressionists. She had never before this encountered an Asian, although she was, as she hastened to inform Mitzko, "most open to new experiences of every sort." There was no dispute or even discussion about sleeping arrangements: Lexi had already chosen and made up the bottom bunk of the double-decker bed with a brand-new set of pink floral sheets and a lace-edged pillowcase. She was also prompt in announcing that—without fail, in winter and summer alike—she showered twice a day; she insisted that she be the first one in the bathroom mornings. Then, with a stick of white chalk from the top drawer of her desk, she stooped and bisected the floor of the room from window to door. "There," she said, surveying her handiwork proudly and glancing over at Mitzko for frank approval if not actual approbation. "See the line? I've cut our living space exactly in half! Fair and square! I'll be on my side; you'll be on yours. That way, there won't be any problems or misunderstandings between us . . ." She smiled—the smile of a girl used to having her own space, her own way. "Okay with you, Mitz?"

"Mitzko—"

"Well, it is all right with you, isn't it?"

Mitzko shrugged. "I guess it is. If that's what makes you happy, Alexis . . ."

"You may call me Lexi—"

There would never be anything between the two. The chalk line would inexorably separate their intimacies, their lives. They would be physical presences temporarily sharing physical space, no more. More than all else, both were relieved to know that. To unburden themselves of any social obligation, of all human interest. Warmth, concern—even basic curiosity—were entirely out of the question. But they were polite to each other, civil, proper and correct. If Lexi wanted to sneak a man into the room (strictly forbidden according to dorm rules), she notified her roommate well beforehand so that Mitzko could arrange to be in the library; if Mitzko needed to study into the wee hours of the morning (something that her roommate never so much as dreamed of doing), Lexi donned her embroidered sleep mask. Everything was trade-off, quid pro quo. It was, as Mitzko once wrote to Fumiko, "a symbiosis made in hell . . ."

Mitzko threw herself into the work. By nature, she was industrious, organized, disciplined; her upbringing had reinforced these qualities. Her studies sustained and propelled her; she sensed that in them lay her destiny. College—and life—offered their diversions and their temptations; she avoided and ignored them. She rose early, long before Lexi ever lifted a blanket; faithfully, almost religiously, she attended classes; she studied when others slept and socialized and played. Her body was not neglected: she swam, ran, and when she could find the time and a partner, played tennis. She never went back to riflery. But she kept the target sheets from camp on one of her shelves.

No one ever asked her to join a sorority, or even considered her joining a remote possibility. She was regarded as aloof, secretive, slavishly devoted to classwork. If fellow students ever thought to describe her, they called her "bookworm," "drone," "asocial." In accordance with the dictates of most societies, the labels stuck. She was generally shunned, abandoned, left to her structure and regimen. Initially, men approached her; they made earnest attempts to take her out. She was svelte, intense: a mysterious female attraction. But she turned them all away. In time, her reputation spared her the trouble of refusing them. She was known unceremoniously as "The Nun."

One Saturday morning, after her shower, Lexi said: "You're really a peculiar duck, Mitzko. Has anyone ever told you that?"

Mitzko was surprised—the two rarely conversed. She had just finished making her bed and looked over at her roommate, who stood wrapped in a towel in the doorway to the bathroom; she was energetically brushing her long blond hair. "What do you mean, Lexi?"

"Well, you don't mix, you don't date, you don't party. You don't belong to a sorority or any campus group. Fact is, you don't do much of anything at all. Except study."

"That's what I came here for, Lexi."

"How absurd!"

For Mitzko, it wasn't absurd at all: it was supremely logical. She had purpose: she knew exactly why and for what she had come to college. She was immersed in learning. Her personal life was something else: she kept it under strict control, all but locked away in some inner vault. It emerged to an extent whenever she got a letter from Komako or—far less often—a short note from Akira who, it was painfully obvious, had marshaled all of his strength to compose it. It also came out when she dreamed—surely against her own volition—of Garrett, or had nightmares about Chuo. And it confronted her when she heard from Fumiko.

Fumiko had written often and regularly at first. She wrote

that she was in constant telephone contact with Bob Berry, who had promised to keep phoning and to write back and even to fly from Detroit out to the coast just to be with her. He planned to visit her during the Christmas break and spend the next summer with her at camp; and who could say what might happen after that? "We're a real couple," Fumiko wrote, in an ecstasy deliciously apparent in her ferocious, floral scrawl. "I know that he loves me," she went on, "and wants to keep me forever. The last time he called, he said: 'Fumiko, I need you.' It made me shiver. It's not only the sex, Mitzko. Sex is just the expression of his love."

But a week later, there was a gloomy letter. "I'm disillusioned," Fumiko wrote. "Bob Berry hasn't called in three whole days." It got worse. Berry stopped calling altogether; he didn't write either. "Maybe he's sick," Fumiko suggested. "Or maybe he was killed in an accident. What will I do then?" But she knew she was deluding herself. "Probably, he met another girl," she wrote. "The bastard." Her letters grew shorter and sadder. She had invested "far too much" of herself in Berry; he had turned out a "cheat" and a "fraud." And, if she were to face the bitter truth, the "sex wasn't that hot either." She had done what a girl ought never to do: she'd "made it all up." Everything was over; she had to face up to the "ugly reality"; the future with Bob Berry was a chimera.

Fumiko was still living at home. She worked in the supermarket at a checkout counter. The job ranged from "depressing" to "gruesome," but she couldn't find any other. She considered looking around for some new lover, but "didn't have the energy." Her passionate summer love affair at camp and its catastrophic outcome had "worn her to a frazzle." However, the very next letter made mention of a young man by the name of Ieyesu. He'd come to the supermarket to buy a loaf of bread for his mother—"Imagine that!" He was a local fellow, and had been in their graduating class. He was tall, husky, "rugged-looking"; he kept his sideburns long and wore sunglasses. Did Mitzko remember him? If things "developed to any degree," she'd send Mitzko a photograph.

In the letter that followed, Fumiko wrote that though they'd only dated a few times, Ieyesu had already mentioned "getting engaged." His father had a good job in a local bank; his mother was a legal secretary; he had three married sisters. At present, he was an apprentice mechanic, but he planned to go to technical school; Fumiko was certain that in the future he'd earn a good living. He had, she wrote, "a lot to learn in bed," but she readily confessed that it was "fun teaching him how," and that in the end he'd be better than the "summertime gigolo" who'd "betrayed her trust." How much time did Mitzko think was needed for a couple to be engaged? How could a woman be sure she was in love? Had Mitzko any idea of why Berry had jilted her? Should Fumiko blame herself in some way? She didn't, heaven forbid, want to repeat her mistakes with her new boyfriend. But was Ieyesu "old enough" for her? Or did Mitzko feel she needed somebody "with experience"? Somebody "more mature"?

Mitzko did her best to answer. Aside from her parents, Fumiko was the only human being with whom she had real contact. She liked getting letters from Fumiko, and responded with interest and empathy. However, her friend's letters suddenly stopped. Mitzko couldn't imagine why. She kept on writing, but there was no response. She had Fumiko's phone number in her address book, but when she called, she discovered that it had been disconnected. Taking pains not to communicate her uneasiness, she asked her parents: they were unable to help. With all the avenues exhausted, she decided to investigate further when she went home for Christmas vacation.

The weeks flew by. Her first set of exams was given; she passed them with flying colors. Characteristically, success only whetted her appetite. Instead of granting herself respite or coasting, she worked all the harder. She rose earlier; went to bed later. Her studies nurtured and inspired her; she wanted to absorb and be absorbed in them. Returning from a date or a party, Lexi often found her bent over her books, her shoulders hunched forward, her dark hair glistening in the brilliant glare of the desk lamp. "Jesus Christ, Mitzko!" she exclaimed on one occasion. "It's three o'clock in the morning on Saturday night! Everybody on campus has been out having a ball—and you're locked away in here, still at it!" She shimmied out of a skirt that, wrinkled and askew, was obviously not being removed for the first time that night. "What the hell's the matter with you? Don't you ever let up?"

Squinting, Mitzko glanced over at her. "You've got it all wrong, Lexi," she said. "I don't ever let down . . ."

As in high school, she attracted the attention of many of her teachers. But she never used the attention to curry favor or to advance her interests unfairly. She wanted to earn what she deserved—no more and no less. En route to a classroom one afternoon, it occurred to her that she was very much like her father. As tending to the land had been holy to Akira, so was study holy to his daughter. Akira had never explicitly told her to listen for the inner voice that would direct her to holiness, but he'd purveyed the message. She had understood. Understood that holiness saved: it saved people from desolation, despair, indifference. She had learned that holiness made life meaningful and coherent. And endurable . . .

Some days before the Christmas break, as a part of her phys ed program, she finished a gym workout and went into the locker room. On a bench, she dried the sweat from her face and neck with a fresh towel and then leisurely undressed.

185

It was late in the afternoon; the locker room seemed empty. As she showered, she noticed only one person down at the other end of the stalls. The silence—as opposed to the usual bedlam—and the privacy made her calm; she soaped herself several times over and rinsed in the hot water until she felt drowsy. Cleansed and relaxed, she turned the faucet off and headed out.

At the entrance to the locker room, the other person who'd been showering—Mitzko had lost all awareness of her—suddenly blocked her path. Mitzko stared. The naked woman confronting her was an occasional tennis partner of hers named Delores—Mitzko didn't even know her last name. She was taller than Mitzko, with firm, conical breasts and hips surprisingly broad for her slim body. She seemed ill at ease in Mitzko's presence, yet she was the one who had forced the meeting. "Are you in a hurry right now?" she asked.

Now, Mitzko was uneasy. The tone of Delores's voice, the thrust of her breasts, the unsettling, indefinable look in her green eyes. Mitzko made an effort to put it all together, but couldn't. "No, I'm not in any particular rush," she replied. "What is it?"

The other seemed unwilling yet compelled to speak; it was as if she were torn between two opposing inclinations. "We've played tennis a few times," she said softly. "And—" She halted.

"And?"

But Delores didn't speak. She had no need to. Her eyes said it all. Mitzko saw her own female body in those eyes—naked and desirable. Saw a look not entirely unlike the one she had seen at times in Garrett's eyes as he undressed or hung over her. She was shocked but not dismayed. She flushed. Involuntarily, she pressed her bath towel to her loins and her chest. The other saw—could not escape seeing—and winced. An expression of humiliation and utter disappointment came over her features. She looked like she wanted to cry or run, or both. Mitzko felt a pang of sorrow for her. "It's all right," she said, managing to smile to prove it. "There's no harm done. Really . . ."

Dressed and sitting side by side in the deserted locker room, they found that they liked talking to each other. "I've been observing you from afar for a long time," Delores told her. "And I thought—"

"Thought what?"

"Well, you don't date. I've never seen you out with a man. In fact—" She broke off, reddened.

"In fact—what?"

"I'm sorry—I talk too much . . ."

"No, you can tell me. I want to know."

"They call you 'The Nun.' They say you're married to your textbooks . . ."

"Perhaps I am. Is it a crime? Should I be punished?"

Delores bent over to tighten a lace on her sneaker. "Well, I got the idea that maybe . . . you preferred women. And I found that I was terribly attracted . . ."

"We can still be friends," Mitzko said.

She was right, they could be. In the few days that remained before the start of the vacation, Mitzko saw to it that she had time for Delores. They played tennis twice. And they met in the cafeteria for coffee during breaks in their schedules. In a very brief period, they talked a lot and grew close. It was ironic, Mitzko thought, that the two of them had drawn closer than they'd probably have if they had been lovers. Each sensed the other's pain; each responded. They did not tax or burden one another; they made no demands. That was the crux. They even agreed to correspond during the weeks of their absence from school. Mitzko would travel for only a few hours by bus; Delores was flying back east, to her family in Boston.

Home was familiar, gratifying, in some ways succoring. But early on, Mitzko knew that she no longer belonged. Her past was there, not her future. Already, her destiny was being shaped in another place. Here on the estate, she was a visitor, a guest, an observer; she had forfeited her rights as a tenant. Though she'd been away for no more than several months, Akira appeared to her to have aged considerably. Physically— and in spirit. He gave her the impression that he was pledged and determined to carry on with his life, but that he was weary. Life had cheated him too often and too harshly, and though he'd tacitly agreed to go on, his struggle was pro forma, born more of inertia than inspiration. In his expressive eyes lurked the terrible sadness that he attempted to hide. He might well fool others, but not his daughter. At this point, Mitzko believed that she knew him better than did her mother. Komako, after all, was his wife, and therefore needed to depend on him, but Mitzko had gained independence and could be more objective.

Sensing her husband's dejection and near-surrender, Komako had become withdrawn, removed, ethereal. That is to say, she had taken a decisive turn inward, a direction that had always pulled at her. Mitzko found her to be elusive, taciturn, even secretive. As was her wont, she kept strictly to her household routines and garden chores, but behaved somewhat oddly during the interim periods. She had taken to whispering to herself and at times spoke aloud disjointedly. She welcomed Mitzko's return from school, but soon seemed to grow uncomfortable with it, as if her daughter's presence were distracting her from some clandestine, compelling purpose. Occasionally, she acted like a woman who is hiding a love affair, but Mitzko understood that whatever her secret liaison, it was spiritual, not earthly. The peculiar change in her mother made Mitzko worry.

"She seems to pray very often now, doesn't she?" Mitzko asked her father.

Akira nodded.

"I see her doing it—she doesn't seem to know that I do."

"Soon after you left," said Akira, "she made herself some kind of little shrine. A candle, a bowl of fresh fruit, a photograph of her departed parents—nothing more. In the evenings, she prays there for hours. I can't lure her away. Nothing that I do or say budges her. So I decided to leave her alone . . ."

"Where is the shrine, Father?"

"It was in the kitchen, on the shelf over the sink. But the day before you arrived, she moved it to our bedroom."

"What do you think of it?"

Akira shrugged. "Your mother has always yearned for a world beyond this one. She claims that she senses it. Perhaps . . . it has simply moved closer to her . . ."

"Does it worry you?"

Akira shook his head. "No," he said. "In a world of incalculable harm, I find your mother's preoccupation quite harmless."

To Mitzko's very actual though unavowed relief, there was no sign of Garrett about the estate throughout the entire length of her stay. She made no effort to find out where he was. On occasion, she caught sight of the general or his wife, at pleasure or in the course of their regulated daily rounds. General Edwards had a new nurse; Mrs. Edwards had new outfits. One night, there was a party, with scores of guests and a dance band; Mitzko shut herself in her room with the window closed and plugs in her ears. She sometimes glimpsed the white mare, mounted by the general's wife in a luxurious riding habit, or at exercise with one of the grooms. But the people were distant to her, storybook characters or mere figurines in a diorama. For her, the center of gravity had shifted to another place, a different world.

The time passed quickly. Mitzko read, mostly for pleasure. She took long walks, visited old haunts and remembered scenes, jogged for miles. One Saturday morning as she was starting out, Akira suggested that he accompany her. She was surprised and delighted—they had spent so little time together in the last few years. "Where will we go?" he asked her.

"To the river."

"Shall we fish?"

"No. Let's just look . . ."

As they walked along the path through the woods, she said to him: "Father, do you often think of Chuo?"

Akira seemed almost to have expected the question. He took hold of Mitzko's arm. "I never forget," he said. "Not even for a moment. Never. He haunts me—but I would not want it otherwise . . ."

On the mossy, sloping bank of the river, father and daughter sat and watched the unceasing flow of the current. They sat side by side and, like the river, their spirits flowed. There was no exchange of words, but it was good for them to be there together: that very fact expressed what they felt. The water was beginning to turn color in the light of the setting sun when they rose to walk home. Akira was on the verge of saying something, but he held back. "What is it?" Mitzko asked him.

"You had . . . a disappointment; it caused you a great deal of pain. Perhaps you thought I didn't suspect. I did, but I didn't know what to tell you, how to help you heal it . . ."

She stared at him in surprise.

"I'm sorry," he said simply.

"I've made my peace, Father."

"We all must."

She wrote to Delores once, and two days before leaving received a letter from her friend. Delores wasn't close to her mother; she'd had a difficult time in Boston and was openly happy that she'd soon be back in school, on her own, and able once again to "talk everything out" with Mitzko. That night, Mitzko dreamed that the plane bringing Delores west had crashed, and that Delores had been killed. "Burnt to a crisp," said the hospital official, turning his back and striding away as Mitzko wept. She wakened without understanding the dream, and all day long had a hard time shaking her apprehension.

The next day, she solved the riddle of Fumiko's disappearance, at least up to a point. She rode into town with Carlos and, while he was completing his round of errands, went to the house where Fumiko's family had lived for years. One of the neighbors informed Mitzko that Fumiko's father moved the family to San Diego, where he'd gotten a better job. But Fumiko hadn't gone with them. Instead, she had eloped with a local boy by the name of—? Here, the neighbor was stumped. "I forget how he's called. But he worked at the garage on Orange Street. And he always wore sunglasses." Mitzko nodded. "Ieyesu," she said. "Do you know where they went?" The neighbor shrugged. "Your guess is as good as mine, dearie." Mitzko thanked the woman for her help and left to rejoin Carlos in front of the bank.

The day of departure came. Like Delores, Mitzko was glad to be going back to school. Her parents—forever beloved, forever respected—were no longer the couple who lived in the snug little house behind the general's great mansion on the estate; now, they were two sometimes perplexing but unfailingly loyal spirits who went with her wherever it was that she elected to go . . .

Chapter 38

After classes on a Friday afternoon, they sat in a not-so-popular little café over behind the music building on Pinelawn Street. Not long ago, it had rained; the sidewalks were still wet and fragrant; here and there, tree leaves dripped. Delores had been talking about her own life and dis-illusionments, when suddenly she shifted the subject to Mitzko. "I don't understand," she said. "A person like you. Warm, perceptive, empathetic. Why isn't there someone sharing your life? Your being without a boyfriend, a lover—it doesn't figure."

Mitzko had been personal with Delores; she trusted her enough to confide in her. But she had never discussed Garrett: she considered it off-limits. Now, she hesitated. Maybe it was time to break the taboo? Maybe Delores—and she herself—were entitled to an explanation? She put her coffee cup down. "There was someone . . ." She looked away, over to the other side of the street where a woman pushed a stroller with a child in it past flowering hibiscus. "Once—"

Delores waited. "Well?"

Mitzko met her friend's eyes; they were curious, challenging, expectant. "It came to nothing," she said.

"I gathered as much," said Delores. "But how? What happened? Who was the person?"

Mitzko lifted her cup, but didn't drink. The old reluctance to speak, the unwillingness to rake up dead leaves, the familiar feelings of bafflement and impotence came over her.

She avoided the eyes that abruptly she thought of as prying. "What does it matter who he was? Or why it ended? It's finished. Dead and buried and never to be revived. That's all . . ."

For a moment, Delores was silent; the barbed wire had scratched but not cut her deeply. She toyed with her napkin. "Okay," she said, forcing a smile. "You don't want to talk about him or the affair. Fine. But tell me: why do you remain alone? Why aren't you with someone else?"

"I don't want anyone else."

Delores drew a deep breath. "He broke your heart. Is that it?"

Mitzko shook her head. "No, that's not it. My heart's intact—very much so . . ." She reflected; searched for the right words. "Sometimes," she said evenly, "in a violent storm, a ship founders on a reef. When the storm's over, it stays there—stuck. Nothing can budge or dislodge it . . ." She shrugged. "That's the way it is with me. I've gone over it a thousand times, but I can't say why . . ."

"It's a pity," murmured Delores. "A waste."

"It is what it is . . ."

Two strangers they had been, but they were genuinely friends. They were sensitive to each other's needs, enjoyed each other's company, relieved each other's isolation. Mitzko had invited Delores into her life; Delores had accepted wholeheartedly. They ate meals together in less-frequented restaurants, discussed books and music, saw an occasional film with each other. They continued to play tennis and rose early to jog together. The friendship deepened; it was balm, sweetness, nourishment. Delores spoke of her affairs and their dissolutions, of the obstacles she'd surmounted, and the desires she hadn't satisfied. Though Mitzko avoided talking about Garrett, she dared to tell Delores about Chuo. She surprised herself. Rather than aggravating the wound, discussing the relationship with Chuo and his death in some ways relieved her. She felt more able to handle the pain. Her intimacy with Delores made her feel more human, more accepting of her humanity. She suddenly realized that since Fumiko's disappearance, she'd been terribly alone.

Then came Louisa. Tall, reed-thin, scarlet-lipped, with the omnipresent scepter of an upheld cigarette. "I know," she'd say in her affected, strangulated tone. "It's poison. But then, so am I." She loved shocking people. Loved scandal and scorn. Loved Delores. "And I love her!" proclaimed Delores exultantly in the locker room after a tennis match with Mitzko. Mitzko stared at her flushed face, feverish eyes, restless hands. "It just happened! Like so! I never expected it, but that's life—" Delores drew a breath and kicked off one sneaker and then the other. "You remember the chamber music concert you couldn't make last Monday? Well, I went on my own. That's where I met her. She overpowered me. After the concert we had drinks—and ended up sleeping together! It was incredible—sensational! Can you imagine?"

Mitzko certainly tried. But the riddle proved insoluble. The suddenness, the sheer adventitiousness of Delores's involvement with Louisa. The abandonment. The almost ruthlessness of the passion. The sameness of sex. It was too much for Mitzko to grasp. Perhaps she would have asked, would have attempted to understand, but Delores by degrees became unavailable. Lousia monopolized her, devoured her. And Delores went willingly along with the enslavement. "I'm a love slave," she simpered during one of their inevitably truncated phone conversations. "Lousia has me in the palm of her hand! So what's wrong with that?"

Mitzko might well have told her, but didn't get the chance. Their relationship had altered radically. Delores either broke or forgot about appointments; telephone calls were interrupted; later on, it became impossible to get through. When they did speak, Delores had little or nothing to say. Delores was correct: Lousia had taken possession of her. In turn, she had succumbed. Somewhere, Mitzko realized, choice was involved, but one would have to thread his way through a labyrinth to get to the bottom of it all. Ultimately, the seduction of Delores, or her obsession, or whatever one elected to call it, was as inscrutable as Mitzko's own fatal attraction to Garrett. One could praise and extol and celebrate such a bind; one could decry and lament and bewail it; one could search for answers or accept it blindly. But one would be hard put to explain. "It's not rational," Delores told Mitzko. "That doesn't make it any easier," Mitzko said, not without bitterness.

Lousia looked and was consummately cruel. She had a sharp wit and a vicious tongue, both of which she used to advantage. She mocked and ridiculed, she gossiped and maligned—all with zest and enterprise. When, by sheer accident, Mitzko bumped into her striding along the sidewalk outside the Student Union, Lousia declared: "Make no mistake about it, my dear: I'm a bitch. I was born a bitch in my heart; I'll always be one. Nothing and nobody will change me. I like it that way—get it? Whoever doesn't can lump it!"

The humiliation and suffering of others amused her, offered her manifest enjoyment. Several days after Delores's confession in the locker room, Mitzko waited for her friend in front of one of the two local movie theaters. Instead of Delores, Lousia—massively rouged and lipsticked and bearing her imperious cigarette like a torch—put in a substitute appearance. She didn't waste any time. "I'll get right to the point," she said, flicking ashes Mitzko's way. "Keep away from Delores. She's mine—and I don't take kindly to trespassers. I'm jealous, and I'm vengeful. If you know what's good for you, you won't cross me!" Mitzko walked away in dismay and disgust. She could not fathom what Delores saw in Louisa or what she got from her. But Louisa's near-hypnotic hold on Delores seemed complete and unbreakable.

In her last telephone conversation with Delores, Mitzko fought to keep her voice from cracking. "I don't understand what's going on, what kind of warped relationship you're involved in. Frankly, it worries the hell out of me; I'm depressed about it. Delores, please tell me what's happened to you—"

"I'm bewitched."

"It isn't a joke, Delores."

"I'm not joking."

"But—"

"There are no 'buts.' Louisa has me. She has me wrapped around her little finger. She can do any damned thing she wants with me."

Mitzko bit her lip. "You're investing yourself in nothing positive, Delores," she shouted into the phone. "You're investing in nothing at all! It's just chimera, illusion, madness, masochism!" Her voice did crack: "Delores—you're a fool!"

There was a pause. Then Delores said: "So are you, Mitzko!"

And hung up.

That was it. Finished and final. Requiem for a friendship. Mitzko was once more alone. There was a void in her life. She would be distressed, frustrated, confounded, isolated. But in good time, the waters would come together. The waters would close, leaving for all the world to see (or to ignore) a lustrous, calm, unruffled surface. She would be accustomed to her solitude again.

Chapter 39

She wanted to avoid seeing Delores at all costs. And since Delores often played tennis and Louisa watched her ("like a hawk," she'd once commented), Mitzko chose to give up the game. To fill the gap, she took a job in the main college library; the extra money it provided was useful as well. Towards the middle of April, she was clearing a table of newspapers that hadn't been returned to their racks, when her eye was caught by a recent issue of her hometown daily. Her shift was almost over, there wasn't much work to do; idly, with far more nostalgia than any real interest, she found herself leafing through it. Suddenly, she froze. It was the photograph in the upper left-hand section of the society page. She bent over it to make certain.

There was no mistake. She was right. Arm-in-arm, on a lawn—she was sure it was the front lawn of the estate—stood Garrett and the blond young woman she'd seen him with at his birthday party. Garrett was in dress uniform; he stood stiffly, properly, with one of his white-gloved hands locked firmly in the primly gloved hand of his companion. Mitzko lifted the paper. Garrett looked staid, settled; she could not discern whether there was still the dismembering sadness in his eyes or whether it had gone. The young woman beside him was elegant and poised; she had sufficient self-confidence not to need to look haughty. The photograph was black-and-white, so Mitzko couldn't tell the colors of her gown and accessories.

Mitzko's eyes dropped to the caption beneath the picture. She read with difficulty: ". . . Garrett Wilson Edwards, the son of . . ." The words blurred, but she struggled on. ". . . Elizabeth Meredith Atherton, daughter of Major General and Mrs. . . ." She scarcely saw: ". . . betrothed on Saturday, the ninth—" She lowered the paper and steadied herself against the table. She lost track of time and of her surroundings until a hand touched her shoulder lightly. It was Mrs. Rodney, the chief librarian. "I'm sorry, Mrs. Rodney," she murmured.

"Sorry about what? It's past your shift. You should've been gone fifteen minutes ago . . ."

Mitzko shook her head. "I didn't realize . . ."

"Are you all right, dear?" Mrs. Rodney adjusted her glasses on the bridge of her nose, smoothed her gray hair. "Is something wrong?"

"Nothing's wrong, thank you."

"Are you sure? Can I help?"

"It's very kind of you, Mrs. Rodney, but I'm fine. I'm just leaving the library now . . ."

"See you tomorrow, then. Bright and early. Remember, it's Thursday, and you have the first shift—"

"Tomorrow. Bright and early."

But it seemed to her that time had stopped, that tomorrow would not arrive. Somehow, she didn't feel devastated—just numb. How queer: she felt as if she'd been frozen into an ice cube! But it was ridiculous; if the truth were to be told, she'd always known that such a moment would come. Komako had warned her. Garrett's desertion at Easter time had confirmed the warning. Mitzko knew then what the future would bring. So why the fuss? Why the benumbing implosion? The feeling that life wouldn't go on?

It did, of course. Hers and everybody else's. The world

turned. The invisible current of time, carrying everyone and everything, flowed. On Thursday morning, bright and early, she was in the library. Doing her job. Nodding to students. Smiling at Mrs. Rodney, who said: "Feeling better today, dear? That's good. I was sure whatever it was that caused your mood would pass. A bad mood always passes . . . if one is willing to give time a chance. Patience and perseverance: those are words we all must learn. I'm sure you agree . . ." Mitzko slipped books into their places on the shelves. "Oh, I do, Mrs. Rodney. We all must learn them."

She took her last final exam on a Monday, and had planned to leave school for home on Wednesday. She thought to be there for several weeks and then leave for her summer job. Through the school, she'd found work as a nature counselor in a camp, not the one in which she'd worked with Fumiko, but a camp up in northwestern Oregon. The Pacific Northwest attracted her; she was eager to go there, excited about the forthcoming season. But on Tuesday, late in the afternoon, she had a phone call from Komako, whose voice she almost didn't recognize. "Come home at once," her mother said. "Your father's very ill."

Akira had suffered a sudden, massive heart attack. By the time he'd received medical attention, there had been considerable oxygen loss to the brain. He was in a coma; the extent of the damage to his brain was still unknown. Mitzko went directly from the bus station to the hospital, where she learned this from her mother. "Can I see him?" she asked. "He's not conscious. He's been unconscious ever since the attack," said Komako. "I want to see him," Mitzko said.

Dr. Princeton, the neurologist, a portly man in his mid-fifties with bushy eyebrows and sideburns, was just leaving the room. "See your father?" he mused, sucking dryly at the stem of an unfilled pipe. "What for?" He shrugged. "Well, if you wish, I won't prevent you. Go ahead in. But make sure you don't stay too long . . ."

She didn't spend much time in the room; it was more a matter of verifying for herself that he was alive than anything else. He looked flimsy—a wan imitation of himself. Uneasily, she stood by his bed. Staring down at him, she allowed herself to touch his cheek, to whisper words she didn't dream he would hear. Then she turned and left. Komako was on a sofa in an alcove at the end of the corridor, and Mitzko joined her. The two women sat next to each other, keeping bitter vigil. It was all they could do.

About an hour later, a petite woman in her late thirties wearing a severely tailored blue suit appeared. Komako scarcely noticed her; Mitzko glanced up. "I'm the psychologist," said the woman. "My name's Harkness. Dr. Ruth Harkness." At once, Mitzko trusted the brown eyes—just a shade darker than the fine-textured hair—and the authoritative yet gentle voice. "My father," Mitzko began, "will he—?" But she couldn't go on.

"Will he be a vegetable?" said Dr. Harkness. "Is that what you wanted to ask me?"

Mitzko nodded.

"I don't believe so. I've seen him several times. There are good signs. Positive signs—" Dr. Harkness gestured. "It's possible for your father to recover. You and your mother can help—"

"What must we do?"

"Talk to him. As much and as often as you can. Bring a radio or a tape-recorder and play music that he likes—"

"But will he hear? Will he understand?"

Dr. Harkness dug her fine-boned hands into the pockets of her jacket. "Keep on stimulating his mind," she said. "It can help to bring him back . . ."

Mitzko and Komako did as the psychologist had advised. They took turns. Eight days after he'd lost consciousness, Akira came out of the coma. Komako's cheeks were stained with tears as she hurried into the alcove, where Mitzko was sitting with Dr. Harkness. "He opened his eyes!" Komako proclaimed. "Thank God! He's back—!"

"Not all at once," Dr. Harkness cautioned. "It'll take some time for him to recover. For speech and recent memory to return. Be patient. Keep up the stimulation—"

Akira was back indeed. Several days later, in late afternoon sunlight from the window swimming with dust motes, he spoke his first words. Mitzko was at his side. She'd had the radio on; she had to turn it down to hear him. "Chuo," he said softly, "I won't let you die here. Come on, Chuo . . . I'll take your gear, you take your rifle. Now, get on your feet—" Then, shutting out the sunlight with shaking hands, he began to sob.

Mitzko didn't think he would ever stop.

Chapter 40

Akira was back again, but not in contemporary time. He was back in the war, back in the army in which he'd enlisted, back in the 522nd Field Artillery Battalion. He was in wartime Europe. In mud and freezing rain and snow. He carried his gear like a pack-horse; he ate K rations; he mailed V letters; he slept in a puny tent or in foxholes; he washed in the water from a helmet; he excreted on the ground. After word of the death of Chuo's young wife and unborn child came, he cradled his friend in his arms. He did everything humanly possible to comfort Chuo: he talked, he reasoned, he pleaded, he sang, he moaned, he grieved the grief of the principal mourner as though it were his own. He would not abandon Chuo, who knew it. And in the end, by sheer will, he roused Chuo from a longed-for oblivion, half-dragging him, half-prodding him forward. But forward to what?

To Dachau.

There, Akira's rambling anecdotes and broken episodes stopped. As if he'd crashed head-on into a concrete wall. His eyes glazed over, his jaw dropped; once more, he went blank. He became a wick around which flamed an invisible fire. The two women were baffled, dismayed, stunned. "It's as if something inside him short-circuited," Mitzko told Dr. Harkness. "Up to this point, he was doing well. Making so much progress. Now, he's clammed up. He's—like a mummy again! What should we do?"

"Keep talking to him," the psychologist said. "Don't let up . . ."

As instructed, wife and daughter worked on with their patient. Gradually, Akira moved into the present. His speech became much clearer, he rambled less, his recognition of Komako and Mitzko didn't blur or waver. He asked relevant questions; he talked about the estate and his work. Haltingly, tentatively, painstakingly, he came nearer to being his old self. He ate by himself, conversed at length without discomfort, was interested in the newspapers and books which were brought to him. But there were motor difficulties. He couldn't walk on his own: Komako, but mainly Mitzko, took him from bed and hospital room in a wheelchair.

Finally, it was time for discharge. Dr. Harkness came by to bid them farewell and good luck. Akira and Komako pressed her hand and gave her their thanks. Komako moved the wheelchair down the corridor towards the exit; Mitzko lingered behind. On a number of occasions, she had spoken to Dr. Harkness about her studies and aspirations; the two of them had become rather attached. As they walked together, Dr. Harkness said: "You're well-suited to the profession you've chosen. Fact is, I haven't seen better. Keep up the good work!"

"I intend to," said Mitzko.

Dr. Harkness took her arm. "You know, we're usually short of good physical therapists here. They aren't easy to find. Who can say? Perhaps one fine day, you'll come on staff . . ."

Mitzko reddened. "Perhaps . . ."

That very afternoon, with Akira safely installed in the house, Mitzko contacted the Oregon camp to inform them that she wouldn't be coming. She wished and intended to dedicate her summer to her father's convalescence. It proved a good move, one that had undoubtedly been prompted by her intuition. Komako loved Akira; she was of course interested in his welfare. But there was something withdrawn about her, some subtle mechanism—of which she herself most probably wasn't aware—which pushed her to escape. She cooked—often lavishly; she cleaned—to the point of obsession; she was out of the house, working in the vegetable garden or hanging laundry or doing endless little chores, more than she was inside. And she had turned irritatingly religious. There were shrines all over the house—one couldn't escape them. In the kitchen, in the dining room, in the big bedroom—even in the entrance hall. "A forest of shrines!" Akira exclaimed with astonishment and despair to his daughter. He thought it bizarre; Mitzko agreed. She wasn't able to condone the process; she didn't bother trying to analyze it: she—and Akira—simply had to accept it. There was nothing else they could do.

So Mitzko was in charge of her father's regimen; she was the mainstay. She'd wanted Oregon, but it wasn't a loss to her. The excursions with Akira in his wheelchair, their discussions about the living things around them, the hours at night when she read to him and he read to her, her satisfaction with his improvement: all of this constituted a rejuvenated closeness with him that filled her life. Oregon could wait for some other summer. If it had to be, even college could wait. Her first duty was to Akira, to his physical and mental health. She had made up her mind.

June went by and then July. Akira had improved enough for Mitzko to address other problems. Late one night, after he'd gone to bed, she sat with Komako in the kitchen. Over undrunk tea, the two reviewed the family's economic future. Akira would never walk again: that was certain. He might learn to pursue some trade or occupation from his wheelchair, but he could not continue working on the staff of the estate. The general had not appeared personally to announce the fact, he hadn't even come when Akira returned from the hospital; instead, he sent Carlos with his message. "What does it mean?" Mitzko asked. "When exactly will my father's salary stop? Can we go on living here, in this house, or will we have to make other arrangements?"

Carlos fidgeted; he was visibly disturbed and anxious about what he was about to say. "I'm very sorry—" he began.

"We know you're sorry," said Komako, touching his arm.

"Say what you have to say," Mitzko demanded.

Carlos bit his lip. "Akira's last paycheck will be for July. And the general would like you to be out of the house by the first of September . . ." He twisted his cap in his hands. "I'm sorry," he murmured once again.

Komako went white. "Leave this house? The gardens? The land? But that's impossible! It will kill Akira!"

Carlos retreated towards the entrance hall. "If there's anything I can do," he muttered, "any way I can help . . ."

"Thank you, Carlos," said Mitzko. "Thank you for coming. Tell the general that we'll be gone by September first, as he wishes . . ."

The two women had agreed not to tell Akira until a new place for them had been found, until all the arrangements had been made. Now, in the kitchen they were soon to vacate, they made plans. They would be compelled to go to town, to a neighborhood such as the one Fumiko's family had lived in; there was really no other possibility. Over the years, they'd laboriously accrued some savings: these would provide for the move and see them through several months' rent. Komako would work: she was sure she could find employment as a domestic, or perhaps in a local store or in the supermarket, or perhaps some shop or factory would hire her. "We'll manage," said Komako, with a fire and with an energy that her daughter hadn't seen since the moment that the general had been shot by Chuo. "We'll get on our feet somehow."

"I'll leave school," said Mitzko.

On the tablecloth, Komako clenched her fists. "No," she said. "You will not leave school until you've finished. No matter what."

Komako seemed somehow to have revived—or, more exactly, to have revived herself. To have dragged herself or clawed or crawled, Mitzko thought, across a bitter, blind place in her life. Mitzko admired her mother's startling comeback, and she put stock in it. Without involving Akira, the two women made their plans. They searched for and found a small but decent apartment in the neighborhood they'd reckoned on, not very far actually from the building in which Fumiko had lived for more than a decade. They put down the security money, as well as the first month's rent; they contacted a local company and scheduled a moving day; they made arrangements with one of the estate handymen to paint the new flat a week before they were to enter it; stealthily, after Akira was in bed and fast asleep, they began to get rid of all the extras that had accumulated over the years. Komako smiled thinly. "Where in the world did we ever get all this?" Mitzko shrugged. The same was true for spiritual acquisition, she thought.

In August, Mitzko got a job as a cashier in the town supermarket, the one that Fumiko had worked in and written about. She was able to do so and to earn the needed extra money because Komako had stopped eluding life and become more involved in caring for Akira. Komako had also purged the house of all its shrines but one; now, she spent scarcely any time praying at it. She never said why, nor did

Mitzko ever question her. "We're going to be all right," she kept repeating. Almost as if it were a new prayer.

One night, just before the two of them separated for bed, Mitzko said: "How did you ever do it?"

"Do what?"

"You know, Mother, bring yourself back. Pull yourself up the way you did—"

Komako reflected. "I reached for the strength," she said slowly. "I reached very deep inside myself. Very deep. I did not know what I'd find—even if I'd find anything at all. But I took a chance. I felt I had no other choice . . ." As if she were immensely relieved, she sighed. "The strength was there, Mitzko. Waiting for me."

Akira now required far less attention. He had taken to carving wood and making toys. For hours on end, sitting in his wheelchair outside the house, he occupied himself with his woodwork. "Chuo taught me how," he once said. The women were pleased and impressed. They believed that he might progress in the pursuit, that he might one day convert the hobby into an occupation. But for the present, they agreed not to suggest such to him; they'd decided that it would be better to wait until after the move.

On Monday of the final week before their departure, they told Akira about it. Supper was over. He was in his armchair in the living room. The light from his lamp fell on the newspaper that lay opened over his lap. He seemed calm, stable, engrossed in his reading. The house was so quiet that the ticking of the clock could be heard from the kitchen. When he finished with the paper, he folded it over and dropped it to the floor. Then he reached for his pipe: he rarely smoked it, but he often chewed the stem. "Like a dog on a bone," he liked to joke.

Komako cleared her throat. "Akira—"

He saw that both women were staring at him. Inches from his mouth, the pipe hovered in mid-air. "What's all this?" he asked. "Why are you two looking at me that way? What's gone amiss?"

"Akira, we must speak with you—" said Komako.

"That's quite obvious. But what's wrong? Is it money—?" Akira jabbed with the pipe stem. "That's it, of course! Money! You two thought that I wasn't paying attention. Or—worse still—that I'd forgotten. That's what's awry, isn't it?" His brow was furrowed; on the arms of the chair, his hands trembled. He was peeved, offended, agitated. "I may not walk," he went on, "but I do think. I have a plan. I've been working out the details for days, maybe weeks. Let me explain—"

Mitzko intervened: "Father, we're moving."

"What's that?"

"We're moving away from here," said Komako.

"Moving? Leaving the house? The estate? Leaving—!?"

"The general asked us to be out by September first," said Komako.

"The general has ordered us out? Ordered us off the land—?"

"We've rented a flat in town," said Mitzko. "We have a moving date for next week. We've been packing. We're almost ready to go, Father."

Akira tossed his pipe into the ashtray. His hands shifted this way and that—he seemed not to know what to do with them. "General Edwards was here? When did he come? I don't recall seeing him or speaking with him. When did all this happen?"

"The general didn't come here," Komako explained. "He sent Carlos with the message. You were asleep; Carlos spoke to Mitzko and myself. He told us we had to go. As Mitzko

208

said, we've made our arrangements. Everything has been taken care of . . ."

"I see," said Akira.

Komako leaned forward. "Do you wish to speak personally to the general? To request that he change his mind?"

"To beg him, you mean . . ."

"Call it what you please, Akira . . ." Komako rose from her place on the sofa. She looked tiny, like a bird weary from flight. Her hair had grayed, her shoulders were rounded, she wore a faded flower-print dress that made her appear fragile. But her voice was firm. "You must decide, Akira: do you want us to arrange a meeting? Do you want to talk to the general yourself?"

"Never!"

On Wednesday, in the supermarket, Mitzko looked up from her cash register and saw a familiar face.

"You don't remember me, Mitzko—?"

"Toge!"

"That's better!" He smiled broadly.

"Toge! It's good to see you! How've you been?"

"This isn't exactly the place to discuss it. When do you finish up here? Maybe we can have coffee or sodas at Mason's?"

He was tall, angular, but he had filled out nicely, and he had shed the awkwardness and patent uncertainty of youth. She was actually quite pleased to see him again. "I'll be happy to have coffee with you," she said. "I can meet you at Mason's. At four-thirty. But I can't stay all that long . . ."

"It doesn't matter."

They spent about twenty minutes filling each other in on what had happened in their lives since high school. Toge had been in San Diego, studying aviation mechanics; he said he'd done very well. "Fumiko's folks moved to San Diego," said Mitzko. "You remember her, don't you?"

"Oh? Naughty Fumiko—I remember her well! You two were good pals. Are you still in touch?"

Mitzko shook her head. "She eloped with some boy from town a while ago; I've not heard a word from her in ages. She's disappeared . . ."

Toge was silent. He looked grave, drawn into himself. Then, meeting her eyes again, he said. "Mitzko, I've enlisted."

"Enlisted? What do you mean? When—?"

"Today—this afternoon. Actually, I left the recruiting office just a little while before I came into the supermarket and met you. I decided . . . to join the marines."

"But why, Toge?"

"There's a war on, that's why."

"I still don't understand . . ."

"What don't you understand, Mitzko?" Toge stared at her. "Your own father was in the service, in the Five Hundred and Twenty-second. People in town remember it. I've heard stories about what he did in the war."

"That was a different war."

"It's my country, Mitzko. My country's at war. I'm going."

Mitzko was silent; there was nothing she could do, except wish him well. "Good luck, Toge," she said. "Come back home safely."

"Mitzko . . . may I write to you?"

"Yes, if you wish. You may always feel free to write . . ."

Suddenly, he leaned forward and kissed her cheek. She slid from her stool and left. Around the corner from Mason's, on the sidewalk, she put her fingers to her cheek where his lips had been. Almost as if she were touching a wound.

210

Every day, she traveled to and from work in an old Chevy with an assistant manager named Frank Allbright who lived with his wife and two small children in a house a mile or two beyond the estate. Frank's parents had been farmers, but they were dead and most of the farm had been sold off. When he discovered where she lived, he promptly offered Mitzko the ride. "It's nice of you to take me," she told him. Allbright shrugged. "As long as we work the same shift, it's no real problem for me."

On Friday, after work, he stopped the Chevy in front of the main gate; Mitzko thanked him and got out of the car. Halfway down the walk, she spotted the figure in uniform. There could be no mistake: she knew at first glance that it was Garrett. Her first impulses were to retreat or to hide. But both were impossible—she was certain he'd seen her. Was perhaps even waiting for her. And the impulses were false, cowardly, unproductive. Why should she run? She had done Garrett no wrong, broken no promises, betrayed no trust. If she'd thought to flee, it could only be from herself. From pain she didn't care to acknowledge as unresolved. So she continued walking in his direction.

He was trimmer than ever, immaculate, elegant—as if he'd been cut perfectly from a stencil. Viewing him at close range made her catch her breath. As always, he looked serious, confident; dedicated: the officer's pips shining on his shoulders were tangible evidence that he was well on his way to reaching his goals. It wasn't a surprise: she had expected no less. Now, their glances met. She searched his eyes. They showed her decisiveness, command, and the characteristic daring—or was it arrogance? Where had what she'd seen in them during their relationship gone? Would it ever return? She wondered if it had ever really been there. But all that was in the past. Altogether, he looked leaner, tougher, more actively combative. As if he were hardening in his father's mold.

"Were you waiting for me?" she asked him.

"Yes."

"How could you be sure I'd come?"

"Your mother told me. I asked her."

She had absolute control of herself now; it seemed at once amazing and natural to her. "Why? Why did you want to meet me?"

"I wanted to tell you—" He hesitated; he was choosing his words. Then he said: "I heard about what happened to your father. I wanted to say that I'm sorry. That I hope he's better—"

"Thank you. My father's doing quite well."

"I also found out that you and your parents are leaving—"

"On Monday."

"I'm very sorry about that as well—"

"You needn't be sorry. We have a place in town. We'll do fine."

He seemed to ignore—or dismiss—the remark. "I wanted you to know that as soon as I discovered you were going, I spoke to my father. I asked him if there wasn't any way for your family to remain on the estate, in the house—"

"And—?"

Garrett cleared his throat. "My father wouldn't change his mind. He wouldn't budge. He refused me."

"I appreciate the effort," she said. "But it wasn't necessary."

He shrugged. "I did what I had to do . . ." His eyes regarded her, more personally now, she thought. "How is school going?" he asked.

"School is fine."

"That's good to hear. I figured you'd do well . . ."

There was an instant of silence—not awkward, but fateful.

Both knew it was time to cut the cord of conversation. To part. To be on their separate ways. Forever.

Suddenly, without having planned or even thought about it, she blurted out: "Congratulations . . . on your engagement! I wish you and your fiancée every happiness!"

She saw not the slightest reaction on his part; he appeared to take her good wishes forthrightly, in stride—just as she'd given them. But as she brushed by him, she believed that in his eyes she glimpsed some strain of what had first drawn her to him. It was a fragmentary perception, only a flash—she couldn't be certain. But what did it matter? She had already closed the door, had locked it securely. And yet, as she hurried away from him towards the home that Akira and Komako and she would soon leave for good, she wondered. Until, with a hand on the front doorknob, she felt foolish. Only a fool, she reflected, would rake a dead fire for flame . . .

Late that Sunday afternoon, after the last of their household goods had been stuffed into boxes and cartons, Akira looked up from his folded and refolded weekend newspaper and said: "Mitzko, please take me out—"

Komako, who'd been up and working since daybreak, was napping; bereft of her tiny figure moving methodically from one room to the next, and stripped of almost everything familiar, the house suddenly seemed desolate and foreign; Mitzko was happy to get the wheelchair from the foyer and assist her father into it. "The house is so stuffy," he said. "It's like a damn jail. I must have . . . some fresh air . . ."

She wheeled him along the pathways and walks that encompassed the estate, pushing the chair past the gardens and swards and buildings where he'd worked and which he'd tended for so many years. Several times over, she attempted to make conversation, but he didn't respond. He sat silent and unmoving, his hands laid inertly on the metal armrests, like a mannikin arbitrarily being shifted from one store display to another. Mitzko had hoped that the excursion would be pleasant, would relax both her father and herself; instead, he was rigid and uncommunicative—and she had become tense. As they neared a side gate in the southern wall, he suddenly lifted a hand and pointed. "Take me out there—"

She pushed him through the gate and onto the dirt trail that wound down to the woods and led ultimately to the river. The setting sun folded drapery of red and gold over the open fields; to the east, the mountains—beginning to blur in the weakening light—looked like waves arrested in motion; birds drifted by in the uncertain colors of the sky. Akira signaled with a finger and Mitzko stopped. She watched her father, followed his gaze as it slowly swept the points of the compass. She hesitated, but in the end couldn't help herself. "You're going to miss all this," she said softly, "aren't you?"

He didn't answer.

She put a hand on his shoulder. "Father, you will miss this land; I know you will . . ."

"It's not my land."

She stood there with him for several moments and then, sensing that he wished to move, pushed the wheelchair ahead, in the direction of the trees. But he said abruptly: "Take me back."

The sun was down by the time they returned to the estate; a mauve afterglow stained the sky, but it was fading fast. She took the wheelchair along the road and entered the grounds through the main gate. On their left, coiling a length of rubber hose, Carlos glanced up. He seemed glad yet at the same time uncomfortable to see Akira. When he started forward, perhaps to grasp the other man's hand, Akira said brusquely: "The ritual's quite unnecessary. Thanks for being my friend all these years, Carlos."

"We'll stay in touch, Akira—"

"Of course."

Just past the gazebo, the central walkway they were on merged with a transverse one. On the latter, a second wheelchair moved: Mitzko and Akira caught sight of it at the same instant. "Stop," said Akira, and Mitzko did. Pushed forward by his nurse, the general glided across the intersection of the paths, the wheels of his chair hissing smoothly on stone. He did not turn his head or stir; he gave no sign of recognition or of even seeing Akira. Like an iron shadow, he was swallowed up in the dusk . . .

Chapter 41

Everything was new, strange, cramped. The apartment seemed tiny, like a sectioned-off shoebox. There were sounds and smells from the neighbors; there was constant noise from the street. Cats positioned themselves on the fences and yowled; stray dogs prowled the alleyway behind the yard and poked in the garbage cans. Cars blew their horns; children screamed at each other without stop. They had rented a first-floor flat to accommodate the wheelchair, but Akira didn't want to go out. "There's nothing outside," he said with disgust, "except filth and racket."

Komako was determined to make the best of it. "You'll get used to things," she told her husband. "Give yourself time."

"She's right," assented Mitzko, uneasy because she was leaving but also because she couldn't altogether agree with Komako's opinion.

Though supposedly it had been settled before they moved, mother and daughter continued to argue about Mitzko's return to college. "You need me here," Mitzko insisted. "Dad needs me."

"We'll do fine without you," rejoined Komako. "In fact, we'll do better . . . because college is where you belong."

"Dad won't adjust—"

"He doesn't have a choice."

By mid-September, Komako had employment as a seamstress. "You see," she said to Mitzko, "I already have a job;

216

our situation is better. I told you things would work out—remember?"

"What about Father?"

Komako was plainly optimistic. "He can certainly keep himself busy. He'll carve, make his toys: I believe that he'll find a market, that it will bear fruit. He'll write in his 'Encyclopedia' and he'll read—I'll see to it that he has plenty of books from the library. He has the radio, and we'll buy a television set in time—" She paused. "In the end, he'll even get into the wheelchair and leave the apartment. There's a whole world waiting outside; your father will want to explore it. I know him. Trust me . . ."

Mitzko felt better, more secure than she'd been initially. At this point, it was difficult for her to make an objective judgment. Part of that was because Akira—always open and direct—had taken to dissembling and to shutting his family out, so that Mitzko couldn't assess his true state of mind. The other part had to do with her fierce desire to return to school. "School will save you," a voice inside her said. She believed the voice; she wanted things at home to be stable and settled, so she could leave for college in peace, with a quiet conscience. Ultimately, she accepted both her parents' injunction that she go back to school. She based the decision on her mother's remarkable rebirth, and on her father's uncanny resilience . . .

Back at school, she felt enormous relief and managed within a short time to rid of herself of guilt that she was relieved. Instead of one of the dorms, she rented an attic room in a three-story frame house on the periphery of campus. The place was perfect: the floor was parquet; there was a large bay window that looked out over the arboretum; the bathroom had a French door with a glass knob and was tiled in blue-and-white mosaic; there was a charming nook in which to cook meals on a hot plate. Because it was so small and a walk-up, the rent was cheap. Mitzko loved everything about it: the privacy, decor, view—even the climb up three somewhat shaky flights of stairs.

Without waiting, she plunged into the work that she relished, into the routine that she found stimulating. In renewing the connection with college, she discovered how intensely she'd missed it. Immediately, she established a schedule from which she wouldn't be budged. She went to her classes religiously, she fixed study periods, she got back her old job at the library, she worked out in the gym, she jogged, and on weekends, she took long walks in the arboretum and through the surrounding countryside. She wrote to her parents regularly, at least once a week; sometimes, she phoned them. From time to time, she caught glimpses of Delores and Louisa—singly and together—and on rarer occasions spotted Lexi, her former roommate, usually with a male escort. But she kept her distance. They had nothing to offer her; she had nothing to give them.

She was absorbed in her life. Only one shadow disturbed it, a shadow that seemed to grow and darken by the day. The war. She didn't give her active support to any of the campus protest groups, whose efforts steadily mounted, but she sometimes went to rallies or meetings. The war bothered her, gnawed at her conscience, disturbed her dreams. She fought hard to keep it from blurring her concentration, from upsetting her equilibrium. At times, she felt desperation approach, but she couldn't allow herself to be carried away.

In November, she received her first letter from Toge. "... This is only training," he wrote, "and it's hard. I have no illusions: being in Vietnam will be a million times harder. I've heard stories. And I've seen some of the wounded. It's horrible. Too horrible to write to you about. But I had to enlist. And I have to go over. Don't ask me why: I don't have any answer . . ."

She surprised herself and wrote back to him. Told him about the move to the apartment in town, about Akira's difficult adjustment. ". . . Mother has proven herself adaptable, inventive, energetic; she's risen to the challenge. As for Father, I really can't say. His mind's clear enough. But his heart is troubled. So far, he's above water. My great fear is that suddenly he'll sink . . ." She described her life in college minutely, down to details of the protest assemblies. ". . . You feel that you must fight in the war," she wrote him. "I feel just as strongly that I have to fight against it . . ."

Being home for Christmas buoyed her. Komako was earning decent pay in the dress shop which employed her; she'd managed to pick up a few jobs on the side. Akira had sold several toys and one or two carvings; he was beginning to look around for outlets. "And he's left the flat a few times," Komako confided. "He doesn't by any means consider this paradise. But he doesn't think it's hell either." The apartment itself was spic-and-span. Komako had made curtains, and bought a carpet for the living room; Akira had fixed up a workplace for himself in the foyer. Neither said anything about the war. So Mitzko didn't raise the subject on her own.

The next semester brought another letter from Toge. He'd finished his training and was "awaiting orders." Though he didn't say so outright, Mitzko knew it meant service overseas. She tried a number of times to reply, but something always seemed to get in the way. Finally—perhaps after he'd shipped out—she wrote a short, stiff, almost formal note wishing him well: ". . . Come and visit with me when you return." she told him. "I look forward to seeing you . . ." But she felt apprehension as she wrote the words; she felt naked fear when she mailed the letter.

Mid-semester, as she entered the classroom, her zoology professor asked that she remain after the session. It was an unusual, if not odd, request; since she had an "A" average in the subject, she couldn't imagine what he wanted. At the session's end, the bell rang; the students left their seats and filed noisily from the room. She hesitated for a moment, then she walked up to the desk, where the teacher was slipping folders and loose papers into his briefcase. He glanced up; she saw him redden; she felt her own cheeks grow warm.

Marc Harrison was an assistant professor in his early thirties. He was slim, stood somewhat above medium height, had black curly hair and green-gray eyes. He possessed a comprehensive knowledge of and an obviously deep love for his subject, which he taught in a compelling, bell-clear, tenor voice. He dressed nattily, was always impeccably groomed, gave off what many of his female students called "electric signals." Mitzko herself hadn't ever received such a signal, but she knew what was meant. She cleared her throat. "You said you wanted to see me after class, Dr. Harrison?"

"I did."

"Is—something wrong?"

He shook his head. "Not at all. Your work in class is excellent, Miss Shiraishi. You're one of my very best, if I may say so . . ."

"Then what is this about—?"

Snapping the lock of his briefcase shut, he said: "I—I'd like you to know that I don't do this usually, that I've never actually done it before—" He broke off, dropped the briefcase to the floor.

"You've never done—what before, Dr. Harrison?"

He stared at her. "It has been my policy never to ask a student out. But in your case, I mean, I—"

She had known from his eyes what he'd say before he spoke; she'd had the time to compose herself. "I see."

"You don't believe me? You think that it's some line I use?"

"I believe you, Dr. Harrison."

He was visibly relieved. "That's great! That shows you have all the intuition I credit to you!" He smiled broadly—the open, flashing, not intentionally seductive smile that had caused so many of her classmates to come under his spell. "Well, Miss Shiraishi, what do you say? Will you go out with me?"

"I'm flattered by the invitation, Dr. Harrison."

"Yes, but that doesn't answer my question, Miss Shiraishi—"

She had no need to consider. "No."

He seemed taken aback, seemed almost not to take seriously what she'd said. "You don't mean that! You—can't mean it—!"

"I do mean it, Dr. Harrison."

"But why—?"

"Why doesn't matter. The answer is no."

She went from the room with an uneasy feeling, leaving him still there. She didn't fear Dr. Marc Harrison. He was a man of integrity; he would never stoop to revenge or engage in harassment. At most, there would be tension between them in class for some days or weeks—and then it would dissipate. She didn't believe he would pester or pursue her. He'd opened himself up, taken one chance: she was certain he'd leave it at that. Harrison was a born gentleman: he would nurse his disappointment covertly; he would respect her right to turn him down. Every once in a while in class, she'd catch his shy, admiring look. But he never pried or questioned; he never bothered her again.

After refusing him the date and leaving the classroom, she tried but couldn't succeed in ridding herself of her uneasiness; nothing she did made it go away. In bed that night, she recalled a story her mother had told her when she was thirteen or so. One of Komako's elementary school teachers in town was a tall, gaunt, silver-haired woman who'd never married. During the course of a discussion one afternoon, a pupil inquired why not. The teacher—who'd died when Komako was still in high school—didn't reply. But on the very next day, she brought a photograph of a young man to class. The picture was passed around, so that everybody had a chance to see it. "His name was Frank," she told her pupils. "At the start of the Great War, he volunteered for service and was sent overseas. I never saw him again, because he was killed in France." She put the picture into her purse and closed the flap. "Nobody else has ever interested me," she said. Garrett, Mitzko reflected, had never really promised her anything permanent. But it didn't seem to matter. Not even his announced engagement to the major general's debutante daughter mattered. There was something in her attachment to him—long ago null and void—that kept her attached. It was something inexplicable, odd—perhaps even perverse. But it was real. It had power.

Her summer at home went by more rapidly than the previous one. Komako was doing very well. She'd been promoted at the dress shop; her salary had almost doubled. She managed all of the household chores before and following work. She didn't complain; she looked younger than she had in years. Akira was a different story. He was uneven, oscillating between exaggerated optimism and despair. "Much of the time, he's morose," Komako told her daughter. "Then I get lost. I don't know how to help him out of it—"

"Do you ever talk to him?"

"I talk until my voice gives out. It does no good. So I give up. You know, there's only so much you can do to make people change."

Mitzko nodded. "There is only so much one can do . . . to make people change," she repeated.

She found a job in the town's main department store. She gave part of her salary to Komako; part of it she put away towards her school expenses in the fall. After work, she spent time with Akira, even if he didn't particularly seem to want her around him. One Friday afternoon, when he'd put the final touches on a beautiful carving, he was in an unusually affable mood. Mitzko approached him, and he readily agreed to a far-ranging wheelchair expedition. She took him out to the periphery of the town and farther, as far as the creek. She'd been there on horseback with Garrett, but she dismissed the memory; it was of no use to her now.

Akira shaded his eyes from the sun; he gazed at the open fields and the distant orchards. At once, he seemed awed and at ease.

For a time, Mitzko watched him silently, then she said: "You miss it, don't you? I know you do, Father. You miss the land . . ."

Akira said nothing.

His daughter was heartened; at least, he did not say—as he'd said the previous year—"It's not mine." She put a hand on his shoulder. "Who knows? Maybe we'll be able to move back one day. Back on the land. Get a place of our own. Plant and water and harvest again—" Bending forward, she kissed his unshaven cheek. "Mother's doing well now. She's even put aside some savings. When I finish college, I'll earn a good salary. Everything's possible. Father, who knows—?"

But her father seemed scarcely to be listening.

They remained by the creek for a while. Akira's demeanor softened; he seemed transfixed by the running water. The sky grew darker, merging mutely with the earth; the first star of evening appeared. It made her think of the fireflies when she was a little girl, and of Chuo and their rambling walks; once again, she throttled the memories. "I think that we ought to be getting back," she said. Akira nodded, and they started towards the far-off, twinkling lights of the town. By the time they got to the street on which they lived, the streetlamps were lit. Akira was calm, mellow, somehow malleable: it seemed to her that he might mold himself into anything, if he wished. As she maneuvered the wheelchair into the narrow entranceway of their building, he said to her: "Thank you for taking me to visit my friend . . ."

"Your friend?"

He smiled. "The creek . . ."

But on the morning of the day she was leaving for school again, she told Komako bluntly that she didn't trust him.

"Not trust him? What do you mean? He hasn't been really depressed in weeks—"

Mitzko shook her head. "He's hiding, Mother."

"Hiding what?"

"I don't know, Mother. But I sense it. There's something precarious about him. Critically unstable. Like a hundred-floor skyscraper that's balanced on the head of a pin. He doesn't want us to notice it, doesn't want us to see. But I'm telling you that something's going on, something dangerous. You'd better watch him carefully—"

Komako embraced her daughter. "You're anxious about leaving . . ."

Mitzko returned her mother's hug. "Maybe you're right," she murmured. "Maybe that's the reason."

But she didn't believe a word of what she said.

★ ★ ★ ★ ★

Alone in his room, Akira rummaged in a drawer and took the worn photograph of Mariko, his geisha mother, out of a black lacquered box filled with war mementos. He held it up to the light. "So . . . Mother, Mitzko, your granddaughter, is abandoning me just as you did," he murmured bitterly.

Chapter 42

At the beginning of November, Mitzko opened the green tin mailbox nailed to the fence and found a letter from Toge; she recognized the fine, precise handwriting at once. Barely returning her landlady's greeting, she hurried upstairs. Sitting on her bed, she opened the envelope. There was a single sheet of paper—only a few lines had been written on it: ". . . War separates the men who fight it from everyone else in the world . . . I doubt that the gap can ever be bridged. I think of you often . . . it helps me to go on. It may sound absurd, but it's true. Please write if you can . . . I'd love to receive more letters from you . . ." The letter was signed, ". . . Your friend, Toge."

She resolved to write to him weekly. She allotted a regular time for the letters and mailed them promptly. The war was intensifying; so was the antiwar sentiment. Search-and-destroy missions, body counts, napalm and carpet bombings were countered by protest marches, rallies, sit-ins, flag and draft card burnings. Mitzko knew that, in the near future, she would be working in hospital wards with the casualties. She dreaded the horror she'd face; she looked forward to the help she would give. Faithfully, almost at the same exact time every week, she seated herself at the little desk in her attic room and wrote as sincerely and positively as she could to Toge in Vietnam. The knowledge that her letters would give him a measure of solace gave her some comfort.

Christmas break was a relatively quiet one in her personal

life. Akira's mood swings seemed less extreme; Komako said that he "was on a more even keel." Mitzko tried to see it from her mother's point of view. But she still mistrusted him; to herself, she called him " 'The Man in the Iron Mask.' " He had stopped his carving and toy-making and taken to repairing clocks. "Why?" Mitzko asked him. "Chuo taught me how to do carving," he told her. "In the army, before we went overseas. I quit because doing it . . . kept reminding me of him. I no longer wish to remember. I want to forget . . ."

"That's impossible," Mitzko countered. "It's not real. I don't believe you—"

"Suit yourself."

There was something obsessive, Mitzko thought, about the way he handled clocks; something she didn't like. "Fanatical" was the unspoken word she used to describe it. He wrote little or nothing in his "Encyclopedia." But he read a lot. Not the newspapers—he "didn't want to know about the war"—but books. "I bring home books in wheelbarrows," Komako said. "He swallows them up." Akira read natural history, but preferred geography. "Exploration!" he exclaimed, his eyes lighting up. "What men the great explorers were! What incentive they had! What daring! What amazing perseverance!" When he wasn't tinkering with the clocks that people in the neighborhood brought to him to fix, he'd "embark on expeditions" to Africa or Indonesia or Antarctica. "Who'd ever dream," he asked rhetorically, "that a man in a wheelchair could go exploring!?" For hours on end, he'd sit in his chair by a window in the living room with his open books and his maps spread across his lap. Once, when Mitzko came to summon him to supper, he looked up in astonishment. "Dad," she reminded him, "it's time to eat." He shook his head. "A pity . . . that you call me back—"

The night before she left, Mitzko dreamed that Akira was

in a huge room, so large that its walls seemed to fade off into infinity. He sat on a decrepit chair in the very center of the chamber, in front of an old workbench. He was in the process of reassembling an enormous clock. The clock was complex; it told the time in a dozen different capitals of the world, the phases of the moon, and more; hundreds of its intricate parts lay scattered over the table and jumbled at his feet on the floor. So engrossed was Akira in the project that he did not notice her entry; she had to grasp his shoulder to announce her presence.

"Where did you get this clock?" she asked. "For whom are you repairing it?"

Akira turned to face her. From the look in his eyes, she understood. It wasn't the clock at all: Akira was trying to repair himself . . .

Chapter 43

Towards the end of February, a letter from Toge arrived—there hadn't been one in several weeks. "... I'm fine," he wrote, "but I'm tired. Everything about me is tired: my body, my mind, my heart. Sleep, whatever we get of it, doesn't help ... I wake up as weary as ever ..." Toge's fine, precise handwriting had deteriorated. There was a sentence she couldn't make out, then she read: "... I've lost all certainty ... except for the certainty of comradeship ..." Mitzko didn't wait for her regular writing time; she put off an assignment and wrote back to Toge immediately. Usually, she said nothing about either the war or the protests. But now she closed her letter by saying: "... Hold fast. It must be over. The people of this country want the war over ..."

She had written—without ulterior motive—to her parents a number of times about how much work she had. In mid-March, she received a letter from Komako giving her the option of not coming home for the Easter recess. "... Your father's doing splendidly," she wrote. "Not only has his clock repair business grown considerably, but he makes it a point to leave the apartment every day. He even leaves the neighborhood. In fact, he's traveled to the library twice already—by himself! I don't know what to say, except that I'm grateful!" Mitzko turned over the page. "... I'm very busy myself. I've been promoted; I'm now managing a shift at the shop. I've been looking around for a new, more efficient sewing machine: I've a pile of work at home that I haven't even begun to tackle. So if you'd like to stay at school during the vacation and get through the work you have, Akira and I will understand it fully. We love you, we want what's good for you—even if it means missing you here in April . . ."

Komako was sincere; Mitzko took her up on the offer. Though she'd pushed her course load to the absolute limit, she was still maintaining a near "A" average and repeatedly making the dean's list. But the strain was telling. Remaining in her room on the deserted campus would enable her not only to catch up, but perhaps even to get ahead. ". . . Thanks for your perceptiveness, kindness and encouragement," she wrote back to her mother. "I've decided that I'll stay where I am for Easter. There's much to do, including getting started on a couple of term papers. Keep sending me good news . . ."

Had she left college for home, Mitzko would have departed on Wednesday. By Friday, isolated and undiverted, she had accomplished an enormous amount of work. That night, around eleven, as first she put her study materials in order and then prepared to go to bed, she decided to waken early the next morning and take one of her "circumnavigational" walks. During the past days, she'd been cooped up in the room and had literally no physical activity. She set the clock-alarm, and slid between the sheets. She was tired; she dozed off easily, and slept without dreaming.

Thoroughly rested, she woke before the alarm went off. She took a quick shower, put on a sweat suit and sneakers, ate lightly, and left the apartment eager for the outing. It had rained sometime during the night—the morning air was washed, unexpectedly fresh. As she moved along the clean sidewalks, lingering raindrops fell from the trees onto her hair and face. The sun hadn't yet risen: the gray-pearl light seemed cobwebby, tenuous. On the tree-lined streets, all of the brick and frame houses were silent; front porches were empty; curtains were drawn over windows; except for a teen-aged boy on a bicycle delivering his morning papers, nobody was around. She enjoyed the aloneness—she had never feared solitude. From deep within her, a pure, living spring gurgled and sang. As always, she listened. What it whispered was vague, but affirmative.

She walked to the outskirts of the town and into the arboretum. Graced with shards, copses, glens and covert nooks, it was a hospitable refuge—even sanctuary—for lovers. Mitzko always walked in it alone; the lovers never bothered her: they seemed remote from her world, like creatures on some distant planet. From the abandoned haven of the arboretum, she went out into the countryside. A dirt road wound past fruit orchards, fields and pastures; occasionally, it came close to a farmyard in which a dog rose lazily to bark at her or a cat scampered to safety at the sound of her footsteps. She saw a farmer mounting a vintage tractor; another herded cows into a barn. Overhead, a small plane appeared to drift with the clouds. The sun was up, the day was flexing its muscles. The walk had given her peace. She turned back.

She first noticed the car as she rounded the corner. It was parked almost directly across the street from her house. She was familiar with all of the cars on the block; never, in the more than a year she'd been living there, had she seen this one. She wondered for a moment, then she dismissed it. Somebody was probably visiting. But on the stairs, it struck her once again as strange. She was inexplicably curious, even uneasy. Inside her room, she went at once to the window and pulled open the curtains. The car, a fairly new sedan, was still there. She stared at it. Everything before her eyes came into stark, singular focus: the leaves on the shingles of the sloping roof below, the bird on the green fence flicking its tail feathers, the elderly man on the near pavement curbing his

231

dog, the car itself. There was something about the car, something she hadn't noticed before. But what? Suddenly, she knew. Somebody was inside it—sitting in the driver's seat. She had no need to speculate about his identity. She was instantly certain. As soon as she saw him, she recognized Garrett.

Her first impulse was to draw the curtains. Instead, she stepped back, out of view. There was a moment of confusion. She took a number of aimless steps and then sat down on the small wicker sofa. Garrett was outside of her house. How long had he been there? What did he want? Why didn't he get out of the car and tell her? It was difficult, but she tried to be logical, to set things in order. Obviously, he'd come to see her. Earlier, perhaps, he'd pushed her bell and gotten no response; perhaps he'd missed her return. Perhaps he'd driven through the night and, waiting for her to come back, had fallen asleep. Perhaps he'd seen her go into the house, but changed his mind about seeing her. But then why was he still waiting there? Why hadn't he left?

Then she realized that none of it mattered, that she was riding on a logical merry-go-round to nowhere. The only issue for her to consider was what she wished to do. He was in the car, she was up in the room; what did she really want? She looked around her room: it was ordered, familiar, safe. She saw her life: it had stability, direction, the formidable peace of purpose. She had closed the book on relationships. Discarded the book called Garrett. She was sure he didn't dare come up to her. Why would she dare go down to him? Both he and she were poised, each on the edge of his own diving board, and each of them afraid to jump.

He wasn't asleep. He saw her come out of the front door; she saw him turn his head to follow her approach. As she crossed the street, he got out of the car and came round the front to meet her. He was dressed in civilian clothing—polo shirt, sport jacket and trousers. He looked fit, well put together, more toughened even than the last time she'd seen him. As always, his eyes were commanding. But something in their expression had altered. He hadn't lost his decisiveness—he had firm control of the rudder—but in his look there was a hint, or a warning, that he might change direction. She had a clear sense of his old war, that noble, moving conflict within him that had so drawn her to him. A man at odds with himself was a man who challenged chaos; that man was a warrior in the fiercest struggle of all. She had always wanted to be a part of his battle, to help him win it. If victory were achieved, she'd believed that it would be for them both.

"What are you doing here, Garrett?"

He looked at her—as though he were composing a photograph—for a time before answering. "Carlos told me where your family moved," he said at length. "I drove into town and found the place easily. Your mother was at work. But your father was home. He was repairing a clock; he interrupted himself. We talked—" Garrett's eyes held her fast. "He knew I was at West Point—he spoke of his own service. He showed me his campaign ribbons. And his uniform jacket. I was moved . . ." Garrett cleared his throat. "I asked him where I could find you. He told me. He even gave me this—" From a pocket, Garrett drew out a folded envelope; he handled it carefully, as if it were some precious relic. "It's from a letter that you sent to your folks. It has your return address." He smiled thinly. "I drove a good part of the night to get here—"

"But why have you come?"

Garrett looked away—up towards the window from which she'd first seen him—and then back again. "Is there somewhere we can talk?" he asked abruptly.

She nodded. "There is."

She took him to the arboretum. Not far from the entrance, there was a nook she knew. She'd often passed it but never entered; it was the sort of place to which you went with a lover. The interlacing branches of pines afforded privacy; it had mossy earth and a flat, lichened rock on which to sit. Mitzko clasped her knees and pressed her chin to them. Leaning forward without looking at her, Garrett spoke: "Since the last time I saw you, I . . . haven't been the same. Something's been eating me. I tried to dismiss it . . . I sincerely believed that it would go away. It didn't. Instead, it got worse. The more I fought it . . . the stronger it became—" He held his head in his hands. "I began to ask myself questions. The answers I got . . . shook the foundations of all I'd been planning, been building so rationally, so carefully. Until— until I could no longer see my way clear to going ahead—" He turned to her. "Mitzko, do I make sense? Do you understand—?"

"Garrett, what do you want?"

He took her in his arms.

She went willingly.

Chapter 44

He stayed with her that night. In the narrow bed, holding her in his arms, he said: "I've dreamed of this moment for so long. But every time I awoke, I forgot the dream . . ." He smiled and then slept. Propping herself up on an elbow, she watched him. He looked peaceful, but she didn't take the peace for granted; she was well aware of the turmoil he'd endured to reach the moment. Understanding his journey, appreciating how far he'd come to be with her were part of her commitment to their union. She hadn't invented the tenderness in him; as one in a flash of lightning views an entire landscape lit, she'd glimpsed in him the self that she so desired. Her questions had always been: did he desire that self as well; how radically would he wrestle to secure it? Akira and Komako had raised her to know that the compassionate self was not easily attainable, neither was its worth readily demonstrable. She had learned from her parents that the world, by and large, saw compassion as weakness, that it was the strong man alone who saw in it an insuperable power. What stirred Mitzko more than the love that Garrett professed for her . . . was his willingness to love. For Garrett, the love was transformation. For Mitzko, it was vindication.

At breakfast, with the morning light streaming in through the window, he said to her: "It began with a pebble, it grew to an avalanche. I couldn't stop it . . ."

"You didn't want to," she said.

He told her that he'd decided to break off his engagement,

that he would drop out of West Point. He said that over the past few months, he'd worked it all through. Finally resolved it. "I'm relieved," he said. "Probably for the first time in my life . . . I'm relieved."

"You're—certain?"

"Certain? I'm absolutely certain! Otherwise, I'd never have come here—"

"All right. You'll nullify the engagement. You'll quit West Point. Then what?"

Between their coffee cups, he took her hand. "I want to be here. Be with you. I'll transfer my credits, go into some other field. Or else I'll get a job. Maybe do both. We'll see. That's the point: the two of us will see. Together—"

"Garrett—"

"Dearest Mitzko. Don't you understand? I want to marry you . . ."

After breakfast, she stood by and watched him shave. Heard the razor scrape his skin. Saw him bury his rinsed face in a towel and dry it. Helped him button his shirt. Kissed his lips. Felt herself in his arms, lightened, soaring. He buckled the strap of his wristwatch. She touched his cheek, as if the physical contact might enable her spirit to pass into his. But physical contact didn't do that, life did. "Have you spoken with your parents?" she asked.

"Not with my parents," he grimaced. "With my father. It's my father that I deal with. The General."

"Have you told him?"

He shook his head. "I'm going now, Mitzko. I'm driving home to talk to him . . ."

"Garrett, then it will not be your home."

"It hasn't been my home . . . in a very long time. I've just realized that recently . . ."

"Do you want me to come with you?"

He took her head in his hands. "Little Mitzi," he said softly. "Thank you, but no. I'll go by myself. This is my war."

"Your peace, Garrett," she said.

From the same window she'd first seen the car, she saw it leave; it pulled away from the curb, ran the length of the bright street, and disappeared around the first corner. She was alone—more accurately, without him. Even more than a sense of his absence, she had an acute awareness of her own—? She scarcely knew what to call it. Completion? Fullness? Effulgence? Being with him infused her, she reflected, not so much with him as with a keener, richer knowledge of her own self. She turned from the window and faced the room she'd shared with him the night long. Somehow, it was different. She was different. The void to which she had accustomed herself—as one learns to live with an amputation or some other handicap—was filled.

During the morning, as she pursued and at times strayed from her studies, she wondered. Was it all real? Would he divert the course of his life as he'd told her? Would he step from the shadow of his father into his own light? Would he thread his way through the minefield at the estate and return to her? She thought so. She believed so with all her heart. But nothing was certain until it was done and finished. He had asked her to marry him—she hadn't answered. When the last shackle was struck off and he asked again, she would consent. No matter what happened, she wasn't sorry that she'd slept with him. The memory of their night together was a lifeboat to carry her on the roughest of seas.

It was an agitated day, a day that wavered between her regular routine of learning and wild anticipation. For brief bursts of time, she let herself imagine their future life: new, untried, extravagantly promising. She kept getting up from her books and papers to look out of the window. She thought she might see his car again. It was silly, she knew. But she couldn't help it. She chided herself, but without really meaning it. She was aware of the change in her. Doing frivolous things was one of a long list of luxuries she hadn't indulged in; daydreaming was another. Her life had been planned, contained: a life of structure, intent, determination. Now, there was expansiveness. Sweetness.

In the afternoon, the day altered. When she glanced at the street, it was gray. Slate-dark clouds boiled up in the sky; some moments after, thunder rolled. As she prepared supper, the storm broke. She had to shut the window, at which the rain slammed with a savage force. A web of blue lightning jumped; the lights in the room dimmed for an instant. She checked in the drawer of her desk to make sure she had extra fuses. Then she sat down to her meal. As she slept alone, she ate alone. With an unfamiliar rush of emotion, she realized it would be different. Her life would be shared. She believed that.

At about six-thirty, as she was putting away the dishes, the phone rang. She ran to pick it up. But it was the chief librarian, who knew she hadn't gone back home for the break. The librarian had recalled some work that had to be done when school resumed. "Forgive me, dear," she said, "I dislike intruding. But I really couldn't help myself. You're not on vacation anyway, are you?"

"It's perfectly okay," said Mitzko.

The storm slackened somewhat. She tried to get back to her studies, but made little progress. Garrett had promised to call her—she kept watching the clock. Just after ten, she closed her textbook. The rain was intense again; it slashed at the windowpane and hammered on the shingles of the roof. Barrages of thunder boomed into the room. It was no use. She was too anxious about Garrett's call, too keyed-up.

Better to sleep now and get an early start in the morning. She undressed and washed and set the alarm for five. As she made up the bed, she heard the phone. This time, it was Garrett. He sounded strange—she could scarcely recognize his voice. "I'm on my way—" he told her.

"Garrett—where are you?"

"I stopped at a gas station. I'm in the phone booth—"

"You sound terrible! What happened?"

His laugh was harsh, explosive. "I told him everything—as I said I would. My father was furious. He forbade me to see you again! He forbade me to leave West Point; he wants me to finish up there and then to 'serve my country in Vietnam.' He said those were his 'orders.' He said he'd 'destroy' me if I disobeyed, if I 'deserted—' " Garrett broke off.

"What did you tell him?"

"I told him to be a general in hell!"

"Garrett—"

"I'll give you details when I come. Wait for me, Mitzi. I . . . love you. Love you with all my heart, little Mitzi—"

A crash of thunder cut him off. The lights went out. "Garrett," she shouted, "don't drive! There's a terrible storm up here! Check into a motel. Or sleep in the car. Garrett! Do you hear me!?"

But the phone was dead.

Chapter 45

He never arrived. She sat on the sofa and waited for him until after two, but he didn't come. Outside, the storm raged with torrential force; when she went to the window, she saw nothing but shifting sheets of rain. At length, she went to bed but didn't sleep. The hours, filled with the pounding of the downpour and the howling of the wind, crawled by. She knew he was overdue, then long overdue. Perhaps, on his own, encountering the bad weather, he had decided to pull into a motel or stop by the side of the road. Her phone was still out, so there was no way she could hear from him. There were other possibilities as well, but she didn't allow them to enter her mind.

Towards daybreak, the storm abated. The wind died down, the rain lessened to little more than a drizzle. She got up and went to the window. It was light enough to see: what she saw were the glistening sidewalks and street, an endless array of puddles, the dripping trees, and the usual line of parked cars. His car wasn't there. She hadn't expected it to be, but she'd looked anyway. She stood at a loss. There was nobody she could call, nothing she could do. Except bear the agony of waiting.

The first word she got was from the radio. The penultimate item on the morning news was the report of a road accident. On the southern approach to town, a car had skidded off the road and into a ravine. The car had exploded; the driver had been instantly killed, burned beyond recognition.

No other details were broadcast. At that point, there was no real evidence that the dead driver was Garrett. No definitive proof. But it didn't matter. She knew that it was he.

She couldn't eat, but managed to get down a cup of coffee, not without burning her hand on the side of the kettle. As she dressed, she heard the news again. It was essentially the same story as before, except for the announcement that the police were trying to identify the driver's body. She switched the radio off and left the room. Going down the stairs, she met her landlady. "Are you well?" the woman inquired, staring at her. "I'm fine," Mitzko replied, hurrying by.

Outside, the sky was still overcast, with threatening cloud masses to the west. Towards the corner, a repair truck stood at the curb, the signal light on the roof of the cab flashing orange; workmen in hard hats were restringing telephone lines. Holding the collar of her coat close to her neck, she made her way quickly across town to the police station. The desk sergeant was tall, gaunt-faced, balding; the metal frames of his glasses matched the steel-bright sheen of his hair. He looked up from the sheaf of documents he was sorting through with the dismal, defensive air of a man who consistently hears the worst. "Well, young lady," he asked, "what can I do for you?"

"It's about . . . the car accident last night—"

He tapped the point of his ballpoint pen on the desk. "The one out on Quentin Road, you mean? Where the car went into the ravine?"

Mitzko nodded.

"What about it?"

"I think I may . . . have some relevant information . . ."

"Then please tell me, Miss—"

She told him what she thought, what she feared. He made notes as she spoke. The sergeant sighed; he touched the pen to his bottom lip. "Just have a seat over there on the bench," he said, pointing. "I'll check around . . . and let you know what I find out . . ."

"Thank you, sergeant."

"Miss—?"

"Yes—"

"Care for some coffee while you're waiting?"

Mitzko shook her head.

She lost track of time. She must have dozed, because— merging with each other—a disconnected series of images flashed through her mind: Garrett's body arching over her as they were about to make love; Chuo, squatting by the creek when she was a little girl, showing her the silver-gold shapes of crayfish in the clear water; Komako in the vegetable garden by the side of the house on the estate; Akira in his wheelchair, staring hungrily into space. And then she saw fire—great, leaping tongues of flame—and in the center of the conflagration she saw Faceless Horror. "Two have burned!" she screamed out. "Whom must I lose next?" The Faceless Horror replied, but she covered her ears to block out the answer.

A hand touched her shoulder. She opened her eyes. The sergeant, looking less comfortable at having lost the protection of his desk, was standing over her. "What did you find out?" she asked.

The sergeant cleared his throat. "Are you a relative, Miss?"

"A friend."

He told her. But she'd known before the words ever left his lips that Garrett was dead.

Chapter 46

She fell into bed and slept. Eighteen . . . twenty . . . twenty-four hours: she'd no idea how long. The sleep had been dreamless. It had been black as pitch. Black as death. The phone wakened her. She ignored it, she wanted it to stop, she wanted desperately to keep on sleeping. But it continued to ring. At length, she struggled out of bed and picked it up. It was her mother's voice. "Carlos was in town," her mother said. "He brought us the terrible news—"

"Mother—"

"Mitzko . . . I'm so sorry . . ."

"Mother . . . I know you are . . ."

"Do you want to come home?"

"No."

"Are you certain?"

"I'm certain."

On the appointed day, she went back to school and back to work. If her life had been one of isolation before, it was now one of hermetic seclusion. She spoke to no one except when it was absolutely necessary, did nothing that wasn't directly connected to her studies or her job. These preoccupations saved her. Had she withdrawn from them, her life would have imploded. She would have been lost. The Faceless Horror in her police station dream would have consumed her in fire.

She'd considered going to the funeral. She wasn't at all sure that Garrett would have wanted it; she wasn't even certain she wanted it. A telegram decided the issue:

DO NOT TROUBLE YOURSELF TO ATTEND
THE FUNERAL OF MY SON, CADET-MAJOR
GARRETT WILSON EDWARDS. YOU ARE NOT
WELCOME. THANK YOU FOR OBLIGING.
                    (SIGNED)
                    GENERAL EDWARDS

Discarding the telegram wasn't enough: she tore it into
shreds and flushed it down the toilet. Leaning against a wall
in the bathroom, she murmured aloud: "You won your war,
Garrett. But you won't ever taste the fruits of your victory—"
For the first time since she'd been certain of his death, she
wept. When she no longer had tears left to shed, she said
softly: "Be at rest, my love . . ."

Sometimes, her studies suffered. She had employed su-
preme power of will to enclose herself in a bathosphere. But
occasionally, the grief broke through. She was blind then,
with no one to guide her. People sensed her pain. There were
those who tried to help: several of her teachers; a number of
her colleagues at work. She rebuffed them all. She wanted
nothing from the outside. What she had to bear, she would
bear alone. What needed strengthening, she would
strengthen on her own. She desired no charity, no pity, no
support, no religious or philosophical comfort; she wished for
no one and nothing to interfere with her. As one trained and
domesticated a wild beast, she would tame her pain. She'd
learn to live with it; it would learn to live with her. That was
what would be.

That summer, she went home for only a single week. "It's
all I can bear," she told her mother. Komako understood.
That was the first time Mitzko went to the cemetery. She was
there only a short while, just long enough to see the grave. As
soon as she identified it, she turned around and went back to

town. She was ill at ease in her parents' flat; she had no connection to or feeling for it. But Akira and Komako seemed to be doing well. During the day, her father was busy with his clock and watch repairs; at night, he read and sometimes wrote. Her mother had more work than she could keep up with; it seemed to buoy rather than burden her. "So what about buying that bit of land and home you once spoke of?" Mitzko asked her. "Will it come true?"

Komako cleaned her spectacles with a tissue and then put them on again. "That's a long way off," she replied. "If ever—"

Both Akira and Komako avoided mention of Garrett's death. Mitzko was certain they sensed her own stubborn unwillingness to share her sorrow with anyone. They saw that she was alive, that she was coping with what had happened on her own. Why would they wish to tamper with the equilibrium she'd so painfully achieved? Then it was time for her to say good-bye. Too overcome with emotion, Komako embraced her in silence. Akira gruffly wished her well. "Be brave," he said. "It's what we humans must do . . ." Mitzko was glad he was vague and didn't say more.

She was relieved to be back in her attic room. It was snug, isolated—it was hers. She had a job for the summer working as a waitress from four to midnight in a local diner. Customers liked the attentive service she gave them; in time, they tolerated her aloofness. She earned a decent salary and made a large amount in tips. The way she did her job used up a lot of energy: that helped her to sleep. She spent her days preparing for her senior year, which would include work in a nearby hospital. She looked forward to the work, believing that she'd be able to understand the patients' pain and respond constructively. "In the cessation of their suffering," she told herself, "my own must diminish . . ."

The summer weeks flew by. Mitzko did little other than study and hold down her job. Occasionally, she found relief, if not refuge, in a film. She sent part of her earnings home to Komako. "Put the money into the land fund," she wrote. "I have all faith that the day when you and my father return to the soil will arrive . . ." In answer, Komako wrote: "Thank you, dear Mitzko, for your faith. And for the money!"

Fall came and the senior year began. As she'd anticipated, theory at this point merged with practical application. Several days a week, she trained at the hospital which served the area. The reality of what she experienced and did moved her from her own private disaster to the catastrophes of others. She found that her expectations were correct, that she was admirably suited to the profession she'd chosen. "You're a natural!" one of her supervisors told her, much as years before her instructor had given her similar praise on the tennis court. The patients lauded her as well; unceremoniously, they asked for her to be assigned to them. She dismissed the applause. What anyone said or didn't say was unimportant, irrelevant. She knew who she was, what she was meant to do.

In the hospital, she was alert, balanced, empathetic, consummately skilled. She felt deeply for the sick, but never succumbed to her feelings. Instead, she channeled them into therapeutic performance. "The hallmark of a true healer," another member of the hospital staff said to her. "Where have you been all this time?" She accepted the approbation graciously. But she was far more interested in acquiring knowledge, in the improvement of methods and techniques. She stepped from classroom to bedside with calmness, clarity and certitude—and with the modest impatience of those who discover they stand on native ground.

The shock, terror and repulsion she saw while training on the wards and in the gym—repressed by day—surfaced in chilling, chaotic dreams. Amputations . . . degenerative diseases . . . paraplegia . . . strokes . . . vied with each other for possession of her mind. Sometimes, the hospital scenes mingled with eerie dream fragments in which Chuo and Garrett appeared. Often, Chuo looked like her father: he wore the uniform of a U.S. infantryman and huddled in the mud in front of a frost-sheeted pup tent. But she saw Garrett without a face. Where his features should have been, there was only a dark hole. "I know"—Mitzko would scream when she saw him—"you aren't Garrett: you're the Faceless Horror!" But he never replied.

At school, her reputation generally kept men at bay. At the hospital, a number of the interns tried to date her. She rejected them all summarily, with a matter-of-fact, uncompromising manner that she'd perfected. Towards the end of the year, a rugged-looking, blond resident—endlessly sought after by nurses and female colleagues—invited her one afternoon to the cafeteria, ostensibly to discuss a case in which both were involved. But it soon became apparent that he had an extracurricular interest in her. She ignored his overtures, then he asked her out directly. "Thank you for the invitation," she said, "but the answer is no."

"Why not?"

" 'Why not' isn't relevant."

"It is to me. I like to know why I'm refused."

"This time you'll have to be disappointed, I'm afraid."

He grew angry—she saw him redden. "I've heard about you," he said in an unpleasant tone. "They say you turn everyone down, that you have no interest in men, that you're cold as ice—a mummy!"

"What I am or am not is of no concern to you," Mitzko told him calmly as she rose from her seat. "Here's my share of the bill—"

His name was Avery Travis. He apologized profusely the next day. Said he was "dreadfully sorry and ashamed." Said he didn't know what had gotten into him. Asked her to forgive him. Begged her to go out with him. She informed him that she didn't hold grudges—and that she didn't go out on dates. He pursued her for the next week or so and then, like all his predecessors, gave up. "I surrender," he told her dramatically, obviously hoping for a last-minute reprieve. She didn't grant it.

Her graduation took place at the end of May. She was third in a class of more than 1200; she received a magna cum laude diploma; she got the school's science medal; she was awarded a special citation from the hospital in which she'd trained. She also had a standing ovation from her classmates. It surprised her completely, and she was gratified. But it had nothing essential to do with what she thought of or demanded from herself. The applause died down. The dean congratulated her warmly. She thanked him and left the dais to embrace her mother.

Akira hadn't felt up to making the trip—Komako had come alone to the ceremony. After the leave-takings and good-byes, Mitzko and her mother left the auditorium and walked to a nearby restaurant. It was a cozy place, with lace curtains and flowered tablecloths. Komako's eyes were shining. "This is lovely," she said.

"I thought you'd like it, Mother."

Wearing apron and cap, the waitress came over to take their orders. As they ate their salads, Komako said: "What about the summer? Have you decided what you'll do yet?"

"I start working as a physical therapist at the beginning of July. In the hospital where I trained . . ." Mitzko smiled. "I was going to surprise you before you left: I'll be at home all of the month of June. Does that please you, Mother?"

The softened sunlight that filtered through the blinds lit the veined leafage of a potted plant and surged onto Komako's face. Her dark hair, marked with slivers of silver, was drawn back and pulled into a bun at the nape of her neck. She wore no makeup; her skin was pale, almost translucent; her lips were carnation-pink. For an instant, there was a haunting air about her—as of vanished youth—and then it was gone. She rested her fork on her plate. "Your father and I . . . will be most delighted to have you with us . . ." Komako meant what she said; she was truly happy. But in her voice and in her eyes were strains of the sorrow and disillusionment their little family had endured.

Mitzko gave up the attic room. It was time for her to go, but there were regrets. For all the pain she'd suffered there, it had been home and haven. She had spent Garrett's last full night on earth with him there. It was familiar, comfortable, lived-in. It took her several days to go through her things and discard what she didn't want, and another couple of days to pack. She had rented a three-room apartment in a redbrick building in the next town over, about twenty miles to the east. The hospital was there; walking to work would take her ten minutes or so. The final day in her third-floor nest was devoted to cleaning: it was an honored principle of hers never to leave a place where she'd stayed dirty. In the tiny bathroom, under the sink, something lying in the corner glittered. She got down on her hands and knees and reached for it. On her feet again, she opened her hand. A gold ring, emblazoned with the American eagle, rested in her palm. It was Garrett's; he had placed it on the sink soon after he'd entered the flat. "My father gave it to me when I went off to West Point," he told her. "I know I'm probably crazy . . . but I don't want to wear it when we make love . . ." She felt dizzy, and remained for some time on the floor where she was. At length, she got up. She put the ring in her purse. As soon as she could, she'd buy a chain and wear it around her neck. She didn't care who had given it to him or what was on it. It had been Garrett's: that was all that mattered.

Her new apartment was on the first floor. It was bright, in good repair and freshly painted in pale apricot; the living room window looked out on a backyard with a lilac bush. It took her no more than a day and a half to set everything in order. Suitcase in hand, she stood in the doorway and looked around. There would be geraniums in pots on the windowsills, rag rugs on the floors, a cheerful clock in the kitchen. The place wasn't finished, but she liked what she saw. She would not live in it with Garrett, but she could live in it for him too. Her eyes misted over. "Listen, " she said aloud, "I'm off to visit Akira and Komako. But this . . . is my home. I'll be back. Wait for me . . ."

Komako welcomed her warmly; she tried to hide her emotions, but Mitzko knew how deeply her mother felt. Akira was overjoyed; he made no effort to conceal it. "Your mother told me about the graduation," he crowed, "down to the last detail! I make her describe it over and over! I can't tell you how proud you make me, Daughter—" He went on and on about what Mitzko had accomplished and what she'd achieve in time. But the exalted mood didn't continue. In the days that followed, he rejected Mitzko's approaches. He withdrew from Komako as well. There were clocks and watches lying around to repair, but he didn't touch them. The daily paper rested unread on his armchair; he had no interest in books or in his journal. Most of the time, he sat in the wheelchair, staring into space. "That's the way it is lately," said Komako. "He's erratic. He swings from one extreme to the other."

"Perhaps . . . he should have some professional help . . ."

"I've suggested that," said Komako. "He won't hear of it."

"I'll speak to him," Mitzko offered. She tried, but her father rebuffed her indignantly.

On some days, Akira left the house and returned several hours later. However, he didn't appear refreshed; instead, he looked depleted. "Where does he go?" Mitzko asked.

Komako shrugged. "Not to the library—that's for sure!"

Towards the end of her visit, Mitzko decided to follow her father. She kept well behind him, so that she was in no danger of being discovered. Akira had great strength—built up over the years he'd worked on the land—in his back and arms. He used it to advantage: the wheelchair moved along the pavement at a swift, steady pace, for the most part carefully, but on occasion interrupting traffic or causing the pedestrians to step aside. Keeping her father in view and herself out of sight, Mitzko trailed after. Akira seemed to know exactly where he was heading, to be navigating a familiar route. He propelled himself past the high school, Mason's, the library, both the local banks, the supermarket where Fumiko and then she had been employed, the green, the sheriff's office—across the entire town! But to where? And for what purpose? She couldn't imagine.

Finally, he slowed the chair down to a crawl and then stopped. To escape detection, Mitzko had to take cover behind a billboard because they'd actually reached the town's outskirts—neither buildings nor people were to be seen. The asphalt road on which Akira had moved for the last several hundred yards led westward, into a vast, barren area of undeveloped terrain; in the remote distance, bunched like a herd of water-buffalo at the horizon, were mountains. It was after four. The sun was low in the sky: like the man in the wheelchair, it seemed weary, defeated, unwilling to give light.

Motionless and staring, Akira sat where he was until darkness fell. When the first few stars appeared in the sky, he swung the chair around and traveled the same course back to the building in which they lived. Mystified and pained, Mitzko followed him. She waited outside until she was satisfied that he'd settled himself and then went in. That night, after he'd gone to bed, she made certain the bedroom door was closed and then spoke to Komako. "I know . . . where he disappears to for all those hours," she said.

"Where?" Komako demanded.

"Nowhere."

"What do you mean?"

"Exactly what I said. He took himself all the way across town to the outskirts. Without his suspecting it, I followed him. When we got to the destination, I hid behind a billboard. I saw him. Nothing's there. Just a street that turns into a road that leads into undeveloped land. He sat in his chair and stared into space. Like a mummy. Like a stone statue. Then he turned himself around and came back. That's what he does when he goes out! I don't understand . . ."

"If he passes the library and the green and the town hall . . . then he goes west . . ." Komako mused.

"Well, yes . . ." Mitzko recalled. "He did go in the direction of the setting sun. Actually, he watched it go down. And when it was dark, he came home . . ."

Komako had been standing at the stove in the apartment's tiny kitchen; she moved into the dining alcove and seated herself. On the table was a small, black, slender-necked vase covered with white that looked like snow powder; it had belonged to Komako's great-grandmother and been handed down to her. Komako always kept one flower in it: this week, there was a pale purple rose. She was silent for a time—she might have been praying, although no one ever saw her pray these days. Her delicate fingers played over the vase's curves. "The farm . . . the land your father and I owned before you were born; before it was taken from us . . . would lie to the west," she murmured. The expression in her eyes was distant; she was reckoning, remembering. "—About three or four hundred miles due west of here, I'd say . . ." She removed her hand from the vase. "That must be—" But her voice trailed off.

"That must be what draws him . . ." Mitzko finished. "That's why he goes across town. That's why he sits and looks to the west—"

Komako nodded.

Mitzko came closer; she touched Komako's shoulder. "Mother—" Then Komako rose and the two women, sharing the same pain, fell into each other's arms and hugged. When they moved apart, Komako was wiping her eyes with the corner of her apron. "They're old tears," she said shyly. "They really should have dried up a long time ago. But they keep on coming back. It's silly. I'm ashamed . . ."

"Tears keep their own accounts," said Mitzko. Without knowing it, she touched Garrett's ring, which hung on a chain around her neck. Komako saw it, but didn't say a word.

A number of times during her stay, Mitzko considered going to the estate. She thought of the trails and paths where she and Garrett had walked and ridden, of the places where they'd talked and made love. For some reason, she couldn't make the decision to go. Then early one morning, even before her parents had risen, she rose and dressed and went to the taxi stand in the center of town. There was a single cab; the driver was dozing at the wheel. She knocked on the window, and the driver rolled it down. "Where can I take you, Miss?" he asked. She couldn't answer him; the words stuck in her throat. "I—I've changed my mind—" she managed to stammer. "I—I'm sorry. Some other time—" As she walked back to the apartment, she discovered that she was shivering.

She realized that all she'd had with Garrett was with her, inside her—it always would be. She had neither need nor desire to return to some haunted castle.

Mitzko slept on a folding cot that Komako had set up in the little half-room where she did her private jobs. There was a sewing machine, a worktable, and there were several clothes dummies, as well as endless bolts of cloth. Komako had offered Mitzko the sofa in the living room, but Mitzko had chosen the snugness of the workroom. Two nights before she was scheduled to leave, just as she was falling asleep, there was a light tapping on a glass pane of the door. At once, she sat up. "Who's there?"

It was Akira. Clad in white pajamas, he glided wraith-like into the room. "I hope I'm not disturbing you—" he murmured.

"It's all right, Father. I wasn't sleeping."

He positioned the wheelchair at the side of the cot so that he was very close; she could feel his breath as he spoke. "I had a dream," he said hoarsely. "I didn't want to tell Komako. So—" He left off.

"Tell me, Father."

Akira nodded. "I dreamed that my mother came to me," he said. "She was dressed all in white. Her hair and her face were powdered white, her fingernails were done in white—even her lips were painted white. 'Because white is the color of truth,' she informed me. 'And I come to you in truth, my son—'

" 'For what purpose do you come here, Mother?'

" 'To sing you a song, my son.'

" 'And what is the song, Mother?'

" 'It is called, "Song of the End." When you hear it, you will be with me, my son.'

" 'With you? How long will I be with you, Mother?'

" 'Forever, my son . . .'

" 'Forever, Mother? We will never again be parted?'

" 'No, we will never again be parted. But . . . you must wish me to sing you the song. Do you want to hear it, my son?'

" 'With all my heart, Mother! Don't delay! Please begin—' "

The next morning, after discussing it with Komako, Mitzko phoned the hospital in which Akira had been a patient. It took some time, but at length she got through. "Dr. Harkness—is that you?"

"Mitzko! It's so good to hear your voice! How are you? I know you must have graduated by now! Are you working yet?"

"I'm starting at St. Michael's the first of the week. That's where I trained during my senior year at school—"

"They're lucky to have you!"

They spoke about rehab for a while, then Mitzko told her about Akira's situation. "My mother and I feel that he's in need of some professional attention. I'd appreciate your seeing him, Dr. Harkness—"

"Of course, I'll see him. Rest assured, Mitzko—I'm sure we'll make progress. But I'm leaving on Tuesday for a conference in London. It'll have to wait until I get back—"

Mitzko's arrangement calmed her mother somewhat. The two women agreed that Komako would keep a close watch on Akira; in case of an emergency, she was to phone Mitzko at once. On the last day before she left, Mitzko took a cab to the cemetery in which Garrett was buried, which was located halfway between the town and the estate. She arrived just after the gates had opened. During the night, it had rained; there were still raindrops on the tombstones, the shrubs were dripping. On the pathways, the gravel was dark. Everywhere, birds were singing. She didn't stay long—just time enough to set fresh flowers on the grave. As she passed his hut on the way out, the caretaker asked if she wished him to phone for a taxi. She shook her head. "Thank you, but I'll walk back. Good-bye . . ." The caretaker nodded indifferently. He was used to good-byes.

Chapter 47

She threw herself into the work at St. Michael's. It was her work, the work she'd been born for. If outside the hospital she found it impossible to socialize, her sense of duty enabled her to relate well to the staff; her innate respect for humanity—reinforced by Akira's and Komako's upbringing—brought her close to the patients. She was highly skilled, deeply motivated, extraordinarily sensitive. And she was indefatigable. "Don't you ever tire?" Avery Travis, who'd finished his residency and had been hired as a member of the rehab team, asked her. In reply, she'd shrugged. "I'm too busy to notice whether I'm tired or not," she told him. "I believe you," he said. And meant it.

Her superiors valued her; her patients loved her. Their love was shameless, spontaneous—as pure as love could be. From behind the citadel walls of her professionalism, she returned it. She felt the suffering of the sick keenly; in her ministering to them, she passed safely through the fire of the pain. No physical maiming or affliction repelled her: she viewed disfigurement as an alteration of form only. "The human body is either exalted or demeaned by the spirit that lives within it . . ." She had said that to herself from the moment she'd begun her training at St. Michael's. As each day passed, she believed it more firmly.

During her work hours in the hospital, she allowed nothing to shock or dismay her. The rehab ward and gym were battlefields; she was a front-line combatant. Head traumas, spinal cord injuries, amputations, the degenerative diseases: they were the enemy. She gave them no quarter, as she gave none to her fear and revulsion. In the quiet and safety of her own apartment, she fought the war against the depression and terror that followed her home. The job drained her physically and mentally, but it never daunted her. At night, altogether depleted of energy or completely wound-up, she found relaxation in music and reading. She joined a local health club; on weekends, she swam in the pool and worked out. Walking and cycling refreshed her as well; on a good day, she could do ten miles on foot or cover four to five times that distance on a bike.

She kept in close contact with Komako. On no account could Akira be persuaded to go to the local hospital to see Dr. Harkness. After several failed attempts to convince him, she drove to the Shiraishi apartment. "As a special favor to your daughter," she told Akira. The visit, as Ruth Harkness reported to Mitzko by telephone, was "not what one might call a success." Mitzko was disturbed. "What happened?" "Your father," Dr. Harkness responded, "is a tough man. A stubborn man. And at this point, I should have to call him an altogether closed man. Heaven knows, I tried . . . but I couldn't get through. However, I'll go to see him again. He's . . . in a lot of pain. I wish I could help—" Mitzko thanked her warmly for her interest and her sincerity. They would keep in touch on Akira's progress. That was in mid-August.

Early in September, Mitzko was awakened shortly before dawn by a phone call from Komako. She said five words—apparently, the only words she was able to speak: "Mitzko, your father is dead—"

Mitzko put the phone down, threw a few things into an overnight bag and took a cab to the bus station; she waited a little more than an hour for the first bus out. Komako greeted her in silence, a silence it was hard for both of them to break. Finally, at the kitchen table, with cups of cold tea in front of them, Komako said: "He went out yesterday afternoon. On one of his usual excursions—or so I thought. I was at the window. I watched him leave in his wheelchair, thinking that it was good Dr. Harkness was coming again. 'As a favor to Mitzko,' she told him, and I believe he was pleased—" She paused to smooth down her hair which did not need smoothing and continued: "I had a great deal of work to get done—for a wedding next week. I paid no attention to the time; when next I looked at the clock, it was past ten. He had never been out so long. I became alarmed—" She turned away, so that Mitzko could not see the expression in her eyes. "At first, I didn't know what to do. Then I knocked at the neighbor's door. She said I should call the police. So I did. They found him on the west-side road, but ten or perhaps fifteen miles past the spot you mentioned. The wheelchair was stopped. They rushed him to the hospital. But it was too late. He'd died of a massive heart attack . . ."

Mitzko took Komako's hands in hers.

"There was a note pasted to the back of the wheelchair. Apparently, it was there for some time—" Komako withdrew a sheet of paper from her apron pocket. "Here—"

The words were in Akira's finest, most careful handwriting:

Dearest Wife and Daughter:
   When my time of death comes, I humbly request that you dress me in my army uniform and, together with my "Encyclopedia of the Soul," which is the diary of my life on this earth, cremate my remains. I wish to depart in fire, as did my friend, Chuo, and my unknown brothers and sisters in

*Dachau . . . Remember me as one who loved you and came
to despise the world . . .*

> *Yours in memory,*
> *Akira Shiraishi*

Chapter 48

She considered herself a veteran. Her confrontations with the enemy—trauma and disease—were always new and shocking, but she was even more adept at fighting and coping than before. She wasn't hard-hearted—by nature never had been and never would be—but she was tough-hided. Once, after watching her work with a paraplegic child, Avery Travis had called her "a woman of iron." His descriptive phrase stuck like, as Mitzko herself said, "a tin can tied to a dog's tail." She didn't mind. It was good to be "iron" in the hospital. There was more than enough time to agonize at home. More than enough time to weep and to wake shivering and uncertain from nightmares.

At the outset, she'd worked in the pediatric neuromuscular clinic one day a week; now, she generally worked three. Her assignments were taxing, often grueling. She had a special way with children. She knew it; they knew it too. No matter what she saw or heard or touched or felt, she was there for them. All there. She could and would be whatever was demanded: nurse, mother, sister—even angel. They asked: to the very best of her ability, her healing mind and heart and hands delivered. She spared her patients nothing that she could give; she gave herself nothing that wasn't vital to her survival. That was her code, the way she viewed her role as therapist.

If she hadn't become friends with anyone, she had at least formed relationships with two or three members of the staff.

It was a natural process, evolving from their cooperative efforts in the hospital. Rosalyn, unmarried and in her thirties, was a hefty, Swedish-looking woman from Minnesota; she was also a physical therapist. Diminutive, swarthy and newly wed, Anita was twenty-three and had been born in the Philippines; she was a pediatric nurse. Samantha was forty, genial, and divorced; she worked as an occupational therapist. Fairly often, Mitzko ate lunch with them singly or in a group; sometimes she played tennis—which she'd taken up again—with Anita; on rare occasions, she went to the movies or to the theater with Samantha or Rosalyn. The alliances did not run deep; none of the three acquaintances probed or pried or pressured. They respected Mitzko's wish and need to protect her private world. Contact with these women was pleasant, unruffling. It took the edge off Mitzko's loneliness.

As well, she'd drawn closer to Avery Travis. She both respected and admired him as a physician. From her experience in the rehab unit, she knew him to be skilled, humane—and modest. After some months of obvious courtship, Travis had become engaged to and eventually married one of the female residents. Travis was patently happy with his wife; he had no romantic interest whatsoever in Mitzko, so she was able to feel relaxed with him. The two of them met quite regularly in the cafeteria and in a nearby diner for meals and coffee. For the most part, they discussed cases they were both involved with; once in a while, they chatted about life in general. Travis could be witty; Mitzko was a lively and responsive partner.

Late one day, in the near-empty diner, after the two of them had lengthily reviewed the painstaking but steady progress of an acute head trauma—a young man of seventeen who'd been thrown from a car in an accident—Travis said suddenly. "You're comfortable talking to me, aren't you, Mitzko?"

"Of course I am. Why do you ask?"

Travis hesitated for a moment, then he said: "But you always talk 'business.' What about your personal life?"

Instantly, she was on guard. In itself, a question could be innocent, harmless, innocuous, but it could readily lead to some forbidden border. From past, bitter experiences, she'd discovered that questions were by nature hydra-like: you answered one and another popped up. She really trusted and liked Travis; he was knowledgeable, genuine, well-intentioned. After time, she'd allowed him freedoms not permitted to others. But she had no wish to open sealed chambers. For some years now, her life had been a balancing act. She didn't want it upset. She had no idea if there were a safety net stretched beneath her, and no desire to find out.

"Come on, Mitzko—don't be so damn frightened! If you won't give me a break, at least give yourself one—"

She picked up her cup and put it down again without drinking. She stared across the table at Travis, still in his green physician's coat, with the stethoscope tucked into a pocket. His dark brown eyes were warm and frank; he had a strong, determined chin. The two of them worked intimately together, sharing the intimate secrets of their patients. They treated physical pain and anguish, coped with mental grief and despair. Travis had proven himself loyal, he had integrity, she could count on him. If he asked something personal, couldn't she respond? Would it be so terrible if she loosened up? He was constantly giving to her. Didn't she owe him something in return?

Mitzko smiled.

"You were looking grim," he said. "That's much better . . ."

"What do you want to ask me?"

He pointed. "That ring . . . you're always touching it—"

Her fingers went up to the chain around her neck. "The ring belonged to Garrett," she said slowly. "We were to have married—"

"But—"

"He was killed."

"In the war?"

"Not in Vietnam—" She drew a deep breath. "But you might say that he was killed . . . in a kind of war . . ."

"Oh?"

"Technically, he died in a road accident."

Travis's dark eyes reflected more than her pain; they expressed his own naked, uninhibited grief. "Want to tell me about it?" he asked.

"Not—now, Avery. Some other time, perhaps . . ."

He nodded; clearly, he had accepted her wish not to pursue the story of her romance with Garrett and his death. In working with Travis, she'd discovered that he was a man of keen discretion. He would dare, yet he wouldn't exert pressure. However, he wasn't finished with what troubled him. Shifting position in the seat, he said: "You're still very much . . . tied to this Garrett, aren't you?"

"Yes."

"To the extent that you don't ever see anyone?"

"See anyone?"

"I mean, romantically—"

"I'm not a 'romantic' person."

"Mitzko, don't fence with me! It's wrong—your isolation is all wrong! It's pernicious, selfish, destructive!"

She shrugged. "I don't agree with you, Travis. I'm sorry—"

"What's gone is gone. Surely, you've learned that by now—if only from your hospital work. You've got to get on with your life. Meet someone. Marry. Maybe even have kids—" He gestured awkwardly. "I don't understand you, Mitzko—"

The story of the grade school teacher who'd lost her fiancé on a battlefield in France came into her mind. She considered telling it to Travis, but decided that she wouldn't. Why should she? What need was there to explain? What he imagined, she had suffered. He meant well, but it all meant nothing to her. She was losing patience. "It isn't necessary for you to understand, Travis," she said brusquely. "As long as I do . . ."

He ignored her. "It's a waste, Mitzko! A damn, shameful waste! You're a person who can give and take, who can share her life. And furthermore, deep down, you know it! Your behavior's—unnatural!"

She shook her head. "It's my nature."

He said nothing in reply. Instead, he looked down at the table, glancing at the napkin on which he'd been doodling during their conversation. The design was tight, labyrinthine; more than anything else, it seemed to express his frustration. She wondered if she'd offended or insulted him. It hadn't been her intention; she'd meant only to defend herself. "Are you angry?" she asked in a conciliatory tone.

He looked up. "Not angry," he said. "Sad."

She was assured; she felt as if her faith in him had been vindicated. "Don't fret about it," she said with a sudden rush of emotion. "Really, Travis—I'm used to me."

That night, in bed, in her spic-and-span, orderly, meticulously decorated apartment, she reflected on what Travis had said to her in the diner. He was both right and wrong. Right to say that she should end her isolation, get on with her life, meet someone and all the rest of it. She had it in her to find somebody and raise a family. But he was wrong to believe that she could. Her natural, undeniable urge was to remain faithful to the memory of Garrett. Travis considered that withdrawal a prison; she deemed it a refuge. Garrett's ring on a chain around her neck didn't choke her; rather, it made it possible for her to breathe. She wasn't cut off from the world—only from the world of potential lovers . . .

After Akira's death, she had invited Komako to come and live with her; her mother had declined. "But you're alone," Mitzko insisted. "If you come up here, we can rent a larger flat—or maybe even a house—and live together." Komako would not change her mind. "I'm not alone," she told her daughter. "Akira's spirit lives here with me." Mitzko went to see her mother on weekends, as often as she could. Komako had left the dress shop to attend to her own flourishing business. The work occupied much of her time; she seemed to thrive on it. She had grown noticeably older. Her shoulders were bowed; she looked physically frail. But some inner strength seemed to shine through her skin. She and Mitzko got along well; they were comfortable with each other, and they were able to communicate easily.

The two women often spoke of Akira; sometimes, they even evoked his presence without uttering a word. Once, on a Sunday afternoon, as Mitzko was getting ready to leave, she asked Komako: "What did you do with Father's journal? His 'Encyclopedia of the Soul'?"

"Akira instructed me to cremate it with him."

"I remember. But—did you?"

Komako stared at her. "I hesitated. I couldn't stand the thought of burning what he'd written, what he'd felt and believed and recorded about his life. I hesitated—"

"But—in the end?"

"I burned it."

Chapter 49

The Christmas vacation ended. As usual, Mitzko had spent it with Komako. It had been peaceful, pleasant; as always, it had given Mitzko a chance to recoup her energy. Work at the hospital was her life, her war. But she needed time out of the trenches. On the bus traveling back, with a cake that Komako had baked in a box on her lap, she dozed off. Garrett's image came to her open mind. It was before West Point. He was on the white mare. The wind blew his hair. He smiled and beckoned to her. He wanted her to ride with him. But she was rooted to the ground. She couldn't go to him. He beckoned, he waved. She saw the flash of his teeth, the fatal call of his eyes. But she couldn't move. She could only watch him spin the mare around and ride away . . .

Since Komako was in good health and spirits, Mitzko had left a day early. The bus pulled into the station just after eleven, so she was able to enjoy a good night's sleep in her own bed. Early the next morning, she rose, breakfasted and gave the apartment a thorough cleaning; then, instead of showering, she had a luxurious bath. As she prepared to go out and do some necessary shopping, the buzzer sounded. She couldn't imagine who it was. Travis had never been to her home; neither Rosalyn nor her other two acquaintances would drop by without phoning beforehand. Puzzled and somewhat apprehensive, she answered the door. In the hallway, stood a short, plump, pretty woman holding the hand of a little girl. For an instant, Mitzko didn't recognize either of them. Then she cried out, "Fumiko!"

and fell desperately into the woman's open arms.

"I was back, visiting my old neighborhood, where I grew up, and I bumped into your mother," Fumiko said through tears. "She told me where you were. What luck!"

While Fumiko's little daughter, who was called Tamiko, sat on the floor and colored on paper with the crayons and markers that Mitzko had rummaged for and finally dug out of a drawer for her, the two women sat close to each other on the sofa, alternately hugging and talking. Often, they laughed; as often, they cried. Fumiko had indeed married the young man she'd run off with. He had finished his apprenticeship and done very well; he now owned his own garage in a town not more than half an hour's drive away. Fumiko had an older boy at home, Tamiko, and she expected to give birth again in the spring. Her cheeks were rosy, her hair was glossy, her breasts were fuller than ever. Her round face beamed with pleasure and with sheer good nature. She was a ripe, blossoming woman. With her chubby hands, she patted her swollen belly. "The fruit of good sex!" she exclaimed.

When it came time to leave, Fumiko made Mitzko promise to call her and to visit. "We live in a big house," she said to her friend. "There's more than enough room for you to stay with us!" Mitzko nodded. "I will," she said. "I promise." At the door, Fumiko paused for a moment. Her eyes took in Mitzko's trim, modest, immaculate living room. From her expression, Mitzko gathered that she found something missing in it. "That fellow," Fumiko said. "The one who lived in the mansion on the estate, who went to West Point—" Her face darkened. Sensing her distress, Tamiko clung to her mother's skirt; Fumiko gently patted her head. "You cared for him, Mitzko," she went on. "You cared for him very much. He disappointed you, didn't he?"

"No," said Mitzko. "He didn't."

Chapter 50

The work was never easy, but Mitzko went back to it easily, readily—naturally. By bent and by choice, the hospital was the main focus of her being. The body odors, antiseptic smells, moans, screaming, bedpans, surgical equipment, blood soaking through bandages, crutches, IV set-ups, oozing stumps, prostheses, walkers, gym paraphernalia, pointedly soothing colors of the walls—the ferocious, unbreakable embrace of despair and hope—all of these were part of the gladiatorial arena in which she did regular combat. By day, in the wards, she had to play by harsh rules: they cut her off from life outside. A child's terrified eyes, spittle sliding down an old man's chin, the faltering steps of a double amputee on the parallel bars: they were the parameters of her world. At work, she was her warrior-self, the woman Travis had described as being made of "iron."

The first day was difficult. She had been assigned to the case of a young farmhand who'd been injured in a parking lot. A driver, mistakenly stepping on the accelerator instead of the brakes, had crushed the victim against a concrete wall, ripping off a leg and smashing a shoulder. In addition to his physical injuries, the farmhand, who hailed from Mexico and spoke virtually no English, had to be treated for reactive psychosis. After nearly an hour of strenuous work with him, Mitzko left the ward and headed for the physical therapy office. She spotted Travis coming towards her. "How are things, Avery?" she called out.

"Hectic," he replied with a grimace. "The usual crop of Christmas wrecks! You know the story: the human body can do and take anything. Except that it can't—"

He smiled back at her over his shoulder. She felt better. It was good being with him—and the rehab team—again. She was suddenly aware of how violently she'd missed all of them. She stopped at the nurses' station to speak to an orderly about the farmhand for a moment. As she was about to go, Claudia, the head nurse, said: "Oh, there you are, Mitzko—I just rang the ward for you! There's a phone call—"

"For me?"

"Yes. Take it on line three—"

Who could be calling her? Fumiko certainly wouldn't phone her at the hospital. It might be Komako: maybe something was wrong, maybe there was an emergency. But it was a male voice—she had no idea whose.

"Mitzko?"

"Yes—"

The caller laughed with undisguised pleasure. "Fantastic! Miraculous! Somebody told me that you worked here—I couldn't believe it! But it's really true—"

"Who . . . is this?"

"I didn't expect you to recognize my voice . . . even though I'd know yours anywhere in the world—"

"Who's talking, please?"

"It's Toge—"

The rehab unit occupied the third floor; Toge was on eight. On her lunch break, Mitzko went up to see him. The nurse on duty pointed. "He's down at the end of the hall. In the sun parlor . . ."

The little lounge had a rag rug, wicker chairs and sofa, lace curtains and a circular table at which three patients in hospital robes were playing cards. In a wheelchair, facing the sun-filled window, sat the fourth patient; his back was towards her. Mitzko stood for a time staring at him, then she reached out and touched his shoulder. He swung the chair around. "Mitzko—"

She knew at once that he was blind. Shrapnel wounds. Shattered eye sockets. Severed nerves. Failed operations. She knew the whole story. Without his having to say a word.

"Mitzko?"

"Toge! I'm so glad to—"

He stretched a hand towards her voice and she took it in both of hers.

"What a wonderful stroke of luck!" he laughed, squeezing her fingers. "Come, sit down next to me. Let's talk. Catch up—"

Blanketed in sunlight which she could see and he could feel, they talked until it was time for her to go. "I've got to get back to work," Mitzko said, rising.

"One more question," he said.

"Okay—"

"Are—you married?"

"No."

"You didn't marry him? The general's son? I thought—"

"He's dead."

Toge shook his head. "I'm sorry. So sorry—"

"I really must go, Toge. But we'll talk again. I'll . . . tell you about it—"

"Promise?"

"I promise . . ."

Since she'd been there for ten days over Christmas, she didn't visit Komako that weekend; instead, she traveled to Fumiko's place. The house was lovely—a redbrick ranch, with a front yard enclosed by a white picket fence; the back lawn was surrounded by hedges of hibiscus and bougainvillea. Fumiko's husband obligingly took the children for a romp; the women sat on the patio, sipping tea and talking. "I met Toge at this hospital this week," said Mitzko, suddenly breaking the train of their conversation.

Fumiko looked perplexed.

"Toge," Mitzko repeated. "We knew him some years ago . . . don't you remember?"

Fumiko thought for several moments. "Oh, that Toge!" she exclaimed. "I remember him now: the boy we knew in high school—"

"He's not a boy anymore, Fumiko. He's a man. He was in Vietnam for over two years. In the marines . . ."

"What's he doing in your hospital?"

"Toge was wounded. He's blind."

"I'm sorry to hear that," said Fumiko. She looked away, to where sparrows flitted fitfully over the lawn. "Give him my best wishes when you see him again . . ."

Mitzko did just that when she visited with Toge on Monday.

"Yes, Fumiko—of course!" He laughed. "She was famous at school. The guys used to tell . . . all kinds of stories about her—"

"She's grown up," said Mitzko. "She's married to a fine man, has two beautiful children, and she's expecting a third. Perhaps I'll bring her to see you one day—if you wish."

"I'd like that," Toge said. He fell silent. Then his lips moved, but no words emerged. Finally, he said: "Mitzko, when I asked you about being married . . . I didn't mean to pry—"

"I didn't take it that way."

"And I want you to know . . . how terribly sorry I am about . . . the death of your friend . . ."

"I know, Toge."

"And—" He broke off.

"Go on, Toge."

"And I hope that . . . we can be friends . . ."

"Don't worry, Toge . . . we shall be friends. It's in the cards . . ."

His lips twisted; she didn't know whether he would laugh or cry. Then he averted his face: she knew it was so that she couldn't find out.

On Friday, when they met, she told him about Garrett's death. He told her how he had been wounded. They talked through supper, far past the time she'd intended to stay, until at length the nurse on duty came to say that visiting hours were at an end. She left Toge in the lounge and went out of the hospital and walked slowly home along the lamp-lit streets. In bed that night, before she dropped off to sleep, the voice inside her told her that something was possible. But she didn't let the voice pursue the subject. She wouldn't go further. It wasn't fear that kept her from proceeding to the end. It was the pain. She was willing to work through the pain— she'd never avoided necessary pain, never in all her life—but she had to do it in stages. This was stage one. The premonition. The foreshadowing . . .

On Saturday, she made the trip to see Komako. Towards evening, as she was preparing supper, her mother said: "I've been watching you all day long, Mitzko. Something has happened . . ."

"Something's . . . happening, Mother . . ."

They didn't discuss the matter further. But each woman was deeply satisfied: Komako, because the change was occurring; Mitzko, because her mother had noticed. Late Sunday afternoon, the taxi she'd called to take her to the station honked from the curb. As she embraced Komako, Mitzko said: "I won't be coming to see you as often as I did—"

"I'm not a child," said Komako. "I'm fine. You really don't have to worry about me . . ."

The two women stared at each other.

"Let me explain—"

"There's no need to, Mitzko. Just let things be . . ."

Before she went to the physical therapy office on Monday, Mitzko took the elevator up to the eighth floor. She found Toge in the hall, talking to another patient. But she didn't succeed in surprising him—he had already turned his chair and held out his hands in welcome. "I heard your footsteps!" he exclaimed.

"How was your weekend?" she asked.

"I missed you . . ."

She realized that she'd missed him as well. But she said nothing.

"I've big news—" he told her excitedly.

"What's that?"

"I have a pass for Saturday. All day—"

She didn't think. She just said: "Maybe we can visit Fumiko and her husband. How about that? I'll phone her and see—"

On Friday night, the voice wouldn't let her sleep until it had spoken. It told her some things she'd suspected, but not believed. It told her to take her life drop by drop, as if she were taking medicine. She listened. She would go forward. It wasn't her nature to retreat, to run away. She felt calmer; she sank her head into the pillow, she closed her eyes peacefully. Sleep held out its hands to her. The way Toge did.

Saturday was beautiful: clean skies, brilliant sunlight, a sweet breeze blowing. Toge was in the window seat of the bus; she was beside him, and their shoulders touched. "Tell me everything you see," he urged. She did: fields, orchards, houses, fences, tractors, signs, dogs at the side of the road. He nodded. "More, more," he insisted. "Don't leave anything out—" She complied. Barns, bridges, trees, wildflowers, birds, lawns, woods, a river with a waterfall catching the sun, hills in the far distance, a snake sliding into grass. She spoke willingly, earnestly, exuberantly. Telling him about the world he was shut out of gave her satisfaction. For the first time since Garrett's death, she felt that she might— but she couldn't finish her thought, couldn't say what exactly it was that she might do.

Suddenly, he took her hand. "Now, come with me—" he said.

"Come where?"

"—Into the Kingdom of Darkness—"

And, locking her fingers in his, he proceeded to tell her how he felt about having been blinded. Rocking to and fro as he spoke, he returned to the moment when he knew for certain that he'd never see again and brought her forward to the present. "There," he said. "I've finished. Now, you know—" Of course, she didn't know. But if he wanted to say that she did, it was fine. She looked at him. His face was turned away; his eyes were scant inches from the pane of glass that brought him nothing. He was silent, ghostly pale. One hand grasped the handle of his cane. The other did not let go of hers.

The visit at Fumiko's went admirably. Toge and Fumiko hit it off at once; they joked and laughed and teased each other. The children liked Toge, Toge liked the children. While Mitzko and Fumiko were inside making lunch, Fumiko's husband and Toge had beers. They spoke easily, as if they'd been acquainted for years. Although he didn't discuss his service in Vietnam or his face and leg wounds, Toge did talk of his enlistment in the marines, and of his rigorous basic training. "I was drafted into the army," said Fumiko's husband. "But in boot camp, I broke my ankle. It never healed properly," he explained, "so I didn't go overseas . . ." Toge set his beer can down. "You didn't miss much," he said. A little after seven, Mitzko got up and announced that it was time to leave. "I'll drive you to the station," offered Fumiko's husband. "Come again soon!" said Fumiko. "We will!" declared Toge. "If I get another pass—and if Mitzko agrees to bring me . . ."

On the ride back, Toge said: "Tell me about all of them—I want to know everything . . ."

She did, down to the smallest detail: about red-cheeked, melon-breasted, fecund Fumiko; her husband, with his slight limp and his affable smile; the older son and his younger sister, Tamiko. "Yes, yes," Toge nodded. "I see them." Night had fallen. The wheels of the bus whirred heavily on the highway. They were in the rear, with Toge's cane propped up against the seat in front. The driver had shut off the interior lights; the two of them were engulfed in a darkness that—like the light—Toge couldn't see. Suddenly, he leaned his body sideways and put his head down on her lap. "Do you mind?" he asked.

"No."

"Sure?"

"Sure."

"I'm not making you uncomfortable?"

"Not at all."

"Now, tell me all about their house . . . and their yard—"

She began to describe them, but then stopped. He was asleep. She looked down at him. His breathing was soft, regular; it flowed from him like a stream. Tentatively, she put a hand on his head. She let it rest there for a time. Then, gently, so as not to disturb his rest, she caressed him. In the comforting, she found comfort . . .

Chapter 51

On Sunday, she went to the hospital. He was in the sun parlor, sitting in a wicker chair in front of the open window. His cane lay on his lap; like the wheelchair, it would soon be gone. She sat next to him. Below and across the street, was a park. Couples walked behind strollers, children chased each other, old men were out with their dogs, balloons floated lazily in the air, a fountain sparkled. Above the treetops, the sounds of carefree time drifted in to them. "Where will you go to live when you're released from the hospital?" Mitzko asked him.

"The VA's going to set me up with an apartment," Toge said.

"I know—but I mean where? In what city?"

"Oh, that. I'm going to live here in town, of course . . ."

"Why do you say 'of course'?"

"Isn't it obvious? Because you live here . . . and we should be near each other. After all, we're friends—aren't we?"

"Yes," said Mitzko, "we're friends."

"Now, tell me what's doing in the park across the street—"

When she got back to her apartment, she told her mother that she'd been to see Fumiko and her family.

"I hope they're all well," said Komako.

Mitzko hesitated. She saw that the phone trembled in her hand. "I went to Fumiko's . . . with a friend—" she said.

"That's fine. There's no reason for you to be lonely," said Komako. But she didn't ask about the friend.

278

"Mother, there's no reason for you to be lonely either—"

"I'm not. I told you: I have my memories—"

"Still—" Mitzko paused. "Perhaps in time, you'll move up here . . ."

In what Mitzko said, something more was, not concealed, but implied. Both women knew it. But neither one said anything about it. Silence was better about what might be.

"In time," murmured Komako, "perhaps—"

Later in the week, as the two of them were eating lunch in the diner, Travis suddenly said: "Well, are congratulations in order?"

"What?"

"Don't I deserve to be the first to know?"

"To know what? What are you talking about?"

Travis lowered his knife and fork. He stared at her. "The entire hospital's buzzing," he said. "Word came down to rehab from eight, but there's not a department or an office that hasn't heard—including the magpies in administration . . ."

"Heard what, Travis?"

"About you and the blind vet! Everyone says that it's serious. You're always up on his floor; people have seen you outside with him. Are you two engaged?" He was smiling, but the expression in his eyes was a sober one. "Is it true? Mitzko . . . Mitzko! Will you finally let me stop worrying about your future . . . and set my mind at ease?"

"We're . . . companions."

Travis hadn't yet touched his coffee. Abruptly, he grasped the cup and solemnly raised it. "Here's to companionship!" he said.

Mitzko didn't mind the talk. She was used to hospital gossip; it had no effect on her. Nobody other than Dr. Avery Travis ever raised the subject with her; all of her colleagues seemed bound to silence. If Toge had heard anything, he never mentioned it to her. She continued to see him. He waited expectantly for her visits, he was buoyant in her company, he was openly affectionate; always, he was sorry when it was time for her to go. But she was under no illusion. She hadn't succumbed to a spell. Beneath Toge's cheerfulness and optimism, there would have to be an abyss of despair and rage. He'd finished his war in Vietnam; he still had another to fight. It didn't frighten her. She was used to war.

Several weeks later, the two of them were in the public park that the sun parlor on the eighth floor of the hospital overlooked. Mitzko had brought with her a straw basket packed with bread, cheese and wine; she would open it later. In the meantime, they lay side by side in the grass. Above her, she saw the sky—the same sky he didn't see. A pair of butterflies sailed over their faces; she described them to Toge. Then a furry, roly-poly puppy wandered by. It licked Mitzko's hand; she introduced it to Toge, who ran his fingers over its head and muzzle again and again. Then came a little girl in a print dress. "Is this your puppy?" Mitzko asked.

"It's mine," said the girl, sweeping it up. "My mommy and daddy gave it to me for my birthday—" She stared at Toge's face. "What's wrong with him?"

"He was hurt," said Mitzko.

"How?"

"In the war," said Toge softly.

"My uncle was killed in the war," said the little girl.

And she ran away with the puppy.

Then Mitzko said: "Let's eat our picnic lunch—"

"Hey," said Toge, sitting up. "That's great! I haven't gone on a picnic since I was a kid!"

Mitzko filled Toge's cup with wine and then her own. She

lifted hers; gently, she touched his hand so that he could follow suit. "What shall we toast to?" she asked.

"To us—" said Toge.

Slowly, they drank and ate. When they'd finished, Toge propped himself up on an elbow. "I . . . liked the puppy," he said. "I liked it . . . very much."

"So did I."

He was silent for several moments, then he said: "I've decided that I won't use a cane. I'm going to get a dog . . ."

The empty wine bottle lay aslant in the basket; a last crust of uneaten bread was rolled up in paper; nearby, on the lawn, sparrows hunted for crumbs. Mitzko watched them for a time and then looked over at Toge. He was sitting up, hugging his knees. Ostensibly, it was a peaceful pose. But she saw the twitch in his hollowed cheeks, the spasmodic quivering of his lips. From the bridge of his nose up over his forehead, purple-red scars crawled like worms. He wore dark glasses; they hid his blasted eye sockets, but didn't cover the ugly network of the scars. The sun was just slightly past its zenith; it was very warm. Nevertheless, he hugged himself more tightly—as if he were cold; he looked like his teeth would begin to chatter. She knew it was the cold he fought against. Death. She could help. And she would. The born healer in her went out to him, embraced him, pledged him support. They would fight together. It would enable him to live; it would fill her void. That's what she felt. But she didn't tell him.

She was lying on her side, her head resting on her forearm. The wine and sun's warmth and smell of the grass made her drowsy. She allowed her eyes to close. The sun, the sky, the park, the picnic basket were gone. She was in his world. Her mind wandered, fell through space. Strange, disjointed images of people and places succeeded each other, merged, blurred, shut out. She was plunging, flying. She crawled like a baby, loped like a lioness. She'd never been born; she had died long ago. Where was she? What was all this? Was she asleep? But she saw him. He was sitting there, hugging his knees against the oncoming glacier. She had to come close to him. Hold him. Tell him. Tell him that life and death were one stream, that every living being swam in the same stream. She had to connect his emptiness and hers. She had to transform the look of terror on his pitiful face. Only she couldn't move, couldn't stir. Couldn't even see his face now. What had happened to it? Had his face disappeared too? Was she once again beholding the Faceless Horror?

She started. Whispered broken words. Opened her eyes. Saw him sitting in place just as he was, with his own face and his own pain. Shut her eyes again against the brightness of the sun. Heard him as he whispered: ". . . I've always loved you, Mitzko. Always . . ."

He believed she was asleep. She let him believe it.

Chapter 52

He was scheduled to be released from the hospital by the end of the month. Henderson, of social services, had several apartments lined up for him; the final choice would be made within ten days or so. He had done exceedingly well on his psychometric testing; Peter Sanchez, the vocational counselor, had informed him that he would be admitted to the university. He would also, in the near future, begin the study of Braille. His future, according to the test scores, lay either in psychology or law. Mitzko asked him which. "Law," he said without hesitation.

They were walking in the hallway on the eighth floor, Toge holding firmly to her arm. "Have you decided which branch?" she asked.

"Criminal," he replied, again without hesitating.

They reached the sun parlor and seated themselves on the sofa. "And now," he said, "for some more great news! Ready?"

"Ready."

"I've got a pass for the entire weekend! From Friday afternoon to Sunday evening! How's that?" He paused, then he said: "Can we visit Fumiko and her husband again? If it's okay with you. I'd really like that—"

"I'll check with her this evening . . ."

Early that evening, Mitzko called. But there was no answer. Then she remembered that it was Wednesday, Fumiko's family evening. They were probably out, having supper in the local mall. Mitzko would have to call back later. But she didn't. Every time she thought about it, something prevented her. She was in a strange mood, agitated and yet calm.

She spent half an hour or so at her window, staring up at the stars. They told her nothing she didn't already know. The rest was guesswork, conjecture—until it was lived. She turned away from the night sky with an eerie sense of imbalance. As if she were on the brink, about to fall. Or fly.

Without phoning Fumiko, as she'd promised Toge, she went to sleep. In the dream that she had, she was about to be married. She was dressed in white, with a white train and veil. The ceremony was to take place outside, at night, on the front lawn of the estate. Everyone who'd been invited was present: her mother and Akira, whose hand Komako held; Chuo, in his army uniform, wearing the patch of the 522nd; Fumiko and her husband and their children; Komako's parents; Akira's uncle, Toshiro; Akira's mother, dressed in a black geisha costume; General Edwards and his wife; the blond young lady to whom Garrett had been engaged. But there was no bridegroom. Even the minister, waiting with his Bible, was there. On the moon-silvered grass of the sward, the crowd stood quietly; the minister craned his head. But no groom appeared.

"Let's look for him—" Mitzko suggested.

They went first to the stable, which was empty; then across country to the creek, which gurgled indifferently; then to the fallen tree in the woods, where birds sang indecipherable song; then to the river, ever rushing into the darkness. Here, the minister said: "Let us kneel and pray—" And when the prayer was terminated, they saw the white shadow on the far side of the water. It came closer. And they saw it was Garrett, astride the white mare. He sat proudly, erectly, straight as a sword. War flashed from his eyes—or was it peace? Nobody could tell. Was he real? Mitzko wondered. Not was this a dream, but was he real? The mare reared on her sturdy hind legs. From the far distance, where the snow-peaked mountains were, mist rolled over the plain. Garrett saluted, turned the mare, rode into the mist and was gone. "Where is the bridegroom?" cried a voice. But no one knew whose voice it was . . .

On Thursday, Toge asked: "What did Fumiko say?"

"I didn't reach her," said Mitzko.

She could see how disappointed he was. "But I have another plan," she said quickly.

"Oh? What's that?"

"It's a surprise."

"A surprise?"

"Yes. I'll pick you up Friday afternoon . . . and then you'll find out . . ."

She got everything ready that evening. A white lace cloth on the table, blue tapers in silver candlesticks, her best dishware and utensils. She spent two hours preparing the food, and refrigerated it. When she'd finished, she showered. In the bedroom, she stood naked in front of the mirror. She appreciated what she saw. He would never see it, but he would appreciate it as well. She got into a nightgown and slipped between the sheets. In the morning, before she went to work, she'd strip the bed bare and put on fresh linens.

At six, just after she wakened, she phoned Komako. "Mother—"

"Mitzko, are you all right?"

"I'm fine—" She drew a deep breath. "Wish me luck, Mother—"

"Good luck, Daughter. In all that you do—"

It made Mitzko feel better.

At about five-thirty, she went up to the eighth floor to pick Toge up. Dressed in a powder-blue shirt open at the neck and navy blue pants, he was waiting for her at the elevator bank, a bouquet of white roses in his hand. She took them from him; he took her arm. "Now, listen," she said as they exited the hospital, "I'll describe exactly where we're going . . . so you'll be able to envision it. Okay?"

"I won't miss one detail . . ."

Ripe afternoon sun filtered down through the trees; it danced on the sidewalks with the motion of the leaves. They walked slowly, like a couple out for a leisurely stroll. Children were about: the boys played ball and tag; the girls chalked boxes for hopscotch. As they passed, a cat ducked under a hedge; a dog wagged its tail at them. Cars, bicycles, and an occasional scooter moved indolently on the streets. She omitted nothing, told him everything. He nodded appreciatively as she spoke. At the last crossing, she stopped. "My building is on the right—the fourth from the corner," she said.

"Your building?"

"I'll tell you exactly how it looks. Come on—"

She had asked him to bring a few overnight things; he put his bag down just inside the door. Describing each room minutely, she led him through the apartment. Then he sat on the sofa and she described precisely how the dinner table was set. He listened raptly. She watched his face as she talked. He did love her. As he said in the park on their picnic, he'd always loved her. She could accept his love. Touching this man with her hands and her heart and her mind would reshape her world. She would see life from another angle, live it on an altered basis. She would dream different dreams. Suddenly, she became aware that the room was silent, that she had stopped speaking to him. But it didn't seem to matter; he was still sitting at the edge of the sofa, leaning forward, listening. Behind him, the window framed a patch of soft evening sky. He held out his hands to her. "Mitzko—" he said in a voice little more than a whisper. "With us—is there light at the end of the tunnel?"

She was unfastening the buttons of her blouse. The chain and Garrett's ring were gone. The night before, she had removed them and put them away in a remote drawer. Toge's hands would never feel them on her flesh. "Yes, Toge," she told him. "There is light at the end of the tunnel . . ."

About the Author

Chayym Zeldis is a widely-acclaimed novelist and poet. His writing has been praised by such distinguished authors as Henry Miller, Elie Wiesel, Jerzy Kosinski, James Michener, Cynthia Ozick, Doris Grumbach, Ernest K. Gann, Mark Van Doren and many others. *The Geisha's Granddaughter* is his seventh novel.

Zeldis has won numerous awards and contributed to leading periodicals; his work has been anthologized.

Zeldis was born in Buffalo, NY. In 1948, he went to Israel where he worked on various agricultural settlements and served in the Israel Defense Forces during the Sinai Campaign of 1956. He returned to the U.S. on a Creative Writing scholarship to the New School University in 1958.

In 1989, Zeldis and his wife, Nina, a Rehabilitation Specialist, settled in Israel. Zeldis teaches Creative Writing and Poetry at Tel Aviv University.